The Weight of Him

Ethel Rohan

Atlantic Books
London

First published in 2017 in the United States of America by
St Martin's Press, New York.

This edition published in paperback in Great Britain in 2018
by Atlantic Books, an imprint of Atlantic Books Ltd.

1 2 3 4 5 6 7 8 9

A CIP catalogue record for this book is available from the
British Library.

Paperback ISBN: 978 178 6491923
E-book ISBN: 978 178 6491916

Printed and bound by CPI Group (UK) Ltd, Croydon, CR0 4YY

Atlantic Books
An Imprint of Atlantic Books Ltd
Ormond House
26–27 Boswell Street
London
WC1N 3JZ

www.atlantic-books.co.uk

In loving memory of Nathaniel J. Bergman

I thought how unpleasant it is to be locked out;
and I thought how it is worse, perhaps, to be locked in.

—Virginia Woolf, *A Room of One's Own*

The Weight of Him

One

BILLY BRENNAN OVERDID IT AGAIN WITH THE FAST food. After, he hurried as best he could along the street, fighting the need to stop and recover—he didn't want to draw any more attention to himself. Strangers looked twice at his massive bulk. He pretended not to notice. Those he knew seemed inclined to stop and chat, but he issued only passing hellos and pressed on. He was in no mood to suffer further condolences and awkward exchanges, all of which set his heart racing.

A woman overtook him on the footpath, walking fast and with force. She must have just come off a foreign holiday or a session of sun beds. Maybe she had slathered herself in that fake lotion. More noticeable than skin the color of mahogany, though, she was sickly thin. Billy had never seen a woman so skinny; her arms and calves could snap like sugar sticks. It seemed impossible she could move that fast, could have the strength to even stand up.

She marched ahead, her arms swinging back and forth with

alarming range, her body jerking in a way that didn't make sense. It was as if different parts of her insides were struggling to get out. Billy felt eyes on him, a group of gawking schoolgirls. They looked from him to the woman and back again, a mix of humor and disgust on their faces. He walked faster, still hunched forward with the full, too-tight feeling in his stomach.

As he neared his car, he spotted Kitty Moore coming at him like a bullet in slow motion. He planted himself in front of a shop window, his reflection a thick column of flesh beneath a head of dark curls. His heart squeezed and released in time to, *Please don't see me.* Kitty neared in his periphery. Billy braced himself. *Keep going, that's it. Don't look this way. Don't—*

"Billy." Her sad tone pressed on his chest.

He swung around, faking surprise. "Ah, Kitty! How are you?"

Her eyes moistened. The gray-black of her loose, knotted bun made him think of a little heap of ashes. He couldn't hold her watery gaze. Felt as though he was trying to breathe through a pillow. Kitty's chapped lips moved, but he couldn't make out her words above the ringing in his ears.

She glanced at the shop's colorful window display and back at him. "I'll let you get along, Billy. You mind yourself, now."

"You, too, Kitty."

Her pale mouth remained open, as if she intended to say more, but she moved off. It was Kitty, of all people, who had found Michael that chill morning back in January. In the five weeks since, Billy had managed to mostly avoid her, even though they both lived in the neighboring village and just a couple of miles apart.

In her wake, his attention fell on the snow globe in the window's center display. The ornament contained a blond girl in a red dress, a black dog by her spindle legs, and a cottage with a navy door and straw roof. Two yellow birds completed the scene, perched on the skeleton of an ice-blue tree. Billy wanted to shake the globe and bring it to life.

Behind him, a tour bus whooshed past, its red and white reflection streaking the shop glass. He tried to remember back to a time when he was small and thin, and able to feel the undertow from passing traffic. His hand pressed the side of his head, as though trying to keep the egg of himself together.

Billy sped over the twelve miles from town in his black Corolla, sucking traces of grease and hamburger from his teeth. As he entered the village, he told himself to slow down and get it together before he arrived home. The car cruised past the pub, shop, church, and graveyard. He pushed away the image of the dark earth heaped over the fresh grave.

Twenty-two houses dotted the village, a mix of gray stone, red brick, and whitewash all listing to the left. The entire scene dappled with weak, wintry sunshine. Its background colored in various greens courtesy of the trees and rolling fields. Another tour bus approached, a silver-haired driver in front and a load of schoolchildren in back. They were likely returning from Newgrange, centuries-old testimony to a time when the country was supposedly heroic and great. The Land of Saints, Scholars, and High Kings. Billy didn't want to think about the sad state of the country now after the end of the Celtic Tiger, with so much snatched from so many.

Home. Theirs was a redbrick dormer bungalow on a land-scaped acre lot. His parents had given him and Tricia the site twenty-one years ago. The wedding present yet another thing his father liked to hold over him. Billy tried not to look, but his eyes went straight to the trees behind the football pitch—those trees, all trees, ruined for him now.

He entered the kitchen. The radio was tuned to that country music station Tricia liked so much, some lament with an American twang playing. Not so long ago, he might have pulled her by the hand into the middle of the kitchen and twirled her around beneath his fingers. She would likely have pushed him away, laughing, and called him daft. Or on another day, in a sharper mood, she might tell him, "Stop, you'll give yourself a heart attack." Either scenario was better than how they tiptoed around each other now.

She stood at the sink peeling potatoes, all five-foot-nothing of her. He was six-foot. She glanced over her shoulder, a strip of potato skin hanging from the peeler like a diseased tongue. "You weren't long. Town must be quiet?"

"Very quiet, I was in and out." He didn't say he'd done little more than stuff himself. Didn't mention Kitty Moore.

"You just missed your mother," Tricia said.

"Everything all right?" he asked.

"Fine, she was just checking in."

A fresh bouquet of lilies sprang from a vase on the table, their smell sickly familiar. The flowers looked beautiful, but seemed tainted, like black age spots in the glass of an antique mirror. That was the way with so much now—tarnished, loaded. Birdsong that sounded like a child screeching. The creak of a door like groaning. Overhead power lines that could string you up.

He read the sympathy card, from Tricia's aunt in New York. "That was very nice of her."

"Yes, God bless her." Ever since they'd lost Michael, in addition to coffee, cigarettes, and sleeping tablets, Tricia had also taken hard to Catholicism. "Although," she continued, still skinning the potato, "I almost wish the cards and flowers, the people, would all stop coming through the door now. It seems endless."

He understood, but the alternative didn't appeal, either—people forgetting, and the everydayness of life without Michael taking hold. He opened the fridge door, despite still feeling full, and scanned the shelves. Every time he entered the house he walked straight to the fridge and looked inside, and every time he felt this strange disappointment, as though expecting to find something else.

As Tricia stripped the last potato bare, her shoulder blade moved faster beneath her T-shirt, bringing to mind a calcified wing. He watched the hypnotic movement, tempted to touch her, but he knew she wouldn't want that. His touch no longer comforted her the way it had in those first few days after Michael. The last time he'd reached for her, she'd flinched and pulled away.

"Did you want a hand?" he asked.

"No, thanks, I'm almost done."

The clothesline beyond the window tugged. Billy refused to look. Michael, at all of seventeen, had left the house in the dark of night, cut down the previous clothesline, and walked to the band of trees behind the football pitch. Billy pictured the rope on the ground, trailing Michael like a snake.

Up and down Tricia's shoulder blade sliced. She had lost so much weight in five weeks. Her straw-colored hair was brittle now, too. A glassy look in her eyes. She added the naked potatoes to the saucepan and walked to the back door with her cigarettes and lighter. She had given up the killers for eight years, but the day they lost Michael, she had gone back on them worse than ever.

In the living room, John, Anna, and Ivor sat together on the couch, still in their school uniforms, their eyes locked on *Dine About Town*, that cooking show the whole family liked. Only now they weren't whole. Billy's attention jumped to the red floral rug in front of the fireplace. They'd waked Michael there in his mahogany coffin with its shiny gold handles and crucifixes. Michael's walnut guitar still leaned against the wall in the corner, just as the boy had left it. The fast food pushed against Billy's stomach, bloating, hurting. He thought about bursting wide open and how good that would feel.

"Did you want a cup of tea, Dad?" Anna asked.

"No, thanks, love. I'll get myself a cup after the dinner." He smiled, hoping to ease the worry on her little face. At twelve years old, Anna cut a miniature of her mother in old photographs—thin, pale, and short, with bright yellow-blond hair, almond-shaped eyes, and plump lips.

He suddenly wanted the children up and out, doing. "It's such a fine evening, how about we all go for a drive before dinner?"

"No thanks," John said, deadpan. At fifteen, he was now the eldest. He bore his brother's likeness, at least physically, and stood tall, lean, and broad. The defiance in his wild dark curls and penetrating blue eyes was all his, though, Michael a gentler and more agreeable young man.

"We're watching this," Ivor said, his eyes never leaving the TV. He sounded younger than nine, his words thick when he spoke, as though every tooth he'd ever lost sat in a pile on his tongue.

"I'll go, Dad," Anna said, trying to please him.

"Ah, no," he said, not letting his disappointment show. "If this is what you'd all prefer to do." He remained with them, telling himself it didn't matter what they did as long as they were together.

The door to the boys' bedroom stood ajar. Billy shuffled past Michael's empty bed and opened the wardrobe, its hinges creaking. He ran his hands over the shoulders of Michael's shirts, and down the empty arms. He pressed Michael's favorite gray sweatshirt to his face, breathing deep. With each passing day, Michael's earthy, almost spicy scent was fading.

Billy recovered and moved into his room. He was looking forward to a long, hot shower and washing away as much as he could. After he stripped, he dropped onto the side of his bed to remove his socks, his stomach heavy on the pale, hairy slab of his thighs. He clapped his hands to the sides of his huge belly and jiggled it. He tried to lift its mound off his lap. He slapped and squeezed its rolls. Grabbed hunks of himself in his hands and twisted the fistfuls of fat till he hurt. It felt good. It felt awful.

He pushed himself in front of the full-length wardrobe mirror. His reflection appeared pale and sickly, older than forty-seven. His eyes looked bruised, too, as if he'd taken punches. The man of himself was hidden behind the droop of his purple, stretch-marked belly. Thanks to the press of the steering wheel, a permanent purple bruise also marked his middle, like a supersized sneer. His breasts hung larger than Tricia's. He raised his arms out from his sides, their sagging flesh quivering like two blue-veined jellyfish. He turned away from the mirror and rushed into his clothes.

In the days after Michael, a social worker had come out to the house. A brunette, save for the single blond curl at her forehead, and her eyes soft and kind. One of her pamphlets maintained that people lost weight with grief. That was true of Tricia, but not of him. He wasn't even getting grief right. He recalled the anorexic woman earlier, trying to escape her skeletal body. He was the opposite, hiding inside his massiveness. He returned to the wardrobe mirror. His reflection stared him down. He raised his hand and made of his thumb and finger a pointed gun. His reflection aimed. Fired.

Beyond the window, the crows cawed, as if mocking. He lumbered across the room, lifted the net curtain, and watched the birds' black flight. The view of the village and the town beyond rarely changed. Except for the birds and the weather. The furling and unfurling of the Meath flag from windows. The sometimes hurtle of an airplane, streaks in its wake like ocean whitecaps.

The haphazard scatter of the buildings in the village made them look thrown down rather than built up, like dice shaken and rolled, landing where they may. Billy's childhood home stood on the hill, the straight line between him and the farmhouse just five hundred yards across the fields. It seemed much farther away. Smoke puffed from the kitchen chimney, as gray as rain clouds. He dropped the curtain.

Billy followed the smell of oil and fried meat to the kitchen. Tricia stood at the stove, prodding the chops with an orange spatula long deformed by the heat. The oil spat and sizzled, filling the small room with the distinctive waft of browned lamb and rosemary.

Tricia moved to the door and called the children. The three filed in and took their places. Billy avoided looking at Michael's empty chair. Tricia plated the food. The meat pink and juicy. The fried potatoes black-gritted and glistening.

She carried more food to the table. So much food, as if she were still cooking for a family of six. Billy sliced open his lamb chop and found himself hesitating.

Tricia took her seat opposite him. "How is everyone?" she asked, trying to sound casual. The social worker had emphasized the importance of checking in.

"Yeah, what did you all get up to today?" Billy asked. The school counselor had said the children seemed to be doing as well as could be expected, but he and Tricia would never again trust the surface of things.

John gripped his knife and fork hard, his knuckles yellow-white. "Why do you both keep asking how we are? All the time now, it's the same old thing—"

"Hardly all the time," Tricia said, still trying at casual. John's attention remained on his meal, but his cheeks flared red. Anna and Ivor looked out from wide, sad eyes.

"Eat up," Billy said gently.

John's knife and fork tore into his chop, as though he were killing it again. He had his grandfather's hard, square jaw. His temper, too. The boy's knife screeched across his plate, making the roots of Billy's teeth hum.

"Take it easy, can't you?" Billy said, too sharp. Tricia's eyebrows shot up. A warning. They had to be careful. They had to do a better job with the remaining three.

The Beatles' "Yesterday" floated out of the radio. Tricia crossed the room and powered it off. John chewed his meat as though still slaying it. Ivor's chubby hand pushed a wad of bread into his mouth, his chin shiny with butter. Anna inspected the lump of potato on her fork. Tricia remained at the window, her back to them and her arms wrapped around what was left of her. Billy pushed away his plate, his dinner untouched. A first.

Tricia returned to the table and mentioned her morning shift at the chemist. Some strange fella had wanted them to sell his homemade potion, a "cure" for rashes related to measles, chicken pox, and the like. "He couldn't understand why we refused."

Anna chimed in about the Sullivan twins in her class, home sick with the mumps. "Their necks swelled like melons."

The banter went around the table. Billy sat smiling and nodding, adding the odd comment. Inside, though, he couldn't stop the churn of panic, awful sensations that had descended after Michael and which were getting worse by the day. The more he ached to turn back time and undo the unthinkable, the more the torment built. As his family chatted, clocks ticked in his head like bombs, their black arms turning wildly forward, carrying them forever into the future and farther away from Michael.

His attention jumped to the vase of lilies Tricia had moved to the counter, in the farthest corner. He could still catch their smell. The slice of the spades filling in Michael's grave started up again in his head, a wet, rhythmic music. He saw his naked reflection in the wardrobe mirror upstairs. He was killing himself—not nearly as swiftly or brutally as Michael, but killing himself just the same.

Two

BILLY HAD SLEPT BADLY, HIS HEAD A MESS OF thoughts, like an overheated radio about to blow. The same questions had chased him throughout the dark. Why had Michael taken his own life? How could he have done that to himself, and to those he left behind? Why hadn't he, the boy's father, noticed that Michael had felt so depressed or scared or heartbroken—whatever it was that ailed him? There must have been signs.

The social worker had said there are usually indications, especially in hindsight, and always reasons, even if they only make sense to the victim. Billy and Tricia had agonized, going over everything for any clue, but nothing stood out. Yes, Michael was sensitive, and could be troubled at times by his various fears—of exams, of the dark, of water, of bridges, and who knew what else—but there had been nothing to suggest any deadly extent to his anxieties. Billy could only imagine the stories going around. Drink, drugs, a fallout with family, friends, a girl. He and Tricia had asked the same questions of everyone they could, but no one could explain. No one could believe.

He burrowed deeper on the bed and covered himself completely with the comforter, letting the darkness swallow him. His hot, damp breath surrounded his head like a welcome fog. The social worker had assured them they had done nothing wrong. "People can be great actors," she'd said. "They can hide a lot." Billy hadn't been able to meet her gaze, knowing how much of himself he'd always hid.

He grabbed at the bottom sheet on Tricia's side of the bed and scrunched it in his fist. During the long, sleepless night, he'd felt her breath on his arm. Two cool streams from her nostrils that he'd counted up to one hundred, two hundred, three. He'd thought about waking her up, but that had seemed unfair. She should get whatever rest she could. He wasn't just being considerate, though. He hadn't wanted her to see him so distraught. So weak.

The ache to have done better by Michael, to have saved him, set on Billy again. There was one thing he could do, at least. His resolve from last night returned. He was done killing himself slowly. He was going to lose his weight, once and for all.

The motor in the fridge made its whirring sound, as though getting a surge of electricity. It seemed to call to Billy, inviting him to plunder its laden, condensation-fogged shelves. Shelves that shouldered roast chicken, creamy coleslaw, bars of chocolate, a block of sharp red cheddar, cheesy pizza topped with meat and mushrooms, and lots more salvation. Billy's empty stomach called back, almost as loud as the noise of the motor.

He glanced at Michael's empty chair, and out at the clothes-line, steeling himself. "Just one scrambled egg, please," he told Tricia. "And only one slice of toast, with the barest lick of butter."

"Are you feeling all right?" she asked.

"I'm back on my diet. I'm going to lose this weight, for good this time."

She worked on his breakfast in silence.

"You don't believe I'll do it," he said.

"I didn't say that."

"But you don't think I will." He had a lifelong pattern of losing and regaining his weight and then some, up until the past five years or so when he'd wearied of the struggle and had given up altogether.

"I'm done trying to figure out what people are and aren't capable of." Tricia fetched her cigarettes and lighter from the window ledge and stepped outside, closing the back door with a sharp click.

A gray-blue ribbon unraveled across the window. Something about that thread of smoke and breath, both having come out of Tricia and now floating up and away, gave Billy a feeling in his throat like food caught. The morning they lost Michael, Billy brought a towel from the bathroom and he and Tricia sat on the side of their bed together, crying into the two ends of cloth. How did they go from that to this? He swallowed hard. Tricia was disappearing on him, too.

Inside Dr. Shaw's office, Billy struggled up onto the exam table. Beneath him, the sheet of white paper made its scratchy sounds.

His embarrassment grew as he wrestled out of his too-small jacket. Shaw moved toward him, his liver-spotted hands gripping the ends of the stethoscope hanging from his neck. The thought rang in Billy's head. *Hanging from his neck.*

After checking Billy's blood pressure, Shaw placed the stethoscope on Billy's chest and then his back, pressing hard to hear the wheeze of lungs through the walls of fat. The skeleton in the corner was missing its left arm. Billy's last visit, it was intact.

Billy gestured with a nod. "What happened to him?"

Shaw, pulling an impatient, confused face, removed the stethoscope's right earpiece.

"Its arm?" Billy repeated.

Shaw gave a soft chuckle. "Would you believe the dog got in and ran off with it?"

Billy could believe almost anything now.

Shaw finished his check of Billy's vitals and moved back to his desk. Billy tried to work up the courage to tell the doctor he wasn't here for a second stress cert, to get more time off work. Shaw reached for his notepad.

"Actually, Doctor, I'm not here for that."

"Oh, no?"

"I want to drop all this weight, and get fit and healthy."

Shaw's gray eyebrows arched and he pushed on the bridge of his glasses. Their family doctor, he had cautioned Billy on his weight many times over the years, and his lectures had largely gone ignored.

"I mean it," Billy said.

"Glad to hear it," Shaw said, moving back to Billy. "I'm sympathetic to your situation, you know that, but it is about

15

time we had a serious talk, especially with everything you're going through. Your blood pressure is high, worrisome in fact, as is your overall condition. There's no easy way to put this, Billy, you're morbidly obese and on a very slippery slope. Headed straight toward hypertension, diabetes, cardiopulmonary disease, and you put shock and grief on top of all that . . . well, I don't have to spell it out."

"No, don't, thanks."

"All right, then. Let's get you up on the scales."

Billy shuddered. This would be his first time on a weighing scale in years. The number would feel like a sentence.

He dragged himself across the room. A detailed, multicolored diagram of the human body filled much of the wall above the tall, metal scale. Billy stared at the map of veins, muscles, bones, and vital organs. A geography of ourselves. Next to the human map, he looked like an entire, ailing continent.

"Best to take off your clothes," Shaw said.

"I'm all right like this."

Shaw looked out over his smudged glasses and leveled Billy with a cool gaze. Billy sighed. He should have known the death of his firstborn would only allow him to get away with so much with a man of the Hippocratic oath. He stripped down to his briefs. The underwear, riding obscenely low, was stretched to its max. His hands twitched to cover himself, but it was pointless. He took a deep breath, as though going underwater, and made to step onto the scale.

"Not there, here," Shaw said, pointing at a digital scale on the floor. Billy realized his weight must exceed the standing scale's capacity.

He stepped onto the digital scale, his breath held. The red numbers did a horrible dance and then stopped at four hundred and one pounds. Billy's heart thumped. He had topped four hundred pounds. Sweat bubbled from his every pore. He blinked, perspiration and the number on the scale stinging his eyes. The cloying smells of must, iodine, and nameless syrupy medicines worsened in the small, airless office. The beige walls moved ever closer. Shaw made a note of the terrible number. Billy did the math in his head, his stomach lurching. He weighed twenty-eight and a half stone. All these years, he'd sworn he'd never sink so high.

He hurried back into his clothes, trying to concentrate on what Shaw was saying about cutting calories and getting exercise. Four hundred and one pounds. The number seemed impossible to come back from. When he was fifteen, his weight had hit two hundred and fifty pounds, an all-new low he had sworn he would never sink past. Over the next several years, five pounds had climbed on top of that, and five more, and five more, till his weight reached three hundred, another number to which he'd sworn he'd never stoop.

Three hundred pounds. That's when people had started to stare. When he could no longer walk with ease. When he'd stopped fitting in regular clothes and on most chairs. When he was no longer seen for anything but his size. Oh, God. What he'd give to be back there now, though, one hundred and one pounds lighter. When he was three hundred pounds, Michael was still alive.

Shaw placed his hand on Billy's shoulder. "Go easy, okay? Start small and take it slow and steady. Build from there."

Billy left Shaw's office in a daze. He'd known, and yet it had still come as a shock—he was a ticking bomb and if he wasn't careful, he was going to put his family through another premature funeral.

Monday arrived, Billy's first day back to work in almost six weeks. The return to routine galled him. Damned if he could ever go back to the way things used to be. Could ever even pretend at getting back to some kind of normal. Yet the children had returned to school four weeks ago and Tricia had returned to her part-time job at the chemist's shortly afterward. It was past time for him to take the plunge.

Before he forced himself into the Corolla and headed to the factory, he walked around the perimeter of his house, sucking at the rain-sprinkled air and goading himself on like his father did the cows. *Get up*. For the fifth morning in a row, he managed to circle the house twice. Delighted, he pushed himself to brave another lap.

He struggled miserably through the third lap, however, his lungs burning and his breath coming in fast puffs, sending up tiny gray islands. Neighbors rattled past in cars and beeped in greeting, disturbing the stillness of the icy March morning. The low temperatures vicious, even for Ireland. Several passersby looked twice, no doubt stunned. The cattle in his father's field also seemed to look at him funny, as if they, too, could hardly believe they were seeing Big Billy Brennan on the move, on foot. Despite the sting of his chafed thighs, he pressed on toward the imaginary finish line at his car, fueled by a fresh burst of determination and the echo of Dr. Shaw's warnings.

In his car, the sheer pointlessness of everything stretched out in front of Billy like the hard road. He continued through the village and over the narrow, snaking tarmac toward town. The fields and hills were blanketed in a white frost that might make some think of God's breath, but all Billy saw was a gloomy, uninviting morning. The landscape seemed to shrink as well. The roads were too narrow, hills too low, and the fields like patches in a quilt. Even his car seemed too compact.

The new, two-story houses with oversized windows and gleaming slate roofs didn't seem to loom as large, either—state-of-the-art homes built during the country's all too brief economic boom. The size and showiness of these luxury properties brought scorn from plenty. Naysayers who said they hadn't let the country's short-lived upswing affect them. Hadn't moved into fancy houses or upgraded their homes, cars, or much of anything else. No, they gloated, they hadn't changed their ways or forgotten their place. Like some. They knew all along the good life couldn't last. Knew people should never get too big in themselves.

Billy fought the urge to turn the car around and go back to bed. He dreaded having to face everyone at work. Yet he couldn't shirk the responsibility any longer. Resigned, he steered the car around the final bend, feeling its tilt.

He parked inside the factory yard, his heart exceeding its speed limit. Two more cars joined him, crunching gravel. He reached for the glove compartment and pretended to search its contents. The two drivers, younger men from packaging, entered the factory. Billy took deep breaths, trying to rid himself of the feeling his head was rising off his shoulders. He pushed open the car door and pulled himself free of the wedge of the steering wheel. He wanted the numb feeling back, the shock that had shielded him those first two weeks after Michael, allowing him to believe, if only for a moment, that none of it was real.

Inside the factory, the machinery hummed and clanked. All about, splashes of workers in blue overalls. Billy hadn't worn the factory uniform in over a decade. His supersized navy sweatshirt and navy elasticated pants allowed him to blend in about as well as he could. A fellow long-timer, Bald Art, rushed at Billy, and within moments everyone had gathered around, pumping his arm and clapping the meat of his shoulders. *Welcome back, Big Billy. Good to see you. Let us know if you need anything. You all right, Big Billy?* He thanked them, overcome by the fresh outpouring, then hurried to his station, his teeth biting hard on his sucked-in lips.

He took up position behind the production line, his right temple throbbing and his stomach rumbling. Tantalizing smells wafted from the canteen, pulling at his insides like calves to the trough. He had again skipped his usual breakfast of fried eggs and meats with buttered toast. Instead, he'd eaten porridge with fresh, sweet strawberries. Already, though, his diet felt more killing than his weight.

He trained his attention on the conveyor belt and the novelty toys coming toward him, a parade of palm-sized, hand-made wooden dolls and soldiers. Throwbacks to a time when more things bore the mark of their maker. Billy's job required him to quality-check the toys and place his inspector's sticker on each product before ferrying it on up the belt to packaging. He knew no one thought much of what he did—even his children had long tired of the freebies—but he'd always taken pleasure in the toys, delighted by the patient, painstaking skill it took to make them, and by the joy they could bring. Now, though, there was too much memory tied up in them.

When Michael was a boy, Billy often brought home the seconds, those defective soldiers deemed not good enough for sale because of gouges, broken rifles, or missing parts. He and Michael had imagined tall stories about the damaged toys. The infantryman, for one, who had a grenade explode in his hands. He went on to become a superstar drummer. There was the lieutenant, too, with only one leg, courtesy of a land mine. He had become a world-class tap dancer.

There was also that time Michael's face had lit up beneath his dark curls on receiving the soldier with a defective eye. "This blind fella, he's a secret government agent, and his hearing is so advanced, he can tell when people are lying."

"Excellent," Billy said. "What'll we name him?"

"Billy the Blind and Brilliant!" Michael said, making Billy beam like a lighthouse.

Another of Michael's favorite seconds was the cavalry soldier with a missing ear. Michael attributed the loss to a mortar attack. After the maimed, deaf soldier recovered, he went on to become a celebrated horse-racing commentator. Michael, lending his voice to the soldier, would fast-talk into the TV remote control or anything else he could pretend was a microphone. His voice galloped in time to the horses, commentating on the entire imagined race.

The boy went so far as to make the thudding sound of the horses' hooves, banging a shoe on his free hand against the floor. Tireless, fired up, Michael recounted the hard-fought hurtle of the invisible steeds and jockeys with great color. Billy smiled, remembering. All that time ago, and he could still hear his and Michael's ecstatic bursts each and every time a horse beat out all the others to win.

John and Anna, and later Ivor, showed no interest in the seconds or in playing with their father at such great lengths. It was a bond only Billy and Michael shared. Billy studied one such second now, his first catch of the day. The soldier, his chin strap missing from his camouflage hat, stood arrow-straight in his khaki uniform, his bayonet aimed toward the sky. Billy had prided himself on having a keen eye and catching these tiny omissions. Now the torment of what he should have seen in his own son crawled in his head like maggots.

Billy's grip tightened around the seconds soldier. He heard Michael talking in a rush, recounting how the soldier had used a pen to perform a life-saving tracheal surgery on one of his comrades. The soldier-turned-surgeon then ripped off his chin strap to hold the makeshift tracheal tube in place during his comrade's transfer from the battlefield to the hospital. His heroism later earned this soldier with no chin strap Ireland's highest military honor, the Medal for Gallantry.

Billy's hand hesitated above the empty black bin reserved for the seconds and their ultimate disposal at the dump. It looked like a dark hole. After two decades of doing the task day in and day out, he found he couldn't throw away the damaged toy. With the toe of his shoe, he pushed the bin beneath the conveyor belt and out of sight. He slipped the seconds soldier into his trousers pocket.

———

Around noon, the factory's owner, Tony, arrived in front of Billy. "Good to have you back, Big Billy." He was wearing the same exaggerated look of sympathy he'd sported at Michael's funeral.

"Thank you," Billy said, also playing his part.

"How's the family?"

"Tricia?" Billy said pointedly. "She and the children are about as well as they can be, thank you."

"We don't know what we can bear until we have to, isn't that what they say?"

Billy didn't try to fill the silence.

"Well, I better let you get back to it," Tony said. "You'll let me know if there's anything I can do? I mean that, now."

Billy nodded, swallowing. Tony had sounded earnest for once.

The lunchtime bell rang out. Billy's stomach roared in response. Right as he headed to the canteen, though, fresh feelings of dread overtook him. He couldn't face everyone at lunch. The mournful looks. The same old condolences and well-intentioned attempts at humor and distraction. He was also afraid he wouldn't be able to withstand the temptation of the steaming, maddening buffet in all its glory. The creamy mashed potatoes. The fat, breaded fish cakes. Those flaky, buttery meat pies. The sugary, jammy desserts. It would be hell in heaven.

Despite all his promises, Billy found himself hurrying along St. Patrick's Street toward Seanseppe's. He entered the eatery through the side door, always with that feeling of being watched. Instantly, the familiar, soothing aromas of meat, hot oil, garlic, and oregano calmed him.

His hunger rose up and chased off the last of his willpower. He was putting in a hell of a day at the factory. The least he deserved was a nice lunch. He would eat something light for his dinner, soup or salad, and tomorrow he would again walk three laps of his yard. Maybe more.

He waited in the shortest of the long lines, avoiding eye contact and the stares of strangers. Dr. Shaw's warnings and his vows to himself wrecked his head. This would absolutely be his final feast.

Armed with his order, he drove to the relative seclusion of the car park down by the quays, away from most of the gawkers and that forever feeling of not wanting to get caught. His hands shaky, he started into the thick, salted, vinegar-drenched chips. The first delicious wad burned the roof of his mouth, but he kept eating. The chips gone, he went at the onion rings, his teeth sinking into the succulent mix of crispy batter and crunchy vegetable. Between bites, he pressed his tongue to the newly formed blister next to his molars, liking its stubborn resistance.

He stretched his mouth around the loaded burger and its mess of cheese, bacon, onions, and coleslaw. He slurped the sugary cola, making rude noises with his straw, and enjoyed its icy swim inside him. He bit into the bread-coated chicken and sucked the oil and crumbs from his fingers. His greasy hands broke the breastbone with a snap, its white meat coming apart like wet teeth opening in song. This was church.

Billy's eyes fluttered with thanks and pleasure. His whole life, he could always count on food. From his earliest memories, he'd loved food's colors, textures, and tastes. The way flavors went off in his mouth. How food distracted. Kept his mind still and his bad feelings quiet. Comforted. Pleasured. Sated. Filled him up. Made him feel in charge. A giant. Food made everything better.

At least it had made everything better. Finished, stuffed, Billy remained parked by the quays. His tongue pressed harder at the burnt bubble of skin on the roof of his mouth, flirting with the verge of bursting. His bloated stomach felt as though it were forcing his lungs up and into his throat. It was hard to breathe. He tried to reverse his seat, but it was already out as far as it would go. He shifted about, pulling his trousers bottoms off his middle and down around his knees. He slumped forward over the wheel with a groan.

Sweat turned his skin sticky. His heart was thumping so hard, he could feel its beat in his palms. Dr. Shaw's warnings went off in his head. Maybe he needed medical attention? What if his heart gave out? This was how someone would find him, stuffed and slumped, his trousers down around his knees. He would die alone, too. Just like Michael. He removed the soldier with no chin strap from his trousers pocket and gripped the toy in his palm. He leaned back against the headrest and ordered himself to stay calm and his breathing to slow.

He felt almost human again and tried to rouse himself. He needed to get back to work. Yet he stayed parked. The clouds had shifted, letting the sun out, and the river glistened gray-blue, the color of Michael's eyes. Billy had always thought it funny that the boy's eyes matched the color of something that scared him so much—Michael terrified of bodies of water and of heights, bridges in particular.

———

When Michael was nine, Billy took the family on holiday to Kilkee. A record heat, the sun had never seemed so near. So much so, as soon as they arrived at the caravan park, they broke with tradition and put off unpacking and settling in. Instead, they headed straight to the beach—everyone giddy and grinning, shiny with suntan oil and excitement.

Billy and Michael entered the water, Billy intending to teach Michael how to swim. Tricia watched from a blanket on the sand, Ivor on her lap. John and Anna played next to them, building sand castles with bright shovels and buckets.

The deeper they moved into the water, the more Michael knitted himself together—his shoulders pulled to his ears, elbows at his sides, and his clasped hands twisted beneath his chin. "I want to go back," he said, his voice shaking almost as much as the rest of him.

Billy finally convinced Michael to stretch out on his back while Billy held one hand beneath the boy's narrow back and the other beneath his slender thighs. "Look at you, floating already."

"Don't let me go," Michael pleaded.

"You're well able to do it on your own," Billy said, only half aware of the three boys playing in the water close by.

"No, I'm not!" Michael said.

"Relax," Billy told him. "I'm not going to let you go until you tell me it's okay."

"Promise?" Michael said.

"Promise. Now, keep your arms and legs straight, and your eyes on the sky, your lungs full of air. That's it, perfect."

The three boys messing about next to Billy and Michael grew

louder, splashing and shouting, trying to push one another underwater. Billy worried they would splash Michael and make him panic. "Take it easy, lads, all right?" he asked. "You're not the only ones in the water." He returned his attention to Michael, telling him to kick his legs as hard as he could. Michael obliged, tentative at first, but then slicing the water fast and strong.

"You're doing great," Billy said. "You're practically swimming already." Michael's small, shaky smile grew. "Okay, let's try this." Billy dropped his arm from beneath Michael's thighs.

"No!" Michael said, starting to struggle.

"It's okay," Billy said. "You're still floating. You're doing it." He had to raise his voice to get heard over the trio of boys—their playacting rougher now, their language and taunts to each other turning nasty.

"I'm sinking!" Michael said, grabbing at Billy's shoulders and trying to get upright.

"No, you're not, you're fine," Billy said, calm, firm. The three boys were almost on top of him and Michael now.

The tallest boy pointed at Billy. "Look! It's a whale!" He and the other two little gits laughed hard.

Billy tried to ignore them. Tried to keep his focus on Michael. "Okay, I'm going to drop my other arm now and let you float on your own, okay?"

"No!" Michael said, his arms and legs flailing.

The boys shouted, "Whale! Whale!"

"I want to get out," Michael said, scratching at Billy's arm.

"It's okay, relax," Billy said, his agitation building.

"Come and get us, whale!"

"I want to go back to Mam," Michael said.

"Wh-ale, wh-ale," the trio chanted.

Billy issued a roar and lurched at the boys, his arms swinging. The three took off, paddling like dogs. Billy gave chase, his thick legs plowing the water. The commotion behind him pierced his rage. He swung around. Michael's arms thrashed at the water and his mouth dipped below the waterline. He made terrible noises, gagging and grunting.

Billy threw himself onto the water and cut through the current. Michael's head disappeared below the surface and burst back into view. Billy reached the boy, but before he could grab hold, Michael went under a second time. Billy plunged with both hands and grabbed blindly. He touched Michael's hair and clasped his narrow shoulders, pulled him above water. Michael coughed and spluttered, unable to draw a full breath.

"You're okay," Billy said. Michael coughed harder, his small body jerking in Billy's grip. "I've got you," Billy said.

Michael's coughing jag ended, but he was still heaving, gasping. Billy tightened his hold on the tops of Michael's arms and looked him straight in the eyes. "Calm down, okay? Everything's all right." He wrapped Michael's arms around his thick neck and towed the boy toward shore.

They stood up in shallow water, the foam lapping at Michael's calves. "All better?" Billy asked.

Michael's face hardened and he punched at Billy's stomach. "Get away from me."

Billy held on to the boy's wrists. "Hey, listen to me. You're all right, okay?"

Michael freed himself and took off. Billy, breathless, chased Michael out of the water and over the hot sand.

Michael reached his mother and dropped into her arms. "Daddy let me go in the water. He promised, and then he let me go."

The rest of the holiday, Michael refused to return to the sea. On the long drive home, Billy followed the same route he'd taken a week earlier, but this time Michael turned panicky as they drove along the cliff road away from Kilkee. The boy cried and screeched, demanding to be let out of the car. "We're going to fall into the water," he wailed. It was the same, too, every time they passed over a bridge.

"What's gotten into him?" Tricia asked, her eyes wild. The boy had never before shown such fear.

Billy shook his head, but inside he'd known. He'd ruined the water for Michael. He'd ruined something between the boy and him, too.

Three

ANOTHER MONDAY. BILLY COULDN'T START INTO A
second week at work and pretending to play at normal.

"You're calling in sick again? That's hardly wise," Tricia said.

Billy forced himself to stir one spoonful of sugar, not three,
into his tea. "I've worked there long and hard enough these past
twenty years. They can do without me for one more day."

She placed a plate of buttered toast in front of him. "Don't
you know I'm on a diet?" he said, sharper than he'd intended.

She snatched the plate back. "Forgive me for forgetting, but
your diets never usually last long."

His jaw clenched. Back in his early twenties, when they'd
first gotten together, he'd lost almost eighty pounds. He'd
managed to keep the weight off, too, at least until three or four
years into the marriage. Then, the constant empty feeling returned and his weight climbed ever higher. Tricia sometimes
said she felt conned. That she'd married one man and ended up
with another.

"This time is different," he said.

"Everything's different now." She set about sweeping the floor, swiping at the same tile repeatedly, as if it couldn't be cleaned.

Billy was eight years old and sitting at the kitchen table with his parents and Lisa. A drop of water fell from the ceiling and onto his father's forehead. Billy almost laughed, but caught himself. His father jumped up, knocking over his chair. "What in blazes?" He held out his hand, catching more water in his palm. With a sick feeling, Billy remembered the bathroom sink.

"Jesus Holy Christ!" His mother rushed out, and upstairs.

His father moved into the hall. "Well?"

"The sink overflowed," his mother shouted down. "There's water everywhere."

His father returned to the head of the table, red-faced. He looked right at Billy. "Which one of you left the water running?"

"Wasn't me!" Billy said, his stomach lurching.

"Well, it wasn't me," Lisa said, calm. Even if the leak had been her fault, she wouldn't get punished. Not really.

Their mother called down for more towels. Lisa hurried to the hot press, and upstairs.

Billy's father shook his head. "Have you no brains at all? Get up those stairs right now and help clean up that mess, and then straight to bed."

"But I haven't eaten dinner," Billy said, trying not to cry. "And there's a new *Flash Gordon* tonight."

His father's arm shot out. "Get, I said!"

Billy's tears pressed harder. "I haven't done my homework, either. My teachers will kill me if I don't do it."

"Don't have me to tell you again—" His father fumbled with his belt buckle. Billy scampered.

Later, in the dead of night, Billy sneaked downstairs, his stomach empty and his chest full of the churn of his heart. His father's voice filled his head. *Have you no brains at all?* Billy only dared open the fridge a crack, afraid its light would give him away.

He removed a tomato, onion, head of lettuce, hunk of cheese, and several slices of ham. *Don't have me to tell you again.* He lovingly carved up a fresh, spongy bread loaf and slathered several thick slices with a creamy mixture of butter, mustard, and mayonnaise. He pushed away a flash of his father's thick fingers going at his belt buckle.

Billy ate, the sandwich making his stomach sing. After, he ripped open a bag of crisps, a burst of salt and vinegar filling the air. Next, he eased the purple foil from a bar of chocolate, revealing the wrapper's shiny silver underside and the dark, sugary slab. With a dreamy moan, he let the savory crisps and thick, sweet squares melt together in his mouth.

No one ever asked, but he'd filled the bathroom sink so he could pretend-shave, in a great hurry to be more grown up, more like his dad. He'd hoped that might at last please and impress the man.

Billy's mother appeared through the back door, bringing in the smell of home bake. Billy eyed the bright yellow bundle in her hand, his mouth watering.

"What are you doing home?" she asked, surprised.

He glanced at Tricia. "I've a bit of a cold."

"A bit," Tricia muttered.

Billy patted the chair next to him—John's, not Michael's. His mother placed the bundle on the table and opened the tea towels. Billy watched the ribbons of steam rise from the two rounds of soda bread, his stomach rumbling. She sat down, her white hair set in faultless curls and her ruddy hands clasped in her lap. Tricia offered tea. His mother, refusing to ever sit still for long, agreed to a half cup.

"Have you a knife, Tricia?" his mother asked, reaching for the bread.

Tricia returned the bread to the cover of the tea towels, their cotton the color of the butter Billy so wanted to spread over at least one thin slice. "You may take this away, thanks. Billy has started back on his diet."

Billy swallowed his disappointment and pushed a look of thanks into his face.

His mother pursed her lips. "It's not for me to say . . ." But of course she would say. "Do you really want to be at all that now, and everything that's going on?"

Billy made some incredulous sound. "You're the very one always going on at me—"

"I'm just saying—"

"Christ, we need a new kettle," Tricia said, moving to the boiling contraption to stop its screech.

His mother said, "I was thinking I could stay here with the children while you two go off on a holiday? Someplace foreign, maybe, Croatia or Budapest. Aren't they all the rage now? Let you get away from everything for a while."

He could tell from the hitch of Tricia's shoulders she shared his reaction to the idea that there was any getting away from it all. There was also the issue of his not fitting in an airplane seat. He wasn't even sure he would fit in two. "That's very kind," Tricia said. "Maybe down the road." She turned brisk. "There is something you can do, though. Anna and Ivor's school walkathon is coming up and they've to get as many sponsors as possible."

His mother sniffed. "That school is always looking for money."

"You don't have to," Tricia said, her voice tight.

"Of course I will. How would it look if their own grandparents didn't sponsor them?" She poised a pen over the pledge sheet. "Remind me how this works?"

"You can sponsor them by the number of laps they complete or give an overall flat donation, whichever you prefer," Tricia said.

Billy straightened on his chair, his thoughts coming in a rush. A fund-raiser. Now, there was a sure way for him to make his diet stick. A way for him to help more than himself with his weight loss, too. He could go public with his diet and get people to sponsor him, for suicide prevention.

"There," his mother said, pushing away the pen and pledge sheet. "A euro each per lap, is that fair?"

"They'll be delighted, thanks," Tricia said.

Billy sat trembling with his idea. He could set a weight goal and people could pay him for every pound he lost. Or, like the walkathon, they could donate a flat amount. He rubbed at his mouth. Michael's death had cut him in two, so he would set his weight-loss goal at two hundred pounds. Half of himself.

The money he raised would help save lives, in Michael's memory. He grew inches on his chair.

Tricia and his mother chatted. Another idea gripped him. For Michael's funeral, hundreds of mourners had formed a procession behind the hearse like a dark flood, following the boy in his coffin from the house and to the church. People crowded villages all over the country in similar processions for the dead. But what if they walked with Billy in their droves to prevent suicide and save lives?

The more he thought on his ideas, the more convinced he felt. He could really do good with this, and make some meaning out of the awful. Several times he began to tell Tricia and his mother, but he couldn't get the words out. Something told him that the moment he spoke his plans aloud, they would be diminished.

Billy hung his head over the blue casserole dish, taking in the intoxicating waft of garlic, beef, and vegetables. His tongue tingled with the spicy memory of paprika. Hungarian goulash was one of his favorites. He refused even a small amount, though, opting instead for yet another bowl of vegetable soup.

He carried the steaming soup to the table, struggling not to spill any. He was shaky all over, a nervous feeling coursing through him. Adrenaline, too. Since his mother's visit, he could think of nothing else but going public with his diet and organizing the march of all marches through the village.

Anna also refused the goulash. "It's too gooey," she said. The light fixture above her head brought out the golden in her hair. Billy could remember a time when Tricia had looked as pretty and shiny.

Tricia caved and allowed Anna to eat cereal instead. She drew the line at added sugar. "You'll rot every tooth in your head, catch diabetes if you're not careful."

The glass of milk paused at John's mouth and he repeated *catch* with a sneer. He looked tired, the black under his eyes recalling the smudges of mascara on Tricia's face in those days after Michael.

"Are you feeling all right?" Billy asked. Too late, he realized the now-familiar question would only annoy the boy.

"Jesus," John said. "I'm not going to kill myself, okay?"

Everyone at the table stopped. Copycat suicides, once unheard-of, were now making national news.

"We would never do what Michael did, all right?" John continued, his voice rising. "Tell them," he said to Anna and Ivor, sitting opposite. Ivor's tongue poked his cheek and Anna's face blazed.

"Tell them," John repeated.

"Stop that," Billy and Tricia said in near-unison, their fright also matching.

"He's right," Anna said, her voice shaking. "You and Mam don't have to worry about us." She elbowed Ivor. "Right?"

"Right, we'd never be that stupid," Ivor said innocently.

Billy and Tricia exchanged a pained look. Anna elbowed Ivor again, drawing a yelp from the boy. "Michael wasn't stupid."

"That's right," Billy said, knowing they had to talk the thing through. "People who take their lives, it's because they're suffering so much in their heads."

"How did he suffer?" John asked, anger and unshed tears in his eyes. "He was the favorite, always got everything he ever wanted."

"That's not true," Billy said. "Your mother and I don't have favorites."

"No, we do not," Tricia said. "And if any of you so much as think you might be going through anything even close to what Michael must have gone through, you're to tell your dad and me, or someone, anyone, do you hear me?"

"Yeah," Anna and Ivor said in unison.

Billy looked at John. "Did you hear what your mother said?" John refused to look at him. Billy struggled to keep his cool. "I need you to answer me, son."

"Yeah, I heard her," John said, harsh.

Popping sounds from Ivor's PlayStation broke the silence. "Put that away, pet," Tricia said. "You know there's none of that allowed at the table." Even before Michael, she'd worried about technology and how the young nowadays thought more of gadgets than they did of people.

Billy pushed away his empty soup bowl and wiped at his mouth with the back of his hand. John made to get up from the table. Billy hesitated. The dinner had taken a wrong turn, but he needed to make his intentions known. The sooner he started to raise donations and awareness, the sooner he would start saving lives. "Just a minute, son, I've something to tell everyone."

"I'm going to be late for training," John said.

"This will only take a minute."

John dropped onto his chair, sounding an exaggerated sigh. Billy's stomach bubbled and spit, as if boiling something. He placed his hand on his thigh, bunching fabric and the solid feel of the seconds soldier in his fist. Ever since he'd pocketed the soldier, he'd taken to carrying it everywhere. He began, his insides thrumming with a mix of excitement and fear. "I've decided to go public with my diet and make a fund-raiser out of it."

"You've what?" John asked, appalled.

"What do you mean, Dad?" Anna asked.

"I'm going to ask people to sponsor my weight loss. You know, the way people sponsor your walkathon. I plan to drop two hundred pounds and to donate whatever money I make to the Samaritans, in Michael's memory."

Tricia's face knitted. "Who ever heard of such a thing?"

"Exactly," he said. "That's why I think it'll be so successful."

"What's the Samaritans?" Ivor asked.

"They're named after the man in the Bible. They pick people up when they're down," Tricia said, her voice seeming to come from far off.

"Do we get to keep any of the money?" Ivor asked.

Billy laughed. "No, son, afraid not."

"Not fair."

"Of course that's fair," Anna said. She looked at Billy, her eyes shining. "I think it's a great idea, Daddy."

"Thanks, love." He drew a breath, deciding to go all the way. "I also plan to lead a march through the village, to call attention to the suicide crisis and to demand more be done to stop it. The march would be an appeal to people in trouble, as well, urging them to seek help before it's too late." He could see it all in his head and it was terrible-beautiful.

He pressed on, even though it was clear from Tricia's dark look she didn't approve. "I thought July twenty-first would be a good date, Michael's six-month anniversary. That gives us over four months. More than enough time. The weather should be nice, and there'll be a great stretch in the evenings. We'll walk through the village and out the main road to the roundabout and back, stop the traffic on all four motorways, make a right statement."

Tricia's fingers pinched the skin at the base of her throat, turning it an angry red. "Marches take place up in Dublin and in other cities, not anywhere like here."

"My point exactly," he said. "Something different, so people will take notice."

"It would never work," Tricia said. "People would be mortified."

"She's right," John said with relish.

Billy quaked with hurt and disappointment. "People will get behind this, wait till you see."

Tricia cleared the table with quick, angry movements. Anna and Ivor looked nervously at her and Billy. John lifted his plate and carried it to the sink. In addition to his grandfather's square jaw and temper, he had his stiff-backed walk, too. Aside from that, though, it could be Michael crossing the room. John walked to the door.

"Have you nothing more to say?" Billy asked.

John swung around. "Like what?"

"Let him go," Tricia said. "He'll be late to training."

Billy held John's furious gaze. "I don't know, congratulations, maybe? Fair play?"

"You want me to get excited, is that it? You wouldn't be doing any of this if Michael hadn't checked out and if you weren't as fat as fuck."

"John!" Tricia said.

Billy sat stunned, his lips parted and his eyes unblinking. John slammed the kitchen door closed. Tricia followed him, calling.

"Don't mind him, Dad," Anna said kindly. "He didn't mean it."

Billy nodded, unable to speak. Ivor seemed oblivious, punching buttons on his PlayStation, sending up rapid gunfire. The boy's stomach pushed against the table. Breast buds poked through his school shirt. Tricia blamed Billy. "Monkey see, monkey do."

"What did your mother say about gadgets at the table?" Billy said, suddenly cross. "Put that away."

Tricia returned and ordered Anna and Ivor upstairs to do homework. As soon as they left, she started in on him. "You couldn't have talked to me first, before you came out with all that in front of the children?"

"I thought you'd support me, thought you'd see the good I can do."

Her blue-veined hand pressed her forehead. "My God, why would you want to bring any more attention on us?"

Billy looked down at his chubby hand on the table, his thick fingers moving back and forth on the wood, as if clawing. She wasn't just referring to the scandal his size had caused them over the years. Her head was also full of accusations out of small mouths and dour faces, people saying Michael was selfish. Weak. Mad. A sinner. Billy didn't know why she cared so much. To hell with those people.

Four

THE NEXT MORNING, BILLY PUSHED ASIDE HIS DREAD and readied to return to work. Yet his late-night fears about his public diet and march nagged. He told himself all of his concerns, all of Tricia's, would be sent running once he got a strong show of support. For that, he needed to return to the factory and spread the good word.

He had almost made it out of his driveway when his father pulled up in his red Nissan. The seventy-eight-year-old strode toward Billy, one of his dark braces dangling off his shoulder and catching above his elbow, as if trying to get away. The old man brought his white head level with Billy's open window, his pinched face shrinking his eyes and exaggerating his crow's-feet. When he spoke, he revealed wet, pink-red gums that took up too much of his mouth. "Quare talk about you carried into Kennedy's last night."

Billy felt the sting of betrayal. John must have mouthed off about him and his plans. "I haven't time for this, I've to get to work."

"Oh, don't let me keep you." His father straightened and slapped the car roof. "You might want to phone your mother, though, and let her know there's no truth to this march and sponsorship business. She's in a right state."

"I won't be phoning her, then, unless you want me to tell her a lie."

His father's expression softened. "You're not in your right mind yet, there's none of us the same. Can't you wait and see how you feel down the road? Get the first year over you, at least, before you go putting yourself and the rest of us through something like this. It's too soon. Too much."

"I can't wait, there's too much at stake," Billy said.

His father curled his hands around the base of the window. "I'm telling you not to do this. You're making a mistake. We'll be all the talk."

"That's all you're worried about, isn't it?" Billy gunned the accelerator and pulled his car around his father's Nissan, coming within a sinew's breadth of the vehicle.

The entire drive to work, Billy seethed. The old man might have looked shaken by what Billy had said, but they both knew he'd spoken the truth. Billy was always all the talk. Even before Billy had become a fat boy, back when fat boys were a rarity, he was considered odd because he hated the family farm, and didn't ever want to work it, or inherit it, either—a prison that would dictate to him for the rest of his days.

No one understood it. "What's wrong with him at all?"

His father would look away, embarrassed, maddened. "I don't know where we got him."

Once, outside the church, when Billy was about ten, he'd overheard his father lament to Willie Birmingham, a neighbor and big-time farmer, "It doesn't look as if herself has another one left in her, either, to give me a right son."

Decades later, and Billy could still hear those words, as fresh as ever inside him.

Inside the factory, Billy hurried toward the black phone on the far wall, his head full of what he was going to say. The phone looked like a glossy insect on the red brick. Maybe it was a sign? Maybe he should rethink all this? No. He couldn't let his dad, anyone, get to him. He grabbed the receiver and pressed Tony's number, fresh fear blooming.

Right as he was about to hang up and let panic win, Lucy, Tony's longtime secretary, answered.

"Hello," he mumbled, his mouth dry and his tongue clingy. "It's Billy Brennan."

"Ah, Billy, how are you? No, don't answer that stupid question. How could you be? How could anyone be? I've been praying for you all."

"I know, thank you. Everyone's been very good. Listen, I was hoping to meet with Tony sometime today? There's something important I'd like to discuss."

"Can I ask what it's about? You know what he's like."

He hesitated. "I'd prefer not to say, he'll find out soon enough."

She put him on hold. He waited, his teeth soldered together.

She came back on the line. "Yeah, Billy, that's fine. He'll see you at three o'clock."

He forced his jaw open. "Can he meet any earlier? Sometime this morning, by any chance?"

"'Fraid not, Billy. The man has spoken."

At lunchtime, Billy entered the canteen on shaky legs. He pressed on past the food counter, struggling to ignore his bully stomach and trying to appear confident and purposeful. As he moved through the long rows of tables, all crowded with food and his fellow workers, he kept his eyes trained on the bulletin board at the back of the room, determined not to lose his nerve.

He hung both flyers, one for the march and one for his sponsored diet, the pins piercing him as much as the corkboard. People were either going to love his plans or think he had gone mad. He stood back to admire his and Anna's handiwork. The flyers would never have turned out so well without her help. For the headings and borders, they'd used dark green ink, Michael's favorite color. The pledge sheet's header read *Give for Every Pound Big Billy Loses & Help Save Lives*. The second flyer read *March Against Suicide & Help Save Lives*.

Both flyers displayed the same color photograph in the top center, a shot of Billy and Michael taken last Christmas, just weeks before everything changed. Billy touched Michael's pixilated face, his fingers lingering on the boy's smile. He swore he could feel heat pass through his fingers and down into his palm.

Vera, a veteran canteen worker, greeted him at the food counter. "How are you holding up, Big Billy?"

"As well as I can, thanks."

"Day by day, that's all you can do."

He swallowed and ordered a triple portion of salad, with extra boiled egg and the vinaigrette dressing on the side.

"Ah, God love you, are you still not well?" He realized she was referring to his supposed sick day yesterday. Embarrassed, he pointed with his thumb to the bulletin board and explained.

Vera's smile split her face. "Well, if that isn't the best ever." She pulled her brown-stained apron over her head and called to Liz, another veteran, "Did you hear what Big Billy is doing?"

"I did," Liz said, smiling, but he worried he saw more uncertainty than support in her eyes.

"Cover me for a sec," Vera told Liz. "I'm going to make a pledge right this minute."

"Thanks a million," Billy said.

He carried his food tray through the canteen, avoiding his usual crowded table, and continued to the far, empty corner.

"Are you not joining us, Big Billy?" Bald Art called out.

Billy turned around. "Can't, sorry." He delivered a sideways nod, indicating the bulletin board. "All that food on your plates will only tempt me." It was partly true. Mostly, though, he didn't feel up for company. He also didn't want to risk having to withstand any more negative reactions to his diet and march.

Bald Art and the rest of the group looked confused. Billy again indicated the bulletin board with a jerk of his head. "Go check it out."

Seated, Billy started into the rabbit food, munching lettuce and crunching cucumber. He pretended not to watch while people gathered in front of his flyers, his hand curled around the outline of the soldier in his trousers pocket. Bald Art, and everyone in the place, it seemed, made pledges and then hurried over, full of congratulations and praise. Billy's face hurt from smiling.

Yet as the clock turned toward the hour and the canteen emptied, Billy's mood sank again. None of this would be happening if Michael wasn't gone.

Inside the men's room, Denis Morrissey availed of the urinal next to Billy. Denis, a numbers man from upstairs, wasn't usually seen about the factory floor and Billy only knew him in passing. "Are you feeling all right?" Denis asked.

Billy wasn't sure if Denis was referring to Michael, his sick day, or his frequent need to urinate as his meeting with Tony drew closer. "Fine," he mumbled.

"I heard about your march and your sponsored diet, and I think what you're doing is brilliant."

Billy blushed. He and Denis had never really spoken before and he didn't know much about him, other than that the thirty-something hailed from Dublin and had moved to town a few years back, after he married Frances Callaghan, but they'd since separated.

"My dad died when I was thirteen," Denis continued. He looked away, facing the wall again. "It's not the same, I know, losing a father and losing a son, not even close, but"—his voice wavered—"I understand death by suicide is a whole different story and takes so much more out of you." He looked at Billy, his eyes damp. "I tell people my father died of a heart attack, but he didn't. He hanged himself."

"Christ, I'm sorry." Billy finished and zipped up. "Let me

just . . ." He raised his hands apologetically and moved to the sink.

Denis cleared his throat. "Yeah, yeah, of course."

While Billy dried his hands, Denis worked the soap between his fingers and lathered and rubbed with the violence of a surgeon.

After, Billy thrust his damp hand at Denis. "Sorry about your dad." The men shook hard. Billy again wished there were other, better things to say to people in mourning. He exhaled, grasping at some new language for grief. "Tell me about him?"

Denis looked taken aback. Then he sad-smiled. "He was a Dublin man, a welder. Made gates, mostly. He had his moods, but he was kind and funny, too, and really smart. The true gold, though, was in his hands. He could make anything. I often think of how he made a living from soldering things together, only to fall apart himself." He recovered and brightened. "This one time, I'll never forget . . ."

Billy listened.

Almost three o'clock, and Billy's meeting with Tony loomed. Just as Billy thought he couldn't stand to wait another minute, Bald Art appeared. "Big Billy, how's it going?"

"It's going." Billy kept his eyes trained on the conveyor belt and its parade of toys. He didn't need small talk right now. He needed to focus on his big speech.

Bald Art watched Billy work for a few moments. "I see you're hard at it, so I'll get right to it. I need to ask you about the missing seconds?"

Billy felt himself pale. All last week, he'd saved every damaged doll and soldier, bringing them home and hiding them in his toolbox in the garage.

"Why don't you turn off the machine, Billy?" Bald Art sounded like one of those TV hostage negotiators. When Billy ignored him, Bald Art reached out and knocked off the power himself.

"What are you at?" Billy said, annoyed.

Bald Art leaned over the conveyor belt, trying to get a good look at the empty seconds bin. Billy got an up-close view of Art's shaved head and its stud of black hair follicles. "There were no seconds for the entire week you were here, and then you went out sick yesterday and the seconds returned. Now you're back, and again there's none?"

Billy shrugged. "Does it matter?"

"What?" Bald Art asked, baffled.

"Does it matter where they go, as long as they don't go to packaging?"

"Well, of course it matters."

Why? Billy wanted to roar. And why was Bald Art going on about the seconds anyway? Didn't he know Michael was gone? Did he really think Billy gave a crap about anything after that, least of all the protocol for the correct disposal of the seconds? The seconds didn't matter, at least not to anyone except Billy now.

"Everything has to be accounted for," Bald Art said. "That's the issue, and right now everything can't be accounted for, can it?"

As hard as Billy tried to stop them, tears stung the back of his eyes. "No, everything can't be accounted for."

Bald Art's round cheeks reddened and he turned flustered.

"Well, now, that's all right. We just need to agree you're going to go back to how we've always done things. Right?" he finished, almost cheerful.

"Right. Absolutely." Billy just wanted this over with.

"Good. No sense in doing things different, is there? Not when the system works so well."

Billy smiled wryly. "Oh, I don't know, I've become a bit of a fan of doing things differently."

Bald Art's frown deepened. "I'm not sure I follow—"

"Don't worry about it. Now go on. I've heard you loud and clear."

"All right, then." Bald Art moved off, but right before he disappeared around the corner, he glanced back. He looked worried, as if afraid Big Billy might have lost more than his seventeen-year-old son.

Billy arrived at Lucy's desk, sweating and breathless. Lucy looked out over her thick glasses. "Did you take the stairs?" The silver neck chain drooping from her glasses shook as she spoke. "The stairs?" she repeated. He nodded, lying. She smiled. "Good man, keep it up." She suggested he drink green tea, too, great for the metabolism and full of antioxidants. He wasn't sure if she'd heard about his sponsored diet, or if she was just giving him unsolicited weight-loss tips, as so many others were prone to do. Either way, he couldn't listen straight.

"If I can do anything for you or your family, Billy, please say the word."

He nodded, his lips pressed together. She punched buttons on her desk console. "Billy's here."

"Send him right in." The crackle of Tony's voice sent a shiver through Billy. Lucy rolled her wrist and nodded encouragingly, ushering him forward. His hand dropped to his trousers pocket, feeling for the soldier. He pushed himself into Tony's office.

Tony came out from around his desk, his arm outstretched. He invited Billy to sit down, but then looked dubiously at the steel chair in front of his desk. He scanned his office, seeming to search for a couch that didn't exist, then looked at the floor, as if about to suggest they sit on the ruined orange-yellow carpet. Billy forced himself into the chair, trying not to grimace as its metal arms scraped over his hips.

"Oh, good," Tony said, sounding much too relieved. He returned behind his desk and dropped onto his swivel chair. He rotated the chair, left, right, left, right, his thumbs holding on to the edge of his desk. As Tony and the chair moved, Billy fought feelings of seasickness. He tried to focus on a spot on the desk, to stop the dizziness, and gasped at the nicotine-poisoned air. Tony often ignored the ban and smoked out his top-floor window, liking to think he was above everything and everyone.

Billy tried to stop breathing so loud. His rapid, wheezing noises sounded much worse than usual, like a car engine heaving to spark. He held his breath. His lungs filled. Filled and protested. Sweat gathered on his eyelids and the back of his neck.

"How are you ever since?" Tony asked.

"All right, yeah." Billy continued in a burst. "I have a bit of an unusual proposal."

Tony's expression jumped to guarded. "Is that right?"

"Yeah, the thing is, I've set a goal for myself, to lose two hundred pounds for charity, for suicide prevention."

Tony joined his hands prayerlike and tapped them against his mouth. When no further response came, Billy considered bolting, but pressed on. "It's in memory of Michael, obviously, and I was hoping the factory might match the donations that come in, euro for euro? It'd be great publicity all round, and it's for a great cause."

Tony pressed his pointer fingers hard to his lips. "Tell you what," he said at last. "I'll talk to my board members and get their take on it, yeah?" He raised his palms apologetically. "Don't get me wrong, part of me wants to say, yeah, absolutely, I'm most certainly sympathetic to the cause, and I'm happy to make a personal donation, but it's another story to involve the factory, especially in these recessionary times." He spread his hands wide, like a priest calling people to prayer. "I'm just being honest here, Billy; if you *don't* reach your goal, and the factory sponsored you, well, it's just awkward all round, you know?"

A shiver rose from the back of Billy's neck and over his scalp. He sat blinking, asking himself if Tony really had said all that. The bastard didn't believe he would succeed. Billy licked his lips, fighting the feeling he'd lost his voice. "I am going to reach my goal, I can promise you that. I'm giving this all I've got, because people are in serious trouble. Did you know there have been over five thousand known suicides in this country in the past decade alone?"

"I didn't actually—"

"There are now, like, ten suicides a week, and most of them are young men. If there was a serial killer knocking off that number of people, everyone would be up in arms, terrified they or theirs might be next, but the way it is right now, no one seems to care nearly enough."

"Hardly no one," Tony said.

"Yeah, okay, not no one, but most people don't seem to care nearly enough."

Tony seemed to squirm on his chair. "Well, I think it's that there's still a bit of . . . well, silence around it all."

Billy pushed back his temper. Before Michael, Billy hadn't known any better. Now it enraged him how people talked, and mostly didn't talk, about suicide. There was still so much stigma and ignorance—the persistent belief by too many that it was a sin, a crime, a sign of weakness, and something shameful to be hidden. He drew a deep breath. He needed to stay calm and stay the course. "My whole life I've never felt this way about anything. I know I'll see this through and that I can do a lot of good."

Pity oozed from Tony's small, dark eyes. "Fair play, that's all I can say. I wish you the best of luck."

"Is that a no?"

"I said I'd talk to my board."

"Yeah, thanks, thanks a lot." Billy pulled himself free of the squeeze of the metal chair with as much grace as possible.

On his way out, Lucy looked up from her desk and said something, but he couldn't hear her through the fog of temper.

Inside the elevator, he looked down at the floor and away from his exaggerated reflection in the silver doors, where he appeared ever more the freak.

That evening, Billy pushed back feelings of guilt and steered the car for home, reneging on his earlier plan to drive to the little-used cove outside the village for a long, brisk walk. He needed to go straight home and eat. He'd taken nothing since the limp salad in the canteen. Starting tomorrow, he would attempt at least a mile of the cove, five times a week.

He should at least place some phone calls tonight, to spread word of his diet and the march. Should put up flyers around the village this evening, too. He'd start with the two places boasting the most foot traffic—Caroline's shop and Kennedy's pub. He could get to the other places in the village and in town on the weekend.

As he neared home, he changed his mind again. He was too knackered to face Caroline or Ben Kennedy tonight. He would go home, eat, watch TV, and fall into bed. Maybe tonight he'd get his first decent sleep since Michael. He blared the radio to drown out the whispers of guilt and the pleas of his empty stomach. On the road up ahead, the wet spot shimmered.

Just last summer, when he was driving Michael someplace, to town, or a football game, or his guitar lesson, Michael had remarked on the optical illusion. He said how it was always getting away. A place like the horizon, he said, that you could never reach. At the time, it struck Billy how he'd seen that wet spot on the road all his life, but had never once thought about it, and here was his son making poetry out of the thing. It hit him now how wistful Michael had sounded, how full of yearning. He should have noticed that then. He should have said something.

The evening sun glared through the windscreen, its strength remarkable for the time of year. Billy fished his sunglasses out of the center compartment. He felt self-conscious in shades and rarely wore them, but this sun was blinding. He especially hated the pinch of the inevitable too-small frames on his large head. The day he'd bought the sunglasses, the salesman, with a smear of ginger hair on his chin, had said the Italian manufacturers smashed and repaired the glass, a process that made it stronger. Billy had liked the idea at the time, but now it maddened him. Why not make the glass strong enough in the first place?

He drove faster, his sunglasses tinting everything he passed in a sepia brown, as though the world were rotting.

Five

LATER THAT EVENING, BILLY ENTERED THE KITCHEN right as Tricia was closing the back door to Deveney. Billy startled. What now? Tricia ripped open the white envelope. The summons for Michael's inquest, Billy realized. She read it first, and handed it to him. Outside, Deveney's car peeled away. While Billy read, Tricia busied herself, dropping the fish into beaten egg and then dusting the slick fillets in flour. Michael's inquest would take place in two months' time, in Moran's Hotel, on the other side of town. Proceedings, in a courtroomlike setting, that would subject Billy and Tricia to the results of Michael's postmortem and the official ruling on his death.

Billy returned the summons to its now-jagged envelope. Moran's Hotel, and not the courthouse, that was something, at least. But there was still the undercurrent of criminality and victim blame to the whole thing—the police, the coroner, the ruling, the order to appear. It was the same with how people said *committed* suicide. As if suicide were a felony and not the last desperate act of someone out of his mind. He placed the summons in the drawer with the rest of the important documents. He wanted, instead, to rip it to pieces.

Michael's final night had fallen dark and chilly. Billy coasted home from the factory amid warnings of hazardous road conditions, and in particular black ice. He arrived into the kitchen, imagining himself safe, and headed straight to the fridge, looking in at everything illuminated and feeling the familiar disappointment. Tricia stood at the counter, preparing beef stew. In the living room, the children's eyes were locked on the TV.

Michael lay on the floor in front of the fire, his bare feet too close to the flames. Billy said, "Careful, there, Michael, or you won't be at the football for much longer." Michael was a star full forward, destined, everyone said, to someday bring home the Sam Maguire. Michael pushed his dark curls out of his eyes. "I'll be all right, don't you worry." Looking back, there was maybe something ominous in the boy's voice.

Tricia announced dinner would be ready soon and herded the four children upstairs to do homework. Michael filed out. Already six-foot and as tall as Billy, the boy stood broad and lean. He also boasted a chiseled face, gray-blue eyes, and a soft, full mouth. His chin was small and recessed, though, and his forehead too high, making his dark hair start too far back on his head. Handsome, some might say, without the burden of being too good-looking.

At dinner, Michael hadn't eaten much. A sick stomach, he'd said. Billy scoffed two helpings of the beef stew, eating fast, his other arm on the table as if guarding his plate. He'd also eaten Michael's dinner, unwittingly devouring his son's last meal. The memory made him sick.

No matter how many times Billy went over everything, there was nothing unusual about that night. Aside from Michael not eating and his saying he didn't feel well. Billy couldn't remember exactly what they'd all talked about around the table. They'd mentioned the weather and the chill that had felt like it was coming for them. Ivor said the full moon looked like a snowball.

"That's a big snowball, Vor," Michael said in his distinctive deep voice. He was the only one who ever called the boy Vor. "Let's hope it doesn't melt." Ivor laughed.

Billy didn't see Michael again that last night until after the football training. Michael returned home late, around eleven o'clock, and joined Billy, Tricia, and John in the living room. Anna and Ivor had long gone to bed. Michael brought in the smell of beer and Billy and Tricia exchanged a knowing look. They'd gotten the whiff off of him a few times over the previous few months and were choosing to turn a blind eye, unless he took to the stuff too hard.

Michael complained about the frozen pitch and how hard Molloy had worked them. John pulled himself from his TV trance and joined in the brief rant with his brother. Billy only half listened, intent on the screen, a rerun of the first-ever episode of *Father Ted*. Billy chortled when Mrs. Doyle scalded Father Ted with the tea.

"It's not that funny," John growled.

Michael remained silent, seeming lost in his own world. Billy howled again toward the show's end, when Father Ted sat trapped at the top of the Ferris wheel.

"You're ridiculous," John said, but he was laughing, too. Michael still seemed far away.

As soon as the show ended, Tricia ordered the pair up to bed. "Michael," she added, "you need to finish your college application. It's due next week." He had his sights set on UCD, to study agriculture. After he graduated, he would take over the farm from Billy's father, and someday inherit the lot.

"Don't worry," Michael said. "I'll take care of it." Had there been a dark edge to his words?

On his way out of the living room, Michael stubbed his toe on the foot of Billy's armchair. He hissed and yowled.

Billy gripped Michael's arm, wincing. "Ow, I felt that. Are you okay?"

Michael laughed through his discomfort. "I stubbed my toe, not you. You can't feel it."

"I can feel it, all right," Billy said, his face scrunched in sympathy.

"That's not a real thing, Dad."

If only Billy had continued the conversation, if he'd said something that might have made the difference. "Night" was all he'd said, his attention back on the TV.

"Night, Dad. Night, Mam," Michael said.

"Night, son, sweet dreams," Tricia said.

If only Billy had looked up at the boy. If he had seen the boy's pain wasn't just in his stubbed toe.

Did Michael know, when he said good night, that he would never see his parents again? That it was their last time together, just the three of them, as it was in the beginning, before John was born? If Michael did know, how, then, could he have left them with so little?

———

Ronin Nevin called in after dinner. He and Michael had been best friends, ever since they'd started school together, at four years old. He'd visited several times since Michael, to check on them.

The three sat at the kitchen table. Billy fought the urge to ask Ronin to get up off Michael's chair and sit anywhere else. It didn't help, either, that Ronin had the same height and build as Michael. The same dark hair and chiseled features. Red, pus-filled acne splattered Ronin's face, though, an affliction Michael had only endured briefly in his early teens. Also unlike Michael, Ronin's eyes were the dull brown of tree bark and his nose looked small and unfinished. He wasn't quite as quick with the wit and easy smiles, either.

Ronin's motorbike helmet and fat leather gloves sat on the table between them. Billy thought of bodiless parts. On the Internet, he'd read that most suicides hang themselves because they want to cinch at the neck and get away from their tormented minds.

Ronin had also received a summons to the inquest. "What are they going to ask me, like?"

Billy sad-smiled. "Don't worry, they won't drill you nearly as hard as we have."

"It's a formality," Tricia said. "We just have to get it over with."

The three stabbed at pleasantries and small talk, but the conversation came around to the same questions.

Ronin shifted on Michael's chair and shrugged. "I wish I had answers."

"You want someone, something, to blame, you know?" Billy said. *Aside from ourselves.*

"On my mother's life, he never said anything to me—" Ronin's voice cracked.

"What's going on with these young people?" Tricia said. "Every day now, nearly, you hear of another one."

Ronin's eyes darted to the floor. "Shocking."

"More needs to be done," Billy said.

As Tricia lifted the teapot from the center of the table, her hand brushed against Ronin's glove, bringing it to life. "Will you take another drop?"

"No, thanks." Ronin stood, making the legs of Michael's chair screech. "It's about time I got going. I've to run an errand for Mam in town."

"Thanks for calling in," Tricia said. "You're very good." She'd be thinking she didn't have Michael to run errands for her anymore. He had been a good lad like that. Obliging.

"I've something for you." Billy moved to the cabinet and removed the two manila folders. He handed Ronin a wad of flyers for his diet and the march, explaining.

"John mentioned it, all right," Ronin said, seeming a bit bewildered.

"I'm sure he did," Billy said darkly.

"I'll leave you to it," Tricia said, and moved up the hall.

"You'll help me spread word, then?" Billy asked. "It would mean a lot."

"Yeah, no bother."

Billy walked Ronin out the back door and over to his motorbike, a gleaming black beauty of a Honda 750. "Tricia was so worried when you got the bike, afraid you and Michael would get yourselves killed, racing over the roads."

Ronin laughed weakly. "She should have known he was no daredevil."

Billy winced. It came to him just how long and deep it had troubled him that Michael was so fearful. Fathers were supposed to make their children feel safe. Supposed to teach their children how to be brave. He looked over his shoulder at the back door and again at Ronin. "Between you and me, is there anything you're not saying, in front of Tricia, like? Anything you think would be too much for us to hear? Because we'd prefer to know the truth, whatever it is."

Ronin scraped at the gravel with his boot. "You know yourself the way. There's no story and every story going round. I've heard everything from he was destroyed with gambling debts to he owed money to a Romanian drug ring. I believe those stories about as much as I believe I'm black." He kicked at the gravel, scattering stones and dirt. "The only person with the answers is Michael. He didn't talk to me before, and he can't talk to me now. Something in him snapped, that's how I see it." He pulled on his helmet.

Beyond Ronin's grief, Billy heard the lad's hurt and anger. He understood how the boy would feel betrayed. Abandoned. A cold feeling came over Billy's lungs, as if someone had cut away the front panel of his chest. He pushed his hand into his pocket and curled his fingers around the toy soldier. "He thought of you like a brother, you know that, don't you?"

"Thanks," Ronin said.

"Are you doing all right?" Billy asked.

"I'll get there." Ronin's voice sounded muffled, and not just from his helmet.

"We'll see you long before the inquest, I'm sure?" Billy asked.

"Yeah, for sure," Ronin said.

Beyond Ronin, Billy could see only blackness. It looked as if his father's farm had been swallowed by the night. The whys rushed Billy again. Michael had had his whole life ahead and it promised to be a good and fine one. He had loved the farm and was set to inherit the lot when Billy's father retired. He would no doubt have also fallen in love, married, and had children. Children he would raise in a dream house he'd build on a site on the farm, just like Billy had. The boy could have had as close to happy-ever-after as it gets. But that was all gone now.

Ronin reached the gate and pulled out onto the road. He beeped in a farewell salute. Billy couldn't raise his arm to wave good-bye. He remained in the yard, picturing Michael on the bike behind Ronin, as in so many times before. As he still should be. What Billy would give to be riding on that bike instead of Ronin, with Michael on the seat behind him. He and Michael would feel as though they were flying, the wind ballooning their jackets, the rush of speed inside father and son flashing like the gleam of the moon off the bike.

Billy would drive and drive, never stopping for anything bad to happen.

Six

BILLY SET ABOUT PREPARING A STRAWBERRY SHAKE
for his breakfast. He whistled as he worked, trying to throw off
the bad mood that had lingered since yesterday and his meeting with Tony, and then the summons, and then Ronin's unsettling visit.

He beheaded the strawberries, sending greenflies racing
over the foliage. He pushed aside the impulse to crush the in-
sects and allowed them to live. John trudged in, his black hair
mussed and school tie undone. Billy looked at the empty space
behind John. He still expected Michael to appear.

Billy poured the seed-studded shake into a pint glass and
braced himself. Anna and Ivor asked if they could have some.
Billy laughed. "Trust me, you wouldn't like it." He raised the
glass toward his mouth, grimacing at the frothy concoction.
Pink bubbles popped like ungranted wishes.

"Ivor should go on a diet, too," Anna said, laughing. She
poked Ivor's stomach, her fingertip disappearing in the boy.

"Shut up," Ivor said, and laced his arms over his middle.

Billy grabbed Anna's elbow, making her ponytail swing. She scrunched her narrow face, more in outrage than in pain, and tried to pull away. He brought his face close to hers, her breath sweet and her blue irises darker with anger. "Don't ever say anything like that again to your brother, do you hear me?"

Anna freed herself and rubbed her stick arm, scowling. "I was only messing."

Billy tousled Ivor's dark curls. "You all right, son?" Ivor pulled away, wearing a glare that matched his sister's. "What's wrong with you?" Billy asked.

"Nothing," Ivor muttered. His face seemed to get rounder by the day. He was going to end up every bit as big as Billy if they weren't careful.

Ivor's scowl remained, as did the hurt in his eyes. Billy, full of yet another plan, moved to the back door. "I'm going to do my few laps of the yard. Why don't you keep me company, Ivor?"

"No way."

"A bit of exercise will do us both good. I've got my—" He stopped himself from saying *diet*. "My campaign, and you've got the walkathon coming up."

"I hate exercise."

"It's just a few rounds of the yard, you'll enjoy it, trust me," Billy said.

"I'm not going anywhere."

"How about we do one lap and then you can see how you feel?"

"I said no, I don't want to."

"One lap isn't going to kill you." Billy cringed at his choice of words.

"No, leave me alone." Ivor rushed from the kitchen and up the hall, leaving Billy standing at the back door, dragging his hand down his face. He was trying to do some good. Why was his own family making it so hard?

Billy left the factory at lunchtime, feeling ever more deflated. He had hoped Tony would have called him up to his office by now, to say he'd spoken with his board members and they'd decided to match donations. Maybe silence was Tony's answer. Billy had, at least, rescued two damaged dolls. He eased them into the glove compartment, to add to the growing collection of seconds he'd hidden in his garage. Despite Bald Art's threats, Billy had continued to bring home the doomed seconds, liking to feel he had power over their fates. That he was saving them.

He placed the soldier with the missing chin strap inside the cup holder, facing him. His stomach sounded its empty noises. He had felt starved within an hour of drinking the strawberry shake that morning and was one of the first to arrive at the canteen for lunch, while the peal of the bell hung in the air. Even after he'd finished the green salad and minestrone soup, he still felt dissatisfied. He wasn't just suffering the physical pain of hunger, either. There was something more. He felt what he could only describe as a grief for food, a keen sense of loss. For as far back as he could remember, food had been his one, unfailing constant.

He hoped the health shop could sort him. He needed

something to kill appetite, burn fat, and build muscle. He had thought to stop into the chemist's and see if Tricia could ask the pharmacist to recommend some pills or potions, but she'd remained cool toward him ever since he'd announced his public diet and the march. She wouldn't be pleased to see him arrive at her work, making noise about his needs in that regard. The pharmacist's expertise and family-and-friends discount weren't worth her wrath.

As soon as Billy entered the health shop, a young sales lad with spiked, peroxide hair pounced. "Can I help you?"

"I'm all right, thanks." Billy wasn't in the mood to explain himself. He needed to be back at work in fifteen minutes and wanted to get in and out. He scanned the shelves and the thousands of products on display. The rushed, frantic feeling worsened, as though he were on a TV game show and playing against the clock—his time running out fast.

The stuffy air and narrow aisles pressed on him. He took short breaths and hitched his shoulders, drawing himself in. A giant in the small space, he allowed himself only tiny movements, paranoid that a full breath or the wrong move would knock items off the crowded shelves and bring everything down around him. His stomach felt as though it were head-butting him. He needed to eat. To eat something substantial. Something that would keep the mouths in his stomach quiet.

He turned back to the lad. "Actually . . ."

The lad talked him through several products, swearing by the performance powder for killing appetite, burning fat, igniting energy, and building muscle. "Hey presto."

Billy chewed harder on a chocolate-flavored protein bar. This lad must be some optimist, to look from a can of powder to him and sing out, *Hey presto*. The breakfast shake had left him feeling famished within a couple of hours. What if it was the same with this "fuel"? He'd never survive. The youth waxed on, claiming he drank the concoction himself. He looked and sounded earnest enough. He also looked lean and strong and muscled.

Billy clapped his hands to his stomach. "I'm not sure there's any shake can satisfy this."

"How much weight are you planning to lose?"

"Two hundred pounds."

The lad's bleached head jerked backward. "Whoa, that's a lot."

"Yeah, tell me about it."

"Well, then, the shakes are the way to go, trust me." The lad rolled up his shirtsleeves and lifted the shirt's front. His impressive biceps bulged, but it was his stomach Billy couldn't pull his eyes from, the taut six-pack covered in colorful tattoos: a yellow moon; a woman's plump, bright red lips; an orange tabby curled in sleep; and written in an arc across the top of his rib cage, *Free Yourself*—each ice-blue letter inked inside a black circle, as if inlaid on the keys of an old-fashioned typewriter. The lad's large hand moved over the two words, his smile sheepish. "Yeah, everyone likes this one."

Billy looked down at the shop's linoleum floor, its mess of faded footprints like ghosts of themselves. Was that what Michael had imagined he was doing? Freeing himself?

Billy left the shop armed with two tubs of the performance powder. He spotted Patrick Keogh getting into his car. He called out to the older man and hurried toward him. Patrick and his wife, Rita, had lost their son a couple of years back, in the same way as Michael. Fergus had been twenty-one, and he'd made his end in Galway Bay. Patrick and Rita had attended Michael's funeral, and days later they sent holy medals and a book of prayers. Their card reassured Billy and Tricia that, as unthinkable as it might seem, they would get through even this. Life would never be the same, Rita wrote, but they would get through.

Patrick leaned against his car, his arms folded in front of him, and listened as Billy told him about his sponsored diet and planned march. Billy's voice trailed away. It was clear from the dangerous red of Patrick's puffed cheeks and the fiery look in his bog-brown eyes that he didn't like what he was hearing.

"To each his own," Patrick said. "But it wouldn't be for me."

"I don't understand," Billy said, confused, panicked. "I thought you, of all people, would get behind this?"

Patrick dropped into his car and slammed the driver's door closed. He spoke through the half-open window. "I won't thank you or anyone else to be reminded of any of it."

He sped away, leaving Billy standing on the street, his heart beating in his throat like slaps.

At his car, Billy fumbled with his keys, and they dropped to the ground. After a struggle, he picked them up. He closed his eyes, taking a second. He couldn't face going back to work. He was late now, anyway. He phoned the factory and took a half day. Tricia need never know.

At the cove, Billy sat on a large rock and changed his shoes, then set off down the strand in a brisk, arm-pumping stride.

From here on out, he would drink two of the performance shakes every day, one in the morning and one in the evening, and in between he'd enjoy a healthy lunch. *Hey presto*. Full of renewed determination, he pushed away thoughts of Patrick. He would succeed on all counts and lose his weight, save lives, and keep Michael's memory alive.

His phone rang. He pulled it from his pocket and checked the screen. His sister. He'd known this call was coming and marveled she'd taken so long.

"Where are you?" Lisa asked.

"I'm exercising."

She laughed. "You're exercising? Where?"

"At the cove." Too late, he realized he should have lied.

"You didn't have to work today?"

"I'm on a half day."

"The cove. Jesus. You could collapse down there and no one would ever find you," Lisa said.

"Yeah, I'm not planning on doing that, thanks, and I'd prefer if you didn't say anything about this to Tricia."

"Yeah, okay." She sounded confused. "Listen . . ."

Here we go.

"I heard about your diet and the march." Her voice sounded a rare state of nervous. "You do realize what that's doing to Mam and Dad?"

He gripped his phone hard. "Yeah, I don't want to talk about this, Lisa. It's a done deal."

"We need to talk about it, Billy. Mam and Dad aside, I'm worried this diet and march are going to be too much for you, and not just physically, either."

"What's that supposed to mean?"

"All that public pressure, William, you're taking on way too much." She knew he hated her to call him William. "Have you checked with a doctor?" she went on. "Made sure it's safe to even attempt something like this?"

"Your concern is touching, really, but I need to go. I was about to burst into a sprint there when you called."

"Lookit, I'll be down at the weekend, let's talk then, yeah? Meanwhile, why don't you hold off on all this?"

"Like I said, it's a done deal."

"So you've already contacted the Samaritans? Cleared it with them?"

"Why would I clear it with them? Aren't I going to give them money? Nobody says no to money."

Her breath huffed through the phone. "You've already put it out there that you're doing this for charity without first talking to someone? There are procedures to these things." She sighed again. "Do you want me to phone them for you?"

"No, that's all right. I'll get my secretary to take care of it—"

"There's no need for sarcasm. I'm only trying to help. I'll be down at the weekend, let's talk then."

"There's nothing to talk about. If you really want to help, you can make a nice big donation." He looked at the unreachable horizon, an illusion like the distant wet spot on the road. Its reminder of the impossible, of the conversations he'd never had with Michael, tormented.

"Billy? Are you listening?"

He fake-panted into the phone. "I'm jogging now, building up to a run, going to break the speed record—"

"Yeah, it won't take much to break your speed record."

"I thought you weren't a fan of sarcasm."

"Lookit, Billy, you can't just ignore how hard this is going on Mam and Dad—"

"This isn't about them, sorry."

"Would you listen?" she snapped. "You know how private they are, how heartbroken. Do you really want everyone's eyes on them again, especially if this goes amuck—"

He turned off his phone and shoved it into his pocket. That's all he needed, Lisa swooping in. She would come down on the weekend and try to take over. Tell him everything she thought he was doing wrong. *If this goes amuck.*

Despite his earlier determination, and the magnificence of his surroundings—white-crested waves and a sea and sky so blue they seemed more cinematic than real—his willpower faded and his ankles and knees felt filled with broken glass. He turned back.

Clumps of sea foam skittered about his feet and tumbled over the dark sand. The same feeling came over him as when children sent up soap bubbles—that urge to catch the strange lovely thing and hold it in your hands. He grabbed at the rounds of foam but the wind repeatedly lifted them out of reach. This was a game he should have played with Michael, to ease the boy into feeling safe around water. Michael would have imagined the rolls of foam were tiny footballs and delighted in the chase. Once they were caught, the boy would marvel at how the sunlight lent the foam so much color, making the bubbles look like round, miniature rainbows.

Billy squeezed his eyes shut. He wanted Michael back. Wanted time back. He would give anything. His eyes flew open and his breath left him in a burst. He dived once more at the rolling foam, but wasn't fast enough. From the rocks, seagulls squawked like scornful spectators. He straightened, giving up the pitiful chase, and limped to his car, his right ankle crippling him.

Inside the Corolla, from the squeeze of the broken driver's seat, he stared out at the sea, tracking its swell and crash. It made him feel a little better, shrinking before the ocean's staggering size and might.

Billy took the long way home, coming at the small woods from the opposite direction and avoiding the village altogether. He walked the now-familiar path through the band of trees, shafts of sunlight shining through the branches. Inside the clearing, he stared at the tree, at the branch Michael had used, as if they might reveal something new. He had returned here several times since that day in January when he'd insisted Sergeant Deveney show him where, exactly. Tricia had visited only once, on the day after Michael left them, and swore she'd never return. "I can't think of him like that."

The noise of a bird somewhere overhead startled Billy. It sounded like a phone ringing in the sky. His hand curled around the base of the branch that had taken Michael. Why here? Why this tree, a *beech* tree? Why no note, no signs, no sense? Why? Patrick Keogh's furious face annoyed his head. *To each his own. But it wouldn't be for me.* Fuck Patrick. All the naysayers. If everyone kept looking away. If no one ever tried to bring about change. He wasn't going to stop. Wasn't going to back down. He would save lives in Michael's name. Make Michael's life and death matter.

Fired up, he searched the ground for a rock. The tree had

claimed his son and in return he wanted to lay claim to it. He picked up a hand-sized, jagged stone. It was warm from the sun, its edges sharp against his palm. He set on the tree, hacking at the bark, to punish and scar it. Above him, the branches trembled and the leaves sighed. He felt movement in his chest, stirrings that mirrored the tree's sway. Something loosened inside him.

As his anger leaked out, his cuts at the trunk took shape, carving out Michael's initials. MLB. Next, he etched a circle around the letters. He worried the circle could be mistaken for a noose and set on the tree again. He cut lines like rays of sunshine.

Finished, he reached his finger into the carved trunk and traced the initials. *Michael Liam Brennan*. With a start, he realized Michael's initials read backward could stand for *Billy Loves Michael*. His skin broke out in bumps. He touched his forehead to the cool of the trunk, his fingers hooked to those three letters inside the sun.

Seven

THE NEXT DAY, TEMPTATION WAS EVERYWHERE. Billy surveyed its latest lure in the tea shop window, his eyes fastening on the fat éclair. His mouth wetted with the memory of jam, fresh cream, hard, thick chocolate, and sweet puff pastry. Just one bite and the pleasure. The relief. The comfort. How much harm could one little éclair do? He dragged himself past.

Rain needled his nose and cheeks, the clouds bleeding into gray-black and their spill falling sideways. Impossible from here, but he swore he could smell the tantalizing waft from Seanseppe's. Thoughts of hot chips smothered in creamy, spicy curry sauce made him almost buckle with longing. A young lad approached on the footpath, wearing white earbuds, his head bopping in time to the music—another of the simple, countless pleasures Michael would never again enjoy. The lad shot him an angry look. *What's your problem?* Billy hurried on as best he could, his body in bits from his attempts at exercise.

He arrived at the stationery shop, breathless. The dim,

musty space boasted a bigger turnover in staff than it did in its tired, dated stock, but he liked to support small businesses. The cashier stood slouched behind the counter, a mobile phone held close to his face. The light of its screen lent his dark cheeks and forehead a bluish tint. The lone customer nodded at Billy and exited, a white-haired man with a broad build and a spring in his step that made Billy think of his father. He was whistling the tune to some ballad Billy recognized but couldn't name. Billy removed the two flyers from his back trousers pocket and moved toward the rear of the shop. The cashier seemed oblivious, enthralled with whatever game he was playing on his phone.

It took several trial runs with various paper weights, and many paper jams later, but Billy succeeded in copying the pledge sheet and the flyer for the march onto the thickest, most durable paper possible. As the machine spat out the copies, he placed the failed pages into the recycling bin, glad they would get another go-around. He watched the clock. He would never make it back to the factory and his conveyor belt in time. He was pushing his luck, and right when he wanted to keep favor with Tony and Bald Art and not cause any more waves. He needed the factory's sponsorship. He also needed to keep saving the seconds.

His jaw locked. Bald Art had made such a stupid, unnecessary fuss about the missing seconds. So what if Billy was taking them home? They were going to be dumped anyway. Billy had thought of Bald Art as a friend. So much for that. His mood hardened. Bald Art needed to keep out of his business. He'd been messed with enough already.

The copier finished, he plucked the stack of sheets from the tray and hurried toward the cash register. Michael's photograph stared up from the warm bundle. Billy thought of a *Wanted* poster and Michael's upcoming inquest. He'd give anything not to have to go. Would give anything to spare Tricia from it, too, but nothing would make her miss it.

"Of course I'm going," she'd told him. "How could I not?" Her fear, and her anger at a heartless legal system that was putting them through all this, had felt like something live in the air between them. He suspected her crackling rage was also aimed at Michael, but he doubted she'd ever admit as much to herself, let alone to him or anyone else.

At the register, Billy reached into his back pocket for his wallet. The cashier lifted the stack of copies, about to place them inside a brown bag.

"Any chance you'd put a couple of these in your window?" Billy asked. "It's for a good cause."

The cashier scanned the paperwork. "Handsome boy."

"Yes, he was." Sweat fastened Billy's shirt to his back. He pictured large, dark animal shapes. A hippo. An elephant. A raging bull.

"He your son?"

"Yeah, got his looks from his mother, obviously."

The cashier's dark finger jumped back and forth between Michael and Billy's pixilated faces. "I see you in him." Pain filled Billy's throat like food he couldn't swallow.

The cashier removed a flyer from the top of each stack, promising to put them in the front window. Billy thanked him and paid, tucked the thick brown bag under his arm. As he walked out, the cashier called after him, a five-euro note held between two fingers and his face split with a large smile. "Good on you, Big Billy."

Billy accepted the money, a warm feeling spreading through him. "Thank you . . . ?"

"Ajadi."

"Ajadi," Billy repeated, liking the feel of the name in his mouth. His stomach growled. "Thank you, Ajadi." He left the shop, savoring the thrill of having impressed someone.

After a bland dinner of brown rice, steamed vegetables, and a broiled chicken breast, Billy placed the flyers inside two manila folders and prepared to leave the house, his head full of Michael's initials in the tree.

"Where are you going?" Tricia asked.

"To put up flyers around the village."

"You're going ahead with it, then?"

"Why are you so dead set against this?" he asked. "I'm trying to save lives, in Michael's name."

"Why does it have to be you? Can't you let someone else take it on?"

"I want it to be me. I want to do good."

"What about what I want? What the rest of your family wants?"

"What do you want?"

"I'll tell you what I don't want. I don't want Michael, everything, to be about suicide now. Tell me you can understand that?"

"Everything *is* about suicide now."

"Please," she said. "You need to stop all this, if not for me or your parents, then for the children's sakes. They need things to get back to some kind of normal around here, and the sooner the better."

She sounded as though she were being tortured. That hurt Billy in a way that was new, in a way he didn't know you could ache. "I'm sorry," he told her. "I can't turn back. Nothing has ever felt so right. If all I do is help save even one life in Michael's name and spare another family from what we're going through, wouldn't that be something?"

She searched his face, her eyes filling. "Yeah, of course it would, but it's the way you're going about it all, it's not right."

"Listen to me. I need you to believe I'm going to see this through, and that it's good and right. I'm not going to fail, not this time, I promise."

They locked eyes. He reached out and touched his fingertips to her cheek, and then dropped his hand to clasp the side of her neck. He could feel the beat of her pulse against his palm. Her hand reached up and covered his. She leaned her head to the side, resting her jaw on his wrist. He drew her to him. As he bent to kiss her, she bowed her head and his lips landed on her forehead, at her hairline. He tasted pear shampoo and her salt.

She stepped toward the kettle. "Do you want a cup of tea?"

"No," he said, his voice pinched with longing and disappointment. "I don't want tea."

Billy set out from his yard, about to haul himself and his sore ankle over the six hundred yards to the village. At his gate, he looked down the long road and wondered if this was all too much too soon. Dr. Shaw had said to start small and go easy. What if his efforts killed him before his weight did? He started out, forcing one foot in front of the other. He couldn't delay any longer. Every second of every day, lives were at stake.

As he walked, the pain in his ankle marked every excruciating step. His right hand held the memory of the rock yesterday. He could see the tree trunk and Michael's initials inside his best attempt at a sun with bright rays. He hadn't recovered from what he'd made of Michael's initials spelled backward. Locals drove past at speed, waving and beeping. The shock they must feel, seeing him walk to the village. He continued, his massive body going from side to side to the sound track in his head. *Mi-chael, Mi-chael.*

He arrived at the shop, almost bent double with the sharp stitch in his side and the agony of his ankle. He leaned against the whitewashed wall to recover. With his cardigan sleeve, he wiped his face and the back of his neck. He could taste more salt on his upper lip. He glanced through the window. Caroline was sitting at her usual station next to the cash register, leaning over the glass counter and scratching at a Lotto card, longing written all over her face.

He had aimed his visit for closing time in the hopes of finding her alone. Any earlier and there would have been a near-constant flow of people in and out, the bell over the door jangling repeatedly: a stranger in to pay for petrol; the delivery of fresh breads and tarts; tourists and foreign nationals needing directions; and the trickle of locals in for whatever staple they had run out of at home. Caroline never appeared to enjoy a minute alone, at least not until the shop door closed at night and she retreated into the house upstairs. There, she seemed to have only the company of the walls, her black cat with the white blind eye, and the TV images flickering across the building's top window like ghosts.

His breathing and pain eased. He entered the shop.

"Ah, it's yourself." Caroline nodded at the scratched Lotto card in her hand. "I won five euro."

"Nice." He removed both flyers from their folders and spoke in a rush. "Speaking of money . . ."

When he finished, Caroline pulled her glasses off her face, leaving two red indentations on either side of her nose. "Well, I never," she said, stunned.

"Someone has to do more than what's being done right now." His voice cracked.

"There's no one doing anything like this, anyway."

"Aren't I all the talk already?" he said, bristling. "I might as well go all-out."

Her cheeks bloomed red. "Now, now, there's no need to be like that, it's just that it's a bit unusual, is all." She brightened. "How about this? I'll give you a flat pledge of fifty euro, would that be all right?"

"Fifty euro is excellent, thanks."

"Very good. And we'll put these right here for everyone to see." She reached for the tape dispenser and attached both flyers to the glass counter next to the cash register. He thanked her again, giddy with success, and turned to go.

Her words stopped him. "It takes a big man to do something like this, no pun intended. Fair play to you." They nodded at each other, the gesture less of a good-bye and more of a salute.

Billy hobbled across the road to Kennedy's, trying to ignore the pain in his right ankle. Above him, stars strained to shine in the pale sky. He stopped at the corner of the redbrick pub and wrapped his hand around the soldier in his coat pocket. It was going to be a lot harder to make his pitch to Ben Kennedy, the man deaf as well as ignorant. It wasn't going to help, either, that everyone in the place would look on and listen. Caroline's parting words repeated in his head, bolstering him. He pushed himself toward the thatched pub, its double wooden doors scarred and flaking, as weathered as so many of the lives beyond them.

Inside Kennedy's, the few punters sitting about looked over at Billy and away again, their expressions empty. He understood their mix of curiosity and hope every time the door opened, something similar to his expectations whenever he looked into the fridge. Only a handful of people dotted the place. It was hard to believe pubs were dying out all over the country. Who would ever have predicted?

He stopped cold. Sergeant Deveney sat slumped at the bar, off-duty and already drunk. The thought of Deveney cutting Michael down from the tree made Billy's head feel as if it were floating. Even before Michael's death, Billy would have crossed the road to avoid Deveney. The man gabbed nonstop about himself and his supposed exploits, talking shite about collaring criminals on a regular basis with Bond-like ease. The eejit. But now Billy's disgust went way beyond Deveney's noise. He couldn't bear to as much as think of the sergeant, let alone be in his company.

He would never forgive Deveney for not sending for him that morning. To think Billy was lying warm and dreamy in his bed while just a few hundred yards away Deveney was supervising the removal of Michael's body. The boy had fallen into the arms of a paramedic, a total stranger, when he could have met the arms of his own father. How Billy would have held Michael. Rocked him. Begged him to come back.

Billy pretended not to see the sergeant and moved to the other end of the bar. There, he waited for Ben Kennedy to make his way over. When Ben finally deigned to serve him, the publican sounded as sour as he looked. "What'll you have?" Billy ordered a fizzy diet orange. "That's akin," Ben said, "to going to the doctor and asking for sweets instead of tablets."

Thumbs Tom, his eight stub fingers all the same size as his thumbs, laughed from a nearby table. "That's a right one. Sweets instead of tablets." He resumed his annihilation of a bag of peanuts, popping a load into his mouth and sucking the salt off his stub fingers. Billy's stomach kicked at him, hungry, and so soon after dinner, too.

Ben placed the bottle of orange and a glass clouded with soap residue on the counter.

"I'll take some ice, too," Billy said.

"Ice?" Ben said, as if Billy had asked for fire.

"Correct."

As Ben shuffled to the ice bucket, Billy made the mistake of glancing back at Thumbs Tom, the man working his stunted trigger finger over the mashed peanuts stuck to his gums. After a quick inspection, Thumbs Tom returned the wet mush to his mouth and swallowed. Billy gagged. Ben slapped the cloudy glass back on the counter, two miserly ice cubes inside. Billy gathered his courage and launched his stuttering spiel. As he spoke, Ben cocked his head to the left in that irritated way of the hard of hearing.

"What's that?" Ben said, forcing Billy to start over and raise his voice ever louder.

"Mother of God, Big Billy," Thumbs Tom said. "You'll be on one of those reality TV shows yet."

Kennedy pointed to the notice board over by the men's toilets. "Stick them up there," he said. Billy moved to the bulletin board with as much grace as he could muster. He felt people watching.

The notice board was a smother of business cards and flyers, advertising everything from massages, babysitters, day care, art classes, walking tours, and more. Billy pinned his two flyers dead center. He turned away, eager to drag himself and his sore ankle home, but his full bottle of orangeade called to him, consolation promised in its sweet fizz and the false sense of fullness it might give him, if only for a short while.

Just as Billy enjoyed a long, cold swig, Sergeant Deveney lifted his half-full pint from the counter and stumbled toward him. *Stay away*, Billy thought. *Stay the hell away*.

Deveney hooked his arm around Billy's neck. "Big Billy," he slurred. "Oh, Jaysus, Billy." He swayed, his head and shoulders dropping forward and rearing backward, almost pulling Billy down on top of him.

"Whoa." Billy dug his good heel into the sticky pub floor, trying to steady himself and Deveney both. Deveney, his head shaking and his eyes squeezed shut, wore the anguished look of someone trying not to remember. He mumbled through ale-wet lips, repeating *terrible* and looking about to keel over, his hand rubbing at the front of his shirt as if he'd spilled drink on himself. Billy pressed his hand to Deveney's chest. "Stop, man, and stand straight, can't you? Cut out your messing."

"Your boy. Your poor boy." Deveney jerked his head toward his shoulder, his eyes staring wide, his tongue sticking out.

Billy shrugged Deveney off, letting out a roar. "What are you at?"

The policeman shook his head, stumbling, mumbling. "No one should have to see that."

Billy slammed his glass down on the counter and grabbed the front of Deveney's shirt. "Don't you ever mention my son again from that morning, do you hear me? Not to me, not to anybody, or by God I swear I can't be held accountable for what I'll do to you." He pushed Deveney away and wiped his hands on the front of his coat.

Kennedy, everyone, stared. Billy, quaking, delivered a final hateful look at Deveney and turned to leave. Deveney lurched forward, as if about to hug Billy, his leaden movements channeling a zombie. "Get away." Billy pushed again at Deveney's front and rushed for the door, his insides quivering and his right ankle feeling as though it would shatter.

He arrived home, the excruciating walk fueled by rage, and struggled into his car. He sped to town in record time. From there, he continued for miles. Then stopped at a chip shop that seemed far enough away. He couldn't risk being seen by anyone he knew.

He parked out front and remained behind the familiar press of the wheel, rage coursing through him. As soon as the chipper emptied, he hurried inside as fast as his bad ankle and tree trunk legs would allow.

"What you want?" the Polish server asked.

Deveney's grotesque pose filled Billy's mind, the policeman's head tilting toward his shoulder, his eyes wide and glazed, his tongue hanging out.

The server spoke again, his impatient voice ringing inside the small shop. "What you want?"

Billy stemmed the roars that wanted to escape him. Roars

to turn back time, to before Michael, before Tricia, before Billy had buried himself in his body. That was how far back he'd have to go, to fix everything.

He ordered enough food to make a lesser man burst. While he waited, two girls entered the shop. About fourteen, they wore that furious, insolent look that seemed particular to their generation. After they ordered, they kept glancing over at Billy and whispering together.

After several minutes, a middle-aged woman in a shiny navy tracksuit appeared in the doorway. Much like Billy's tracksuits, the two stripes on the sides of her polyester pant legs had turned a dirty white. With her matching orange-blond hair and thin black eyebrows, she was obviously the taller girl's mother. "What's taking so long?" The girls sauntered over to the woman. "It's fatso's fault," her daughter muttered.

The three whispered together, a sound that mimicked sandpaper at work. Billy called to the server, the man hidden in the back, cooking Billy's huge order. "Can you hurry up, please?"

Billy parked inside the vast bog. Fields and fields of peat, where nothing ever decayed, everything was preserved. Soil that saved. Alone in the dark, he devoured the chips with shaky hands, each hot, succulent chunk gritty with salt and drenched with sharp vinegar. Next, the spice burger with its crunchy outer coat of bread crumbs, and the lush, soft inside of beef, onions, herbs, and spices. The two pieces of battered cod he pushed into him also, the oil smearing his chin and hands. He moaned out loud with pleasure.

He worked his way through the box of chicken, more oil

and bread crumbs and herbs and spices. He felt disgusting now. Loathed himself now. He ate faster, barely chewing, barely breathing. Not even tasting. *Get it into you, you fat fucker, you.* Between mouthfuls, he gulped the chilled Coca-Cola, a shock to his teeth after the heat of the food. Nothing, though, could stop the server's voice going off inside his head. *What you want?*

As a boy, ever since he'd set about burying the wrong son inside himself, his parents, everyone, had harped at him to stop eating so much. He hated how others thought they knew when he'd had enough. He never felt he had enough. Not even when Michael was alive had he ever felt he had enough. If Michael were to come back right this second, even then he didn't think he would feel he had enough. He brought the side of his fist down hard on the dashboard, making the contents of the glove box rattle. What the fuck was wrong with him?

Eight

BILLY STRUGGLED ONTO THE UPTURNED DIRTY-white bucket used to slop cows. He grabbed at the rope hanging from the rafters and pulled the noose over his head, its fray hard and itchy against his neck. He couldn't breathe right. He stepped off the bucket, letting out a wretched sound. The rope broke. He tried again, and again, but every time he stepped from the bucket, the rope broke.

Michael watched from the straw-strewn floor in the corner, his back pressed against the barn wall and his arms clasped around his knees. He struggled up from the ground, shaking his head and wiping the straw from the back of his jeans. He moved toward Billy, his arm reaching for the noose. "Here, Dad, let me show you."

Billy awoke with a gasp. His skin wet. The sheets wet. He felt a sharp pain in his chest and pressed his palm to his heart, afraid he was having an attack. He'd had a bad dream. That was all. He breathed in and out, the tension in his body starting to loosen, the pain in his chest subsiding. He was all right.

Or maybe he wasn't. He could still taste the vinegar and cold grease from last night's pig-out. The server's voice chased him. *What you want?* The image of Deveney stumbling and mumbling inside Kennedy's, and the appalling pose he'd struck, also knocked about Billy's skull. That Ben Kennedy, too, treating Billy like he was some kind of imbecile. And Thumbs Tom's crack, about Billy being on reality TV. Ha, ha.

Billy's thoughts quickened. What if he did go on TV? Not in a reality series, but in a documentary about suicide and its aftermath? A vein in his jaw pulsed. What if he made the documentary himself? If he got those left behind after suicide on camera, to let people know the pain. The horror. The senselessness. Along with his fund-raiser and the march, a documentary would really get the nation's attention, and could save countless more lives.

He pushed himself off the bed and put on his trousers. When his hand glanced the soldier, the rush left him and that awful ache set in. He removed the toy and moved his thumb back and forth over its painted face. Some part of him half expected the tiny fella to come alive.

Billy flinched when he heard Lucy's voice crackle over the speakers—an announcement about a car blocking the loading dock. He breathed a sigh of relief. All day he'd waited with dread for her to summon him to Tony's office. If Tony called him into his office today, to give him a yes or a no on matching donations, either way Billy would feel ever more terrible about his epic fail at the chip shop. His stomach cramped.

He'd only allowed himself three performance shakes throughout the day and hoped to go for a long, hard walk after work, too, but his body was deteriorating fast. His head felt like it would split from the pain. He also felt faint and shaky. More than his hunger and the lack of sleep, though, his efforts at exercise had really messed with his body. He felt beaten up.

A stomach-staple operation would be so much easier than all this torture. That would feel like cheating, though. Besides, he doubted people would donate nearly as much money if he lost his weight due to surgery and not sheer determination. Then there was the expense of the operation. Money they didn't have. They hadn't taken out life insurance on the children. Hadn't wanted to ever consider it. His stomach cramped again.

He squatted over the toilet bowl, the fruit-filled shakes running through him. The bathroom door groaned open. Embarrassed, he clenched and wiped hard at himself, even though he didn't feel finished.

As soon as the room cleared, he exited the stall and washed his hands in a rush, eager to leave before anyone else joined him. Too late; the bathroom door again made its eerie noises, bringing in Denis Morrissey and his toothsome smile. The men exchanged nods and Denis unzipped. "How's everything going?"

Billy tried to sound upbeat. "All right, thanks."

If Denis noticed a smell, he didn't let on. "Did I see you have a bit of a limp?"

Billy mentioned his attempt at exercise. "The will's there but the body's not cooperating."

"Take your time and go easy on yourself, Rome wasn't beaten in a day."

Billy laughed at the familiar phrase made strange. He watched Denis wash his hands, going at them again like he would never get them clean enough. The sound of water returned Billy to the rain on the day they had buried Michael, his son's coffin disappearing beneath the shovels of wet dirt. His ears filled with a high-pitched sound.

"Are you all right?" Denis asked.

Billy, dizzy, clammy, reached for the tile wall.

Denis gripped Billy's elbow. "Whoa, there. Do you need to sit down?"

Billy blinked back the blur of dizziness. His heart chugged and his empty stomach sounded its death rattles. He pressed his hands against the cool tile and lowered his head between his arms.

"Should I get help?" Denis asked.

"No, I'm all right." Moments passed, Billy blinking, breathing. Just as he thought he felt a little better and they could both get back to work, the words spilled out. "I'm afraid I'm not able for all this—that I won't lose the weight and I'll let myself, everyone, down."

Denis patted Billy's back, sticking his shirt to his skin. "You don't have to go this alone, you know. There's plenty of groups you can join."

Billy shook his head. He'd already tried group meetings over the years. All that measuring and counting calories, the constant talk of food, recipes, and cheat tips—he'd left feeling ravenous, and even worse about himself. He'd hated, too, how he was always the biggest one there and how all the others had looked at him with either fear or relief, and sometimes even delight. *At least I'm not as bad as him. He makes me look good. Please, God, don't let me end up like him.* The sweat oozed from Billy. He couldn't attend a meeting with a bunch of smaller versions of him and listen to everyone go on about how hungry they felt, how deprived, how guilty. All that and still they'd be thinking how much better off they were than him.

"What about Overeaters Anonymous?" Denis asked. "There have to be OA meetings here in town—"

Billy shook his head again. "Stop, please."

"Come on, what's the harm in trying?" Denis said. "I've been a member of AA for ten years and I swear by the group meetings and the Twelve Step program. OA uses the Twelve Steps, too, I'm sure, and they work for practically everyone."

Fresh hope came over Billy. His vision cleared and his head stopped reeling. Denis might be on to something.

The doors to St. Michael's Church were locked. Billy again rattled the handles, hoping. He looked up and down the street, for someone to ask for information. He'd searched the Internet and had driven fifty miles to find this Alcoholics Anonymous meeting, hoping to ensure he didn't run into anyone he knew. If AA could help alcoholics of every make, shape, size, and color, then surely it could help other kinds of holics, too.

He checked the doors again. He needed this meeting. Needed to get inside the church and out of sight. How would he explain himself if he was caught? That would really set tongues wagging. *He's addicted to the drink as well as the grub.*

He heard voices, and followed the chatter, taking him around the side of the church and into an open courtyard.

People stood talking and laughing, smoking and holding paper cups. He scanned the group, but was half blind with fear and couldn't take in their faces. Behind them, the door to a long, whitewashed annex stood open. He pushed on through the courtyard.

The large, crowded annex appeared to be a dining room, with its high ceiling, low-hanging brass chandeliers, and the banquet tables pushed against the walls. Despite the number of people sitting about on metal chairs—there had to be seventy or more—Billy's eyes went straight across the room to the woman sitting behind the desk, her back to the oversized fireplace and its thick wooden mantel. He pushed himself toward her.

"Do I need to sign in?" he asked, his voice faint.

"This your first time?"

He nodded.

"Nora," she said. He nodded again, unable to get his name out. She pointed to a table next to the doorway. "You'll find all the literature over there."

He hesitated. "Take a seat anywhere you like," she said. He moved to the empty back row and dropped onto a chair next to the aisle. It was only after he sat down that he realized he'd chosen the seat farthest from the exit.

Nora appeared next to him. "We have a little kitchen in the back, feel free to help yourself to tea or coffee and . . ."—she blushed—"and biscuits, if you want. Come on, I'll show you."

He followed her into the next room, filling with fresh fear over meeting someone he knew.

A handful of people stood about the small kitchen, fixing

hot drinks and side plates of biscuits. He reached for a green tea bag, glanced at the shortbread treats, and turned away. After a struggle, he succeeded with the lever on the hot water dispenser, identifying much too much with the scalded tea bag.

He returned to his seat just as Nora called the meeting to order. He couldn't make out her words, she was speaking so low. Every so often the group responded in a loud chorus, making him flinch. He couldn't make out their response, either. *Aye*, perhaps? He seemed to be the only person in the room who hadn't a clue what was going on. What was he doing here? This was a mistake. He was nothing like these people.

The man seated next to Nora said, "Hi, I'm Tim—"

"Hi, Tim." The room's loud chorus again startled Billy.

"I'm an alcoholic. January fifteenth, 1995."

The woman next to Tim spoke, "Hi, I'm Claire—"

"Hi, Claire."

On and on it went, up and down the rows. Billy understood the drill by now, but couldn't get out the words to join the refrain. The introductions moved closer and closer, a line of gunpowder on fire. He wanted to run out of the room but couldn't stand up. When his turn came, he looked at Nora, his eyes pleading, and shook his head. She frowned. He nodded to the woman next in line.

"Hi, I'm Teresa . . ."

Several in the group stared at Billy, some looking confused, others disturbed. He bowed his head and cupped his hot green tea, grateful to have something to hold on to.

The introductions at last over, Nora invited questions and discussion. One young lad said he'd joined AA two years ago. The way he pushed his dark hair out of his eyes and pulled on the tip of his nose conjured Michael. He said he could never have imagined all the good that had come into his life with sobriety. "I'm free now."

The middle-aged man with a flattened nose and cauliflower ear said his sponsor had repeated the same advice in his early days of sobriety: "Don't drink. Go to the meetings." He'd wanted to punch his sponsor, he admitted, but it had turned out to be the best advice of his life. Billy wondered what advice, what help, might have changed everything for Michael.

The meeting ended at last. On his way out, Billy risked a quick stop at the literature table, eager to know the famous Twelve Steps. They worked for everyone else, so why not him? As he grabbed at the paperwork, Nora reappeared, asking if he'd found himself a sponsor. When he admitted he hadn't, she took his elbow. "Let's introduce you to Tracy, she's wonderful."

He pulled his arm free. "I'm sorry, I don't think I'm ready for this."

Someone clapped his back. He spun around, facing another overweight man—his size nothing next to Billy. "Hey, you're new," the stranger said. "You looked pretty tense sitting over there, you okay?"

To Billy's horror he heard himself say, "I'm terrified."

The man hugged him, the intimacy stunning Billy. They pulled apart and the man's hands remained on the tops of Billy's beefy arms. "Don't be terrified. We're all friends here, family. You're in the right place, trust me."

Billy allowed himself the fleeting belief that at last he had found someplace where he belonged. Where he could be saved.

———

Billy quick-stepped free of the church annex and hurried onto the street.

"Mr. Brennan?" A pale, waifish girl stepped toward him, her black coat covered in apricot dog hairs. Her own long, wind-swept hair was several shades lighter, a yellow-blond. She looked vaguely familiar, and then, with a tiny jolt, Billy recognized her. She was one of the last girls Michael had dated. At the funeral, she had shaken Billy's hand and said, "I'm so sorry, Michael was lovely, he really was." Billy had held back on the usual firm handshake he would give, and not just because she'd seemed so bony and brittle. What she'd said had weakened him.

"Sarah," she said. "I was a friend of Michael's."

"Yes," he croaked. "I remember." She glanced behind him to the open door of the annex and the people pouring out. "Do you live around here?" he said, to distract her. She explained she lived in town and was out this far to see a friend. The em-barrassed way she said "friend" made him realize she was visit-ing a boyfriend. He felt what he knew was a ridiculous spark of annoyance, as though she were somehow cheating on Michael.

He rolled the AA pamphlets into a cylinder, trying to appear unfazed. Another jolt went through him. He and little Michael would make toy telescopes from rolled sheets of paper whenever they played army with the seconds soldiers. Michael would look through his paper tube and with great theatrics shout, "The cav-alry is coming! The cavalry is coming!" Billy's heart felt squeezed. Michael had always imagined the big rescue.

"Well," Sarah said. "I should get going. Good night."

"Good night." He watched her walk away, and then rushed after her, calling. She spun around, her tiny shoulders stooped and her hands pushed deep into her coat pockets. It struck him that she looked like Tricia. "I'm sorry," he said. "I have to ask again. Is there anything you can tell us about why Michael might have done what he did?" She shook her head. "Please. Anything you can think of? Anything at all?"

She shrugged. "The last time we met was in town, shortly before Christmas. Michael was coming from his guitar lesson and seemed fine. We didn't really say all that much. We'd only ever gone on a few dates together and we'd parted friends, but it was a little awkward, you know? We said hi and 'bye, really. I'm sorry."

The awful ache inside him wouldn't let up. "Have you heard what others are saying? What their theories are?"

She hitched her shoulders and looked at the ground. "There's always going to be talk."

"So what's the talk?" he asked.

"It's really not my place to say. It's all just gossip anyway."

He stepped closer and gripped her elbow. "Please, I've already heard about the gambling and Romanian Mafia nonsense. Is there anything else? Anything at all? It would really help."

"I think sometimes he felt stuck, you know?"

"No," he said, his right eye twitching. "I don't know."

"I don't think he was so sure anymore about the farm and going to college, not to study agriculture anyway."

"What?" Billy heard the thin pitch of his voice. "But why didn't he say something?"

"I don't know. I'm just guessing. Everyone's just guessing."

"Did he ever say anything to you about it?"

"No, not really. I mean, sometimes he'd say he was fed up,

all right, so tied to the farm and everything. There was this one evening, a few of us were hanging out, having a laugh, and Michael was annoyed he had to leave to do the milking. Once, too, he said something about preferring to play his guitar on the streets of Dublin rather than go to college there, but he never made it seem as if any of it was that big a deal."

Billy's fingers pressed the bones in her elbow. "Is there anything else? Why didn't you tell us this earlier?"

"Like I said, I'm only guessing. I'm sorry, I need to go."

He watched her disappear around the corner. Sarah, everyone, they were all only stabbing at answers. He wouldn't tell a word of this to anyone. If Tricia, any of the family, even suspected Michael hadn't wanted to take over the farm, they would turn it into Billy's fault, say Michael was following his lead. *Monkey see, monkey do.* That claw tightened around his heart. Was it possible Michael hadn't wanted the farm, either? If that was true, wouldn't Michael have told him? The boy should have known that Billy, of all people, would have understood.

Billy pushed back the realization that Michael would have felt under ever greater pressure to take over the farm and keep it in the Brennan name because Billy hadn't. That chill stole over Billy's chest, as if his lungs were laid open to the stinging air.

One evening in December, just weeks before Michael's death, Billy sat parked outside St. Anthony's Hospital beyond town, waiting for Michael to finish up a mini-concert he and a few of his fellow music students were performing for the staff and patients, to bring some Christmas cheer. It wasn't long after five o'clock, but night had already fallen.

While Billy watched for Michael in the dark, he munched on a bag of salt-and-vinegar crisps. He had a stash of treats forever in the car, sweet and salty snacks that whetted, then killed, his longing. And so it went, day after day, year after year, whetting and killing and whetting.

The crisps finished, he enjoyed the linger of salt and vinegar in his mouth, wondering what Tricia had made for the dinner. A Thursday, it would likely be a stew. He hoped for lamb. Across the car park, youngsters burst through the hospital's glass doors, their voices high and animated. They scattered in various directions, some headed to the street, others to the various lines of parked cars.

Billy spotted Michael. He'd know the boy's walk anywhere. Michael was chatting with some girl. She was petite and ropy, with a bright yellow scarf around her neck. They hugged briefly, and she headed to the bicycle rack. Michael continued toward the dark rows of vehicles.

Almost at the Corolla, Michael called out uncertainly, "Dad?"

Billy turned on the headlights and cracked open his window. "Yeah, right here."

As soon as Michael sat in the passenger seat, Billy started teasing him. "So who's the girl?"

Michael shook his head, embarrassed. "No one."

"I don't think it's the guitar you're interested in at all," Billy joked.

"No, it is, it is." Michael had been playing guitar for over a year by then and was putting as much time and hard work into it as he was the farming and the football, maybe even more. The boy chattered on, saying his guitar teacher, a graduate of some fancy music school in Boston, had pulled him aside during the intermission. "He reckons I'm a natural. Said I should take voice lessons as well as the guitar. He thinks I could really be someone."

Billy scoffed. "And how much would all that cost? He sounds like a bit of a cowboy, if you ask me, is only after more money."

Michael turned up the radio volume. Billy let him sulk. Kids nowadays thought they knew everything. Billy quickly tired of the silence between them, though. He liked their chats. "Well, how was the concert?"

Michael shrugged. "Yeah, good."

"Give us a bit more than that, can't you?" Billy said, cajoling.

"We sang carols, mostly, but we revved them up a bit, made them contemporary." Michael's enthusiasm returned. "We gave a mad rendition of 'Fairytale of New York,' too. Everyone loved it." He laughed. "They made us sing it twice, and then a third time for the encore."

"Many there?" Billy asked.

"About a hundred, maybe more."

"What? No way."

"Yeah, I know," Michael said. "It was deadly."

Billy sniffed theatrically. "You got your musical talent from me, you know that, don't you?"

"Yeah, right," Michael said, laughing again.

"I'm serious," Billy said, sounding mock-offended. In truth, they had no idea where Michael had gotten his musical ear or talent, but it was most certainly not thanks to Billy.

Messing, Billy launched into "Fairytale of New York," butchering the song with gusto.

"Jesus." Michael covered his ears.

Billy kept on, sounding worse by the second. Michael soon joined in. Billy quieted, letting Michael finish the song. The boy had a raw, haunting sound to his voice, as if he knew losses, and a burning ache, far beyond his years.

That night, it took Billy a long time to get to sleep. Out of nowhere, tears. He could hardly believe he'd helped make someone as fine as Michael, as full of feeling. He replayed Michael's singing in the car in his head, at the edge of sleep at last. But what finally sent him into a deep, sated slumber was the memory of Michael's single word in the dark car park, when the boy had wanted to be sure of him.

"Dad?"

Nine

BILLY STEPPED ONTO THE NEW DIGITAL SCALE HE'D
purchased, one with the mortifying capacity of four hundred
pounds. He stepped off, and back on, double-checking. Three
hundred and ninety-three pounds. The flood of relief almost
doubled him over. He had lost eight pounds, the equivalent of
four bags of sugar. Eight slabs of butter. A mound of potatoes.
He felt a rush of thanks.

He'd messed up big time the other night at the chipper, but
never again. Everything else he was doing, the shakes, diet, and
exercise, they were all obviously working. He pumped his fist in
the air. When had he stopped believing in himself? When had
he started to believe he had no willpower, no strength? Forget
that. He still had willpower. Still had strength.

During breakfast, Lisa texted to say she would arrive
shortly. He cursed under his breath, drawing a shocked look
from Anna. "Sorry," he mumbled. Lisa was the last thing he
needed. He finished his porridge and strawberries in a rush and

moved to the computer. After an Internet search, he walked out back to phone the Samaritans' local branch. The line rang out. He checked his watch. Not quite ten o'clock. He paced up and down the yard, waiting.

The call would be a waste of time. Of course the Samaritans were going to say yes to whatever monies he raised—but anything to keep Lisa quiet. Besides, he also wanted to ask them if someone high up in their ranks would participate in the march and give a talk afterward in the hall, all of which he'd record and include in his documentary. He redialed the number.

A woman answered, her voice clipped but kind. "Samaritans, can I help you?"

"Hello?"

"Good morning, how can I help?"

He hesitated, picking his words. "I'm doing this charity thing, to raise money for yourselves, and someone said maybe I had better clear that with you first? That there might be some paperwork I should complete?"

"That's wonderful, thank you, we appreciate every cent. I don't believe there's any paperwork necessary . . ."

He smiled to himself. Lisa and her meddling, her always needing to be right.

"Let me put you on hold for a sec and I can double-check. I'd like to be clear, though, before I get off the line, you're not having any kind of emergency? You didn't want to talk about anything else?"

"What?" He sounded a single, sharp laugh. "No, no, nothing like that." His other hand held the side of his head.

She placed him on hold, and moments later returned. "Yes, that's confirmed. There's no paperwork or clearance needed.

We'll take every cent, arm and all." She laughed. Then, "What is it exactly you're doing?"

He considered lying. "I plan to lose half my body weight, two hundred pounds, and I'm asking people to sponsor my weight loss."

"Goodness, that's . . . that's unbelievable. I don't think I've ever heard of anyone doing anything like that before." He heard a sudden wariness in her voice. "Hang on a sec." She placed him on hold again. The moments stretched. A minute, more, passed.

"Hello? Are you still there?" She sounded guarded. "Listen, I was just talking to my colleague here, he's been volunteering a lot longer than me. He suggested you phone our head office on Monday and talk to them."

"What's there to talk about?"

"Well, what you're doing, it's a bit . . . risky, like."

"I don't understand? Everything was grand a minute ago?"

"If anything went wrong, like."

Billy stopped himself from blurting, *You mean if I drop dead*.

She gave him the number of their Dublin office. "Talk to them, they can best advise you."

He ended the call. He would phone the Dublin office on Monday, all right.

As he walked to the back door, the breeze moved the clothes on the line. He stopped, watching the eerie dance. His father had replaced the clothesline the day after Michael did what he did. At first, Billy had felt grateful; the empty space where the clothesline used to be—with its two short, butchered ends remaining—was awful to see. But even this replacement line rankled. It had to bother Tricia, too. Destroy her a little more every time she used it.

Billy returned home from town, finding Lisa's shiny black BMW parked in his usual spot. He would enter the house and face her soon enough. First, he would take down the now-empty clothesline. Tricia must have scrambled to bring in the wash before Lisa's arrival. That was his sister, all right. Such a perfectionist, she made everyone else feel inferior. The taut, empty clothesline seemed like something sketched midair. It looked like it sliced the world.

He dragged his new purchase onto the lawn and ripped open the cardboard box with his bare hands. He removed the various parts and set about assembling the umbrella clothesline at the far corner of the lawn, next to the garage. Merely a matter of screwing together the center pole and locking it into the weighted base. From the kitchen window, they wouldn't even be able to see it.

Tricia and Lisa appeared at the back door. Tricia walked toward him, hugging herself. Lisa remained in the doorway.

"Great idea, thanks," Tricia said.

"I should have thought of it sooner."

She nodded, indicating the rope clothesline. "Will you take that down now, please?"

"Gladly." After a struggle, he unknotted the rope from its hook on the garage, and, after a second struggle, from its hook at the house. Michael mustn't have been able to undo the knots in the previous clothesline. That was why he had used the kitchen knife. All that time to think, to change his mind, and still the boy had ended himself.

Billy held the lump of rope in his hands, wondering how the police had disposed of the clothesline Michael had used. He pictured all the ropes every suicide had ever used the country over.

The whole world over. He saw them burning in a single, gigantic bonfire. Horrific testimony to all that unnecessary waste of life. He decided against throwing the rope away. He wanted to watch it burn. He wished he could have set the rope Michael had used on fire. He would have watched it blaze to nothing.

Tricia nodded toward the band of trees behind the football pitch. "Now all we need to do is bulldoze that lot."

He half laughed. "Don't tempt me."

She smiled, the thin curve of her lips small and sad.

Back in the house, Tricia pushed Ivor's hand away from the plate of biscuits. "They're not for you."

Billy shot her a sharp look, which she missed.

"Ivor, why don't you and Anna go outside and play?" Lisa urged. "The adults want to have a little chat."

"They're all right where they are," Billy said, hating how she liked to make a production of everything.

"Let them go," Tricia said.

"Come on, Ivor." Anna flicked her blond hair over her shoulder and pulled on her brother's arm. The two disappeared up the hall and into the living room, Anna all bones and Ivor all rolls, two miniatures of their parents.

Lisa licked chocolate and biscuit crumbs off her fingertips, her nails polished red and her dark curls tamed into a bun, showing off her thick eyebrows and creamy complexion. Her large, silver hoop earrings glinted under the lights. Billy looked away from her bare arms, the fake-tanned limbs looking varnished and hand-crafted. At fifty-one, she could still draw whistles and comments on the street, something, she claimed, she hated.

He placed two eggs in the saucepan to boil, and fixed himself a cup of green tea.

"So," Lisa began. "You've already gone public with your diet and this march?" She bit into another chocolate biscuit. He thought of the coil of clothesline on the backseat of his car, imagined the rope tied around his hands, stopping him from reaching for the biscuits.

"Were there not other options you could have looked into?" she continued. "Something that would help others without all the spectacle?"

"Spectacle?" Billy said.

"You know what I mean."

"Do I?"

"Stop it," she said.

"Stop what?"

"Did you talk to the Samaritans?" she asked.

"Yeah."

"What did they say?"

He tried not to let his face betray him. "What do you think they said? They said they'd take my arm and all."

"What about medical supervision? Have you gone to see Dr. Shaw?"

"I've seen him, I know what I'm doing," he snapped. He knew Shaw was never going to approve of how hard and fast he wanted to go about everything. Shaw would want him to slow down and go easy. That wasn't an option. Lives were at stake.

"That's something, at least," Lisa said. "Tricia tells me you've been starving yourself, though. That's a huge shock for your system, and it's also how you've failed every other time. This has to be a change of lifestyle, Billy, not a crash diet. You know that."

The gall of her, treating him like a child, a total eejit. All his life, it was the same old thing, as though he was the wrong brother as well as the wrong son. Trembling, he fired his spoon across the kitchen, hitting the far wall and splattering tea onto the pale blue paint. Lisa and Tricia both startled and stared at him wide-eyed.

His anger ebbed to embarrassment and he spoke in a rush, trying to hold on to his temper and the strength it lent him. "You know what I know, Lisa? I know it always has to be your way or no way. Well, not this time." He swung around and barged out the back door.

Billy returned to the yard, relieved to see Lisa's car gone. Tricia stood leaning against the back wall.

"Is she long gone?" Billy asked.

"Not long enough," Tricia said. He gave a small laugh. Smirking, Tricia dropped her cigarette butt and squashed it with her shoe. "She means well."

He nodded at the killed cigarette. "Would you not give them up?" he asked gently.

She looked into the distance, her face hard again. "We all have our crutches."

His lower jaw slid to the right, setting his teeth on edge.

"I will go back off them eventually," she said, softening. "Besides," she said, gruff again, "they're too fecking expensive." She pushed off the wall and returned inside.

He looked at the umbrella clothesline, and at the empty space where the old clothesline used to be, asking himself why he hadn't swapped it out much sooner. Why Tricia hadn't in-sisted. Maybe to punish themselves.

Tricia reappeared at the back door with a plate of leftovers for the feral cats, her cheek bulging. She had taken to sucking a mint after every cigarette, an attempt to mask the reek of burnt tobacco. As soon as she dumped the leftovers into bowls, the cats descended, their noises like children crying.

She knew he hated her to bring the cats around, full of fleas and disease. It had started with one mangy creature many years ago, a white and black kitten on the verge of starvation that Tricia had nursed back to health with a doll's bottle. Now the number of feral cats sometimes climbed to as high as seven or eight a day. His father said Billy should take a shotgun to them. "Survival of the fastest."

Tricia made mewling noises and the cats called back to her. When Michael was a baby, Billy would whistle and Michael would also purse his lips, blowing only tiny saliva bubbles. It made everyone laugh.

Back and forth the noises went between Tricia and the cats, as if in lively conversation. Some days it seemed she talked more to those cats than she did to anyone else of late. Not that she'd ever been all that talkative or outgoing. She didn't like to get too close to people. Once, after a few drinks, she'd said, "It all ends in tears."

When Tricia was nine, her mother died of throat cancer, and it was left to Tricia, the oldest girl, to take care of her father and five siblings. Her father had died about three years back, that horrendous motor neuron disease, and over the past two decades all but one of Tricia's siblings, an older brother she wasn't close to, had emigrated down under, to Melbourne. She'd known much more family death and broken bonds than Billy ever had, and then on top of all that, Michael.

She kept her attention on the cats. "That's it, eat up."

"You know you're only adding to the problem?" he said.

"What do you want me to do? Let them die?" Her words hung in the air and she hugged herself. He understood how now, more than ever, she'd feel the need to keep things alive, especially those creatures with the odds stacked against them.

She kept her attention on the cats. They ate fast, devouring every last scrap. "Everything must have built and built in his head until it got to be too much somehow. Do you think that was it? Could it really be that simple? That terrible?"

"Yes," he said with a rasp.

She flapped her arms, shooing the cats. "You're done, go on, go."

She returned inside. Billy stayed in the yard. One cat remained, a large gray and black tabby somersaulting over the grass and holding hard to a dead bird in its paws. Over and over the two tumbled. Then the supposedly dead bird took to the air, gliding more than flying, and traveling dangerously low, but still managing to make its escape.

As Billy reached the back door, the bird further confounded him and flew back into view. The second it returned to the lawn, the cat pounced. Billy charged, shouting.

He stood over the bird on the grass, breathing hard. There was no blood or sign of injury, but it was dead this time for sure. He bent down and cupped it in his hands—its body blue-black, its neck brown, and a single white stripe in its inky tail. He couldn't understand why it had returned. Suddenly angry, he fired the tiny corpse into the far field. For long moments afterward, its warmth stayed on his hands.

Ten

AT BREAKFAST, ANNA SLICED AND QUARTERED HER grilled tomato, spilling its juice and green seeds. Her knife rushed to rescue her eggs and sausage from the bleed, saving them from cross-contamination. A picky eater, every meal with her was a production. Had been right from the beginning.

Billy pulled his attention away from her mouthwatering breakfast, remembering long-ago nighttime trips to the supermarket to get various kinds of baby formula for her, his large hands grasping at any and all mixtures that might get her to sleep through the night.

Mostly, though, he stacked his basket with food for himself and would savage biscuits, bars of chocolate, sliced cheese and deli meats, and bags of sharp, salty crisps in his car in the dark. Anything to fortify himself before his return home and Anna's inconsolable screams, Tricia's frantic pacing.

He would try his best, but nothing he could do would soothe Anna. Back then, she had only ever wanted her mother.

Michael, on the other hand, had always favored him, right up until that day in the sea in Kilkee.

"What are we doing today?" Anna asked, pulling him back to the table.

"We're going to your granny's," Tricia said. "Auntie Lisa is cooking dinner for us."

"Yes!" Ivor's arms shot straight up by his head. Lisa was an even better cook than Tricia.

Billy suspected Lisa and his parents planned to stage an intervention. He almost looked forward to facing them. They were in for a shock if they thought they could sway him. He wasn't backing down. Not this time.

"First, though, mass," Tricia continued, "and after mass you're all coming straight home to clean your rooms, and if that's not done there's no dinner at Granny's." Various groans and eye-rolls went up.

"We can't clean today," Ivor said. "You're not supposed to work on Sundays." A bite of too-hot sausage bounced amid a mess of scrambled egg on his tongue. Tricia had sworn off any more meat at breakfast, but seemingly Ivor had thrown a tantrum in the supermarket.

"You better remind the priests of that commandment," Billy said. "No one ever worked harder on a Sunday to make money." Tricia leveled him with a cold look.

Billy switched to a safer subject and touched his fist to John's bicep. "Ready for the big match?"

John nodded, his expression hard. "You better believe it, we'll annihilate Clooskey."

Billy pushed away an uneasy feeling. It would be hard to witness John play today, with Michael no longer on the field next to him. The team retired Michael's number and Billy had placed the jersey in his coffin. Tricia also sent Michael off with a professional family photograph and four handwritten letters. John had refused to write a letter, or to put anything else in the coffin with his brother.

"It'll be a great match," Tricia said. She would also see Michael's ghost on the pitch this afternoon.

Later, when the children left the kitchen, Billy moved around the table and placed his hand on Tricia's bony shoulder. "Are you all right?"

"You need to try harder with John. I worry about him, about all of them."

"I'm trying harder with everything, in case you hadn't noticed."

She stood up. "We better hurry, we don't want to be late for mass."

Billy took a hankering to walk to the home place, wanting to follow Michael's footsteps through the fields, a well-worn path the boy had often traveled to the farm.

"No, thanks," Ivor said.

"Yeah," John drawled. "I'll pass."

"Sorry, I can't walk in these shoes," Anna said. She was sporting little black heels.

"You go ahead," Tricia said. "I'll drive them."

Billy hid his disappointment and moved to the gate and into the field. He pictured Michael singing his way along the trodden path. The boy had likely looked to the trees and sky every so often, watching the birds wheel over the world. He probably tried to get the birds to sing back to him. Billy started to whistle, to drown out the sound of Michael's singing in his head. Sometimes he loved to hear it still. Other times it was too much. The only response came from his father's cows, sounding their impatient noises.

At the crest of the hill, Billy's childhood home came into view. Constant smoke puffed from the kitchen chimney. It didn't matter if the weather dawned warm or wretched, his mother kept the fire going in the range year-round. Not just to cook, boil the kettle, and heat the old, draft-filled house, but because she liked to sit and look in at the flames. She imagined whole stories inside the leap of orange, blue, yellow, and red. He remembered the coiled clothesline still hidden in his car. He had yet to burn it.

Any other day of the week, Billy's father could likely be found in the rust-red barn behind the house, drawing out the turf or scaring off the birds and their squirts of shit. There, or his father was down in the fields with the cows, checking on those about to calve, those that were sick or stricken with bloody, infected udders, and those among the big-eyed brutes with any hint of personality, be it strength, stubbornness, or force of kick. These feisty beasts were his father's favorites, and he'd clap each on her broad back and shake his fist in her face, talking in tones twisted with affection and goading.

Billy entered his mother's kitchen and its tormenting smells of roast beef with all the trimmings. His mother greeted him, her air cool. She returned her attention to the children and asked about mass and school, and Anna's dance lessons, Ivor's chess lessons. Lisa marched everyone into the dining room and told each where to sit. Billy was put at the far end of the table, opposite his father.

"Come out to the milk shed," his father said. "There's something I want you to see."

"The dinner's ready," Lisa said. "You can show him that later."

"It'll only take a minute," his father said. "You, too, Tricia."

The three entered the empty shed and its heavy smell of cattle and overripe milk. His father led Billy and Tricia across the straw-strewn floor and down to the back wall, a pine shelf there that looked new, and on it some kind of ornament. When had his father ever displayed anything in the milk shed?

"Lisa got it done," his father said. Billy studied the bronze Wellingtons, his throat closing. Etched on the gold plaque on the sculpture's base, *Our Michael, Boots No One Can Fill.* Billy's hand reached up and clasped a bronze ankle. His fingers and palm tingled. He remembered the similar sensation in the canteen, when he'd touched Michael's photograph on the flyer. He couldn't stop the horrible sound that ripped from him.

Tricia touched her hand to his back. "It's lovely," she said, her voice faint. She and his father stood in silence, waiting for Billy to recover. Billy snuffled and rubbed at his eyes and nose, his hand robbed of the tingling sensation.

Billy's father appeared to hesitate, but couldn't seem to stop himself. "We weren't sure if you would want us to order a second sculpture for yourselves, knowing how you feel about the farm?"

Billy's jaw hardened. Of course he'd like one, too, but he couldn't bring himself to ask. Instead, he would create his own shrine to Michael. Something extraordinary.

When they returned to the house, Lisa asked if they liked the sculpture. Even in this, she insisted on praise.

"It's lovely," Tricia repeated.

"Lovely," Billy said with less feeling.

During the meal, the stilted conversation stretched past the point of a hungry focus on food and started to feel uncomfortable. It didn't lessen Billy's unease any that he had to watch everyone else scoff his favorite meal while he downed chicken stew. Tricia had made the dish just for him, all-natural and low-fat, with no salt or potatoes. Her efforts well-intentioned, but the meal was as good as tasteless.

Billy's father held a forkful of beef, gravied potatoes, and mushy peas at his mouth. "A pity, Billy. This is only gorgeous."

"Daddy!" Lisa said.

"What did I say?" his father said.

Billy, refusing to give his father any satisfaction, struggled to look nonchalant. The old man's attention jumped to John, a look of fondness coming over him. Billy's chest constricted. His father was setting his sights on John now. The old man made mention of the match, kickoff just a couple of hours away. John again bragged about how easily they would win. He seemed to give no thought to Michael's great loss to the team, to everyone. Tricia complimented Lisa on the delicious dinner, making Billy's sister look almost as smug as his father and John.

When Billy was a boy, his family rarely sat together around the table, aside from Christmastime. He could still see, could almost smell, those long-ago scrumptious Christmas dinners—steaming slices of turkey and honey-baked ham, sausage stuffing with fresh herbs, mounds of mushy peas, mashed and roast potatoes, buttered carrots and parsnips, and all smothered in a dark, rich, delicious gravy. He'd loved Christmas. Not Santa Claus and the presents so much, although all that antici- pation and excitement could make his insides quiver for weeks. No, it was the Christmas dinner he loved most of all.

For the Christmas dinner his family sat together in the din- ing room, at the fancy mahogany table. All four of them wore colorful paper hats pulled from crackers—gold-sheathed tubes that made the sound of shots and let the smell of sulfur hang in the air. Never had his family seemed to have so much as they did on Christmas Day. The food. The presents. The fun.

After the dinner and a dessert of his mother's sherry trifle and whiskey-soaked Christmas cake, Billy would help his father clear the table and do the washing up. While they worked, Billy's father would tell him stories, mostly about the history of the village and its families and their holdings, right down to the number and breed of animals. Billy's favorite stories were his father's memories from childhood, when he talked about catching frogs, or getting caned in school, or rid- ing on barebacked donkeys till they bucked so hard they threw him off. Billy listened to his father's every word, rapt. Never had he felt so close to the man, so close to being the right kind of son.

St. Stephen's Day, they would regather in the dining room and eat the leftovers—without paper hats for the second go- around, but still with the food, chatter, and laughter. Every other day of the year they ate at the kitchen table. Those days, his mother fed Billy and Lisa their dinner when they came home from school. His father ate his dinner alone, much later in the evenings, whenever he finally came in from the farm. Maybe that was when Billy had first started to hate the farm, when he'd realized how much the land and livestock took his father away from them.

His mother ate every meal at the kitchen counter, standing between the sink and the fire roaring in the range. She said she hadn't time to sit still. For years, Billy sat in the heat and smoke of that turf-fueled kitchen, thinking if he just stayed eating, just stayed sitting long enough, his mother would join him. But she never did.

The main course finished, Anna and Ivor took turns trying to fire peas into the other's mouth. "Stop that," Tricia said. "You'll choke yourselves." She turned crimson, her words lingering. Lisa rushed up from her chair, clearing the table while taking dessert orders.

Pavlova, Billy's all-time favorite, was on offer, as was Neapolitan ice cream with strawberries. He refused both. His stomach sulked and kicked. Ivor wanted some of everything, his flesh straining against his Sunday shirt and pouring over his good trousers.

"Choose one," Tricia said.

"Why can't I have both?" Ivor asked, slapping the curls out of his eyes.

"Choose one," Tricia repeated, her voice firm. He chose Pavlova. "A small amount," Tricia told Lisa.

"Not fair," Ivor said.

The desserts arrived. Ivor compared his small portion to Anna's and John's. "How come they get more than me?"

"I think someone's eyes are a little too big for his belly?" Billy's mother said.

"They get more because they're older than you," Tricia said, her voice thick with the lie.

Billy's insides tightened. There was no point in making the boy feel bad. "Is there more fresh fruit?" he asked. "Give him some fruit."

Ivor clacked his fork against his plate in temper. "I don't want fruit."

"Then you don't know what's good for you," Billy said, unable to hide his annoyance.

After dessert, John rushed off to ready for his match. Lisa ordered Anna and Ivor outside to play. They protested, wanting to watch TV instead. "Go on, now," Lisa said. "Get out and get some fresh air and exercise." Billy winced at how she'd emphasized *exercise*. "You can feed grass to the new calves," she finished.

Ivor's face lit up. "Can we give the calves names?"

"No," Billy's father said. "They're livestock, lad, not pets."

"Yeah, go on," Billy said, locking eyes with his father. "You can give the calves names."

"Cool!" Ivor hurried out.

"Wait for me," Anna said, following him.

"You need to take control of that boy," his father said. "He's headed for trouble."

"Ivor's grand," Billy said, steel in his voice. "You leave him to me."

His father harrumphed, as if saying, *See where that got you.* Billy's right arm twitched, wanting to swing for the old man. He forced down his tea, trying to keep his hand steady. Just let his father, anyone, say one more stupid thing. Lisa rabbited on about the now-daily scandals surrounding the banks, saying how not every bank and its employees should be condemned as criminals.

Billy jumped at the chance to cut at her, especially in front of their parents. "Those bank executives are nothing but swindlers. They gave out loans to people they knew they were crippling financially while making themselves rich, and then they bankrupt the entire country. They should all be tried and sent to jail. And out of principle, you should quit."

She cracked a laugh. "Why would I quit? I've done nothing wrong. And who, I ask you, would pay my mortgage and the rest of my bills if I did?"

"Don't be stupid," his father said. "If everyone at the banks quit, how would the country go on?"

The room stayed silent. *Stupid* repeated in Billy's head. He fought the urge to drive his fork into his forearm. His father spoke, his large head lowered like a bull's. "I see you put those posters up in the shop and in Kennedy's."

Now it's out. Now we have it. Billy rushed toward the fight. "That's right, and at the factory, too. I plan to put up flyers anywhere and everywhere I can."

"Sure, go right ahead, can't you," his father said. "Plaster the Brennan name all over—"

"That's the plan," Billy said.

The color left his father's face. "I don't know what's gotten into you."

"Glorifying what you shouldn't be, that's all you're doing," his mother said, the bitterness coming off her like sparks.

"What am I glorifying?" Billy said, shocked.

"You bringing all this attention to suicide and . . . and

obesity, well, it's only going to make it all the more attractive to people, isn't it? Everyone nowadays wants to be in the limelight, get their five minutes of fame."

"My God, Mother," Billy said, his hand so tight around the soldier in his pocket he felt his knuckles would burst through his skin. "Are you listening to yourself?"

"Am *I* listening to myself?" she scoffed.

"That's enough, Maura," Tricia said sharply.

Billy felt he was falling in on himself. Felt his mother had ripped out his vertebrae. She didn't know the first thing about him if she thought he wanted to be the center of attention, if she didn't get how hard all this was for him. He'd made his body like this to swallow him up, to disappear. And now here she was accusing him of wanting the limelight? He struggled not to up-end the table and bring everything crashing down around them.

Tricia looked at him kindly. "Come on, let's go."

Just as he thought he'd charge for the door, a different feeling came over him, a kind of strange calm. "No," he said. "We'll stay until the match. Unless we're no longer welcome?"

"Of course you're welcome, stop that," Lisa said.

"Stop is right." His father picked at his teeth with a broken matchstick.

Billy looked at his mother, the heat of her temper still flying at him. She lifted her proud head. "This is your home, isn't it?"

He didn't answer.

As most everyone predicted, their team won. John's teammates carried him off the pitch on their shoulders, his strong, sinewy arms pumping in victory and his smile lighting up his face.

Billy's father shouted, "Good man, John."

Billy also cheered, vying to be louder and more animated than his father. "Well done, son. You go, boy." He caught himself searching the pitch for Michael.

Most everyone headed to Kennedy's. Billy's mother hated pubs and continued home. She had to have been the only woman at the match in heels, pearls, and with a floral scarf pinned at her shoulder with a jeweled brooch. Billy snorted to himself. And she'd accused him of wanting to be front and center.

She hadn't said two words to him during the entire match and didn't say good-bye, either. See if he cared. He remained on the side of the road, watching her navy Fiat shrink toward home.

"What's the holdup?" his father called from Kennedy's doorway. Billy quick-stepped across the road as best he could. He wished his father wouldn't watch.

Ben Kennedy served up their drinks, surly as ever. Rumor had it the publican had a gold tooth somewhere in the back of his head, but it was hard to substantiate the claim when no one had ever seen him laugh that hard.

Nancy Burke appeared next to Billy, inches of her gray roots showing. She addressed his father, pointing to Billy's flyers on the bulletin board. "Isn't he some man?"

His father looked into his pint, his head jerking with embarrassment, and delivered his sharp laugh. "At this rate, he'll be jumping out of airplanes next."

Nancy cackled. "Oh, that's a good one." Billy put his pint of ale to his lips and drank it down in three swallows, his eyes turned to the ceiling and its yellowed, peeling paint. He drifted up there, while his mammoth body remained in place.

"Have you donated yet?" Tricia asked sharply, pulling Billy back into his body.

"I have, of course," Nancy said, chastened. She slinked back to her table and the company of her sisters, the identical twins Margaret and Martha. The three leaned in close, whispering together, their mouths going like seagulls' beaks plucking at something rotten.

Billy tried to catch Tricia's eye, to indicate his thanks, but she was downing the last of her cider. She had tied her hair into a rare messy bun and it made her face look less severe. Made her eyes brighter, bluer. Desire flooded his crotch, so strong it was almost pain. It had been years since they'd had sex—ever since his size had put him outside the realm of such things. He called to Kennedy for another round.

The second wave of drinks gone, his father offered to buy more. Lisa refused. "I need to head off. I have an early start in the morning." She asked Billy to walk her out. He hesitated, thinking he'd taken enough abuse for one day.

They reached her BMW and she turned to face him, the sunshine bringing out the hazel in her brown eyes. "I wanted to tell you how impressed I am. I can see how determined you are, how much all this means. Michael would be so proud."

His eyes welled and he looked down, seeing the impression his shoes made in the gravel, as though he were sinking beneath the stones.

"I'm worried about you, though, we all are," she said.

He shifted his feet on the gravel, trying to get away from the sinking feeling. "Yeah, well, you don't have to be."

"I don't want you to get any more hurt than you already are."

122

"I'll be all right, don't you worry." He looked to the green hills, his tongue poking his cheek.

"I know you mean well with all this, but—"

He pointed with his thumb to the pub. "I should get back."

She looked wounded and rushed on her sunglasses, got into her car. He rapped his knuckles on the driver's window. She lowered the glass and he tried to make light. "So how much are you going to sponsor me for?"

She pressed her head against the driver's seat, giving a small laugh. "Tell you what, if you do this, if you really lose half of yourself, I'll donate a thousand euro."

He tried to mask his shock, in case she changed her mind. "Seriously?"

"I've no children, no pets, and it's a great cause . . . and you're my one and only sibling." She opened the glove compartment and removed her checkbook.

"Fair play to you, sister." He wanted to say more, but couldn't get the words out.

"Don't call me that, makes me feel like a nun." She ripped out the unsigned check and handed it to him. "I look forward to putting my autograph to that."

"Trust me, I look forward to that, too."

"Of course, maybe on principle you don't want a banker's money?"

"Money's money," he said, deciding not to push his advantage. Besides, it hadn't felt nearly as good as he'd expected, to have something over her at last.

"I miss him," she said.

"I know you do."

"I still can't believe it."

"I know." He slapped the roof of her car. "Lookit, go on, drive safe."

Alone on the road, he glanced up. The sky looked white and blank, like nothing was ever there.

Eleven

BILLY HURRIED ACROSS THE LANDING IN HIS UNDER-
wear, and into the bathroom. He weighed himself first thing
every morning now, and last thing every night—and sometimes several times throughout the day. Three hundred and
eighty-eight pounds. Thirteen pounds off, despite his pig-out.
Two pig-outs, he realized with a guilty start. The night at the
chipper, and that first day back at work when he'd gone to
Seanseppe's. Thirteen pounds, though. And in little more than
three weeks. The shakes, rabbit food, and walking might be
hellish, but they were working. He stepped off the scale and
back on, did a little dance with his arms and hips.

He moved to the oval mirror above the sink, and turned
his head left and right. He maybe looked a little less puffy in
the face, and perhaps his jowl wasn't quite such a wattle. He
pinched the fleshy wad. Definitely less chops. He turned his
body to the left, and to the right, trying to check more of himself in the small mirror. He'd have returned to his bedroom

and the full-length wardrobe mirror, but didn't want to inspect himself in front of Tricia. Some of his elation fizzled. He'd thought she would support him more, that she'd be cheering him on. He pushed back his shoulders and forced a smile in the glass. Thirteen pounds, and soon fifteen, and twenty, and thirty. From here on out, he wouldn't be stopped.

Denis joined Billy in the canteen. They stood out among the scatter of navy overalls sitting about the tables, Billy in his signature, supersized navy tracksuit and Denis in a faded denim shirt and jeans. Between his clothes and his gelled hair, Denis looked more like a member of a boy band than a numbers man from upstairs. He had also opted for the green salad with chicken breast and vinaigrette dressing. "I'm going out in sympathy with you."

Billy looked at his newfound friend with thanks, experiencing that same start of surprise he got whenever he found things in the wrong place—his car keys in the fridge, that barn owl flying in full daylight, that time he'd discovered Ivor hiding underneath his bed when the boy should have been at school. Billy could chat and joke away with people in the village, town, at the factory, and the football matches, but having as close a friend as Denis had fast become felt strange and thrilling. Nerve-wracking, too. He worried he'd somehow mess it up.

"How's it going?" Denis asked.

"It's gone actually, thirteen pounds and counting."

"That's brilliant, well done." Denis high-fived him. "You're going to do this, you're going to go all the way."

Billy grinned. "Yes I am."

"What else is going on?" Denis asked.

Billy hesitated, but then confided in Denis about the AA meeting. "When it came to my turn to introduce myself, my mouth felt cemented shut."

Denis winced. "You should probably have said something, all right."

"What was I supposed to say?"

"You could have kept it vague, maybe said you were struggling like the rest of them and trying to find your way?"

Billy munched on his lettuce, wishing he'd thought to say something nearly as good as that. Denis chuckled. "Just as well you didn't get talking to that sponsor they wanted to set you up with. You would have had some job trying to explain to her what you were doing there."

Billy stopped mid-chew, another brilliant idea taking shape.

"I know that look," Denis said, amused, wary. "What now?"

"You could be my sponsor—"

"What? No way," Denis said. "You need to go to an OA meeting and get someone there to sponsor you. Do this on the up-and-up."

"I can't. Not yet, anyways. Maybe down the road. For now, you have to do this for me. I can't fail, there's too much at stake."

"It wouldn't be right. There's an honor code to all this—"

"What's more honorable than helping me stick to my diet so I can help save lives?" Billy said.

"Alcoholism and overeating, it's not the same—"

"Addiction is addiction, how hard can it be? Come on, it's all for the greater good."

"I don't know," Denis said, faltering.

Billy grinned. "Thanks, sponsor."

———

A long line of smoking vehicles clogged O'Connell Street, road works blocking an entire lane. The car clock read ten after four. The Samaritans' head office closed at five. *Move*, Billy willed the traffic. Thoughts of Michael's upcoming inquest made his right eyeball twitch. He would feel like even more of a hostage inside that makeshift courtroom in Moran's Hotel.

He'd cut out of work at three o'clock, citing a migraine. He didn't want that and the long drive to be for nothing. Tricia would go mad if she knew. He had worked at the factory for twenty years, though, and prior to Michael had rarely taken a sick day. That had to count for something. Besides, he really was getting a mother of a headache. His eyes returned to the car clock. Fifteen minutes after four. Cars honked and drivers shouted, adding to the clangor of a distant jackhammer. His head felt caught in a vise.

Pedestrians took advantage of the stalled traffic to cross against the lights. A brunette passed in front of his windscreen, her pale, freckled legs long and bare, her breasts jiggling. As she reached the pavement, he spotted the cut above her right ankle, as if the strap of her shoe had bitten into her. He imagined easing ointment onto her wound, imagined her smiling and murmuring thanks. She disappeared into the crowd. That lonesome feeling came over him again, that voice telling him he would end up alone.

On Marlborough Street, his luck changed and he found easy parking. He arrived at 112, an impressive redbrick building with oversized windows. He leaned next to the doorway, re-rehearsing his speech. The cool, hard brick felt good against his back. Just as he'd readied himself, a middle-aged woman passed, her skirt suit dark and fitted, her legs skinny above high heels, her lipstick a splash of cerise. Tricia used to wear a lot of cerise, in particular a cap-sleeved, short-hemmed dress from their dating days that he'd loved. It seemed so long ago, another life.

The woman doubled back and asked if he was okay.

"Yeah, grand, thanks," he said, embarrassed.

She looked to the front door of the Samaritans. "Are you going in?"

"Yeah, I'm just taking a sec."

"Go on so," she said. "I'll watch."

He looked back when he reached the doorway and she nodded encouragingly. "Go on. Good luck." He thanked her again, realizing she thought he was on the verge. His throat thickened. She'd seen him. She cared.

Sheila Russell stood behind her glass desk, all curves and generous breasts. She invited Billy to sit down, indicating the chair opposite. To his relief, this chair had no arms. He sat down and Sheila waited, her lips thin inside her round, pale face, her hair limp and copper. He was so nervous his own lips were tingling and the tops of his fingers had numbed. He launched his prepared speech, telling her about Michael, his sponsored diet, and his phone conversation with the Samaritan volunteer from his local branch. "Everything was going fine until I told her how I was raising the money."

"I'm not sure I understand her concerns, either. I think what you're doing is wonderful."

He had thought he was going to have a fight on his hands and felt almost disappointed.

"I presume you're doing this under the care of a doctor?" she asked.

"Yes I am." He felt himself blush at the lie.

"Excellent."

His hand moved to the soldier in his trousers pocket. "One more thing. I'd like the money I raise to go directly to help young men in trouble, in Michael's name."

She hooked her hair behind her ear, its underside more brown than copper. "We don't normally allot donations by age or gender—"

"But you can?"

"Well, yes, I suppose we could set aside your monies to specifically target—"

"Wonderful, thank you." He sat trembling with satisfaction, and a growing sense of power. Even his headache had eased.

He told her about the march and asked if she would walk, and give a talk afterward in the hall.

"I could certainly arrange for a local volunteer—"

He shook his head. "It would mean a lot if you could attend. I hope to get a great turnout to this march and really call attention to suicide awareness and prevention. For that, I need to go as big as I can, and you're going to attract a lot more people than any volunteer." Sheila opened her mouth to respond, but he pressed on, quivering with adrenaline. "Which brings me to another project I'd love you to participate in, too. I plan to make a film, a documentary that will put a spotlight on the national epidemic suicide has become and call for more preventative action to be taken. It'd be key to get you on board for that, too."

She laughed. "You don't do things by halves, do you?"

"Except myself," he said. She looked confused, and he clapped his stomach with both hands. "Two hundred pounds."

Her face turned bright red. "Oh, yes, I see."

At the meeting's close, she came out from around her desk and shook his hand. He thanked her repeatedly.

"No," she said. "Thank you."

He strode out of her office, feeling tall and broad, solid and strong.

In the garage, Billy settled at his workbench. Hardly a workbench, really. More a scarred oak table he'd brought down from his father's shed how many years back, to do he didn't know what with. He had taken the table rather than asked, and his father hadn't seemed to notice its absence. Billy couldn't remember his reasoning at the time. Maybe it was simply the satisfaction of taking from his father, without getting caught, without blistering blame.

Billy had never used the table, but had always liked how it gave a certain shape to the garage, making it feel more like a work space than dead storage space. He could never see himself actually sitting at the table and working at much of anything. Until now. Now he planned to make a magnificent shrine to Michael. One that would well surpass the bronze sculpture of Michael's Wellingtons in his father's shed. He would make a miniature village for the seconds dolls and soldiers—an alternate universe where the tiny version of Michael, and the entire tiny Brennan family, would live and thrive.

Days earlier, he'd cleared the oak table of its stacks of old paid bills, dirty rags, various nails, screwdrivers, and light bulbs. He'd also moved the blue gas lantern that had never worked, and more of the forgotten and broken. He'd reluctantly thrown away the unsalvageable and created space for the rest of the miscellaneous on new wooden shelves he'd made and mounted on the wall, about the only carpentry he'd done since school. Then he'd repainted the stained, gouged tabletop in a rich dark green, as though bringing it back to life.

He opened his metal toolbox, revealing his horde of seconds dolls and soldiers, all arranged in neat rows. The damaged toys seemed to stare, as if waiting for his next move. He removed the first five toys and placed them on the workbench—three soldiers, one with an arm missing, one with a gun missing, and one with an inferior eye, and two dolls, one with a half leg and the other with a single cheek painted bright pink, the other cheek an empty, varnished ivory. The toys were tiny versions of him, Tricia, John, Anna, and Ivor. He added the soldier with no chin strap, reuniting tiny Michael with his tiny family.

Billy moved about the garage, searching among the boxes, bags, bric-a-brac, and old furniture for a wooden, stand-alone easel that had belonged to Michael. Back when Michael was ten or eleven, he had loved to paint. Billy seemed to recall an upside-down rainbow, a spotted alligator with black fangs, and a green owl in a white tree. The phase hadn't lasted long, Michael's interests turning instead to music, his studies, the football, and the farm. Billy swallowed hard, remembering how his father used to sit Michael on his lap, even before the boy could walk or talk, and drive him around the farmyard in his red tractor, saying, "You're a right Brennan. You're going to be a right good farmer."

Billy at last found Michael's easel behind the old blue-painted sideboard that had stood in their dining room for years, before Tricia replaced it for something better. He removed the folded sheet of paper from his shirt pocket and taped it to the easel. After an Internet search for the most beautiful villages in Ireland, he had printed out this color photograph of Inistioge in Kilkenny. Inistioge sat nestled in the Nore Valley and boasted the remains of a Norman castle and monastic priory. Period homes and traditional cottages lined the streets, most whitewashed and several others covered in red and green ivy. More trees than people populated the village and its environs, clusters of firs, poplars, redwoods, chestnuts, and giant weeping beeches. He knew of the weeping willow, but not the weeping beech. As if those melancholy, copper beeches weren't enough, the River Nore ran alongside the village, right under a majestic eighteenth-century stone bridge with ten arches—magnificent images both, and both representing Michael's two greatest fears.

Billy placed a length of wood on the table and set about cutting and sanding it. He would first make the base for the miniature village, and then a thatched, whitewashed cottage to house the six tiny Brennans. After, he would build thatched cottages for the rest of his growing seconds community, and then make the ruins of the castle and priory. He would paint the river and create the stone bridge from clay, and also re-create the trees and wooded hills, and the meandering roads and walkways. He would make a wonderful new world, and there, he would teach Michael to not be afraid.

Twelve

THE DAY OF MICHAEL'S INQUEST FELL. BILLY, Tricia, and John arrived at Moran's Hotel, dressed in their Sunday best. To everyone's surprise, John had insisted on attending, and looked about as ill as Billy felt. The three hurried toward the entrance, hoping they wouldn't meet anyone.

They paused inside the hotel lobby, trying to locate the makeshift courtroom. A receptionist with a tall black beehive sat behind the desk, but they didn't want to ask directions and dally in plain view. They would get this fiasco over with fast, put it behind them, and never make mention of it again. Even as Billy told himself these things, some force felt as though it were gathering inside him and would erupt through the top of his head.

They charged forward, Billy in the lead, half blindly following the signs. His anger and anxiety climbed. It was beyond wrong for the government to put them, anyone, through this, forcing them to listen to details that would burn inside them for a long time afterward. So help Billy, if anyone in here said "committed" next to "suicide." He never used the term now. Never wanted to hear anyone else use it, either. Suicide wasn't a crime. Its victims weren't criminals.

He couldn't decide if it would be better or worse if the autopsy revealed the presence of drugs or high levels of alcohol in Michael's system. He even had wild thoughts of the coroner saying the results showed Michael was dying of some fatal disease or had suffered some personality-altering seizure, thereby explaining why he'd done what he did. Billy had other mad thoughts, too. Like the court revealing Michael hadn't taken his own life after all, but was murdered. All these horrible scenarios would be easier to accept than not knowing, than Michael seeming to have had no other reason than that provided by the expert guesses of social workers and the police. They all said Michael had to have suffered unbearable anguish and utter hopelessness, and saw no other way out.

A woman called out Billy's name. He spun around, seeing Delia Murray. A florist, she had supplied the flowers and wreaths for Michael's funeral. "Ah, hello, there, how are you?" she said. "I've thought of you all often." The three Brennans mumbled embarrassed hellos. "This is a pleasant surprise," Delia continued. "What brings you here so early?" Billy wasn't sure if she was making idle small talk, or fishing for news.

He, Tricia, and John looked at each other guiltily. "We're here for a meeting," Billy said.

"I see." Delia looked unconvinced. Her attention remained on Billy, as if she was trying to figure out what had changed about him. He'd lost twenty-nine pounds.

Delia raised the green watering can in her hand, looking pleased with herself. "I do the flowers here."

"Very good," he said.

"Well, I'll let you get on with it," she said. "Best of luck with everything, now."

They hurried down the corridor away from her. "Do you think she knows?" Tricia whispered.

"Who cares?" John said.

"We're here," Billy said, breathless. He pulled open the heavy wooden door.

Two tables stood at the head of the empty room, spaced several feet apart and covered with starched white cloths—the makeshift judge's bench and the witness stand. A lonely-looking jug of iced water sweated on each table, a stack of glasses next to them. Behind the tables, two red-velvet chairs with thick wooden arms, and in front, a dozen gray plastic chairs arranged in three rows. Billy, shaking, checked the time on his mobile phone. Twenty-five minutes before the hour.

"We shouldn't have come so early," Tricia said.

"Where is everyone?" John also sounded rattled.

They sat in the front row and waited. Tricia's pointer finger picked at the skin next to her thumbnail. "I'd kill for a cigarette."

"You've time," John said.

"It might start early." Her fingernail dug at her thumb, drawing blood.

"It's not going to start early," John said.

"Let your mother do what she wants," Billy said.

"I want this over with," Tricia said. "Before I get sick all over the place."

Billy fetched her a glass of water from the witness table. "What are you doing?" she said nervously. "That's not for us."

136

"What are they going to do?" Billy said. "Arrest me?"

She took a long drink. "Thanks."

These were the things to notice, Billy thought, a thirst quenched, a kind word, a seat beneath them, and warmth out of the cold. That was how they would get through this.

Fantastic smells wafted from the hotel's kitchen—fried foods, roasted meats, and creamy, herbed sauces. A lid opened on Billy's stomach, letting out a wail. He felt starved. He needed to eat. To stuff himself. At the very least, he deserved a little treat. No one could blame him for breaking out today, of all days.

He could be in and out of the hotel restaurant in minutes, could put away a burger, chips, and Coca-Cola in record time. No one need ever know. He could make some remark to the staff about it being for John and Tricia, then he could scoff the lot in the car. His mouth wetted and his eyelids turned heavy. He could taste the salt and grease and meat already. A little treat would calm him. Fortify him. After, he'd get right back on track. He'd never again cave.

The door opened and Sergeant Deveney entered. Billy's stomach bucked. He hadn't seen the policeman face-to-face since that night in Kennedy's. Now the fucker had ruined his planned treat, too. A short, white-haired man with small round spectacles followed Deveney, a thick file of papers under his arm. Billy, Tricia, and John stood to attention, a sweat breaking on Billy that rivaled the condensation on the two water jugs.

Deveney nodded his hellos and introduced the coroner, Mr. Feeney. Feeney's small eyes slid over Billy's bulk and then darted to Deveney, as if to say, *You weren't joking.* Billy pulled on his open cardigan, trying to drag the front panels around his drooping sides and middle. Twenty-nine pounds gone, but he couldn't get any more give out of the garment.

Feeney offered his condolences. "I know this is difficult," he continued, "but we'll move through everything as quickly as we can, all right?" Billy and Tricia thanked him. John hung back like a distrustful dog.

Moments later, Kitty Moore arrived. She looked frightened, and as pale as her putty-colored coat. Billy still couldn't get his head around the fact that the stubborn seventy-two-year-old had braved that freezing January morning to take her usual early ramble through the woods, little knowing what she would find.

He linked Kitty's arm, guiding her to a chair, feeling her tremble. She and Tricia chatted about the loveliness of the hotel, and the perfume of the purple hyacinths out front. John sat with his elbows on his knees, his attention trained on the patch of gray-and-black-striped carpet between his feet. He worked his lower jaw left to right nonstop with unnerving speed. Billy experienced a fresh spike of panic. What if things ever got to be too much for John, too?

"You all right?" Billy asked.

John nodded. "Yeah, you?"

"It'll be good to get this over with."

"Yeah." John's attention returned to the striped carpet.

Beyond the large windows, the sky sheathed itself in a magnificent blue. Beneath it, the world marched on. Billy again wondered how Michael could choose to leave it all.

Ronin Nevin completed the gathering, dressed in his black leather biker suit, his gloves and helmet in his hands. Like the rest of them, his face looked whitewashed. Feeney called the inquest to order. Billy's tongue fastened to the roof of his mouth. The pits of his shirt and the crotch of his underwear turned damp. He wished he could take off his cardigan, but didn't want anyone to see the full size of him, or the cling of his shirt to his rolls, its dig into his grooves. Worse, he'd had to cut slits in the shirt's side seams, to just about make it fit. When he was sitting, bubbles of fat bulged between the shirt buttons. He tugged again at his cardigan, trying to hide himself.

Feeney invited Sergeant Deveney to take a seat at the table next to him and deliver his report. Billy reached for Tricia's hand, her palm slippery in his.

Deveney moved behind the table and glanced nervously at Billy. Billy recalled his parting threat inside Kennedy's, warnings of what he'd do if Deveney ever again mentioned Michael and that morning. Billy sat straighter on his chair, pleased the policeman seemed afraid. People rarely took Big Billy Brennan seriously.

Deveney's words rushed out like bats. He gave the date, time, and location of the discovery of Michael's body. With the aid of the paramedics, Deveney cut Michael down and the boy was pronounced dead. The estimated time of death was between two and five A.M. His findings were consistent with death by suicide.

Every time Deveney opened his mouth, Billy felt as if the sergeant were sucking the air from his lungs. Blood filled Billy's head to bursting and pushed against the back of his face. He struggled not to jump up and shout, *Stop!* Tricia rubbed at her eyes and nose with the tattered remains of her tissues, struggling hard to quiet her breathless crying. John's foot bounced faster on the carpet. Divine smells from the restaurant filled the suffocating space. Billy was going to lose his mind if he didn't get something to eat. Deveney kept on talking. Why couldn't the policeman shut up? Hadn't he said enough already? Michael was gone. By suicide. There was nothing more to say.

Billy shook with the need to let out all the breath and pain and noises stuck inside him. He should be allowed to interrogate Deveney. To ask the only questions that mattered at this point. Why hadn't Deveney sent for him that morning? Why hadn't he let Billy be the one who caught Michael when he fell from that tree?

Feeney excused Deveney. As Deveney rose from the red-velvet chair, the words burst from Billy. "Why didn't you send for me?" Deveney dropped back onto the chair.

Tricia pulled on Billy's arm. "Don't, Billy."

"I'm sorry, Mr. Brennan, it isn't procedure for family to ask questions," Feeney said.

Deveney blurred in front of Billy's wet eyes. "I could have been there with him. You could have easily made it happen, so why didn't you?"

Deveney seemed pinned to the chair, speechless.

"Answer me!" Billy shouted. Tricia pulled on his arm, shushing him.

Deveney's face, his entire body, slackened. "Trust me," he rasped. "You didn't want to see him."

Tricia's hand jumped from Billy's arm and covered her mouth. John, looking crushed, placed his arm around her shoulders. Billy's stomach lurched.

Feeney cleared his throat. "That will be all, Sergeant Deveney, thank you."

Once Deveney returned to his seat, Feeney called Ronin to

the stand. Billy couldn't stop shaking. He rubbed his hand over his face, struggling to keep himself together.

Ronin placed his helmet and gloves on the white tablecloth, again bringing to mind bodiless parts. Billy's stomach heaved. He was going to be sick. He touched his free hand to his middle and pleaded with his insides not to betray him. Not now. He had to see this through.

Ronin confirmed he had seen Michael on that last night. He, Michael, and some of the other football players had gathered behind the village hall to chat and mess around, drink a few cans of cider. "Michael only had the one, two at the very most, and he never touched anything else, no drugs or anything, he wasn't like that."

Pain shot through Billy's chest, thinking of all the things Michael was.

"Would you say, Mr. Nevin, there was anything unusual or out of character about Michael Brennan that night, or at any time leading up to his death? Did you have any cause for concern?" Feeney asked.

"No, none. I'm as in the dark as everybody else."

Feeney excused Ronin, and called Kitty to the stand. Ronin returned to his seat, his head down and his Adam's apple working hard. As Kitty approached the table, Tricia's crying intensified. Billy tightened his hold on her.

Kitty started and stopped several times, her voice shaking. She confirmed she had found Michael's body on the date and time given, and had immediately phoned 999 from her mobile.

"And you stayed with the—" Feeney looked down at the file next to his clasped hands. "With Michael Brennan until the police and paramedics arrived?"

Sergeant Deveney stood up amid the empty rows of chairs. "That's incorrect, Mr. Feeney—"

Feeney raised his hand. "Mrs. Moore has the stand now, thank you."

"Beggin' your pardon, Mr. Feeney." Sergeant Deveney sat down, his face beetroot.

"No, sir, I didn't stay," Kitty said with a small sob, her eyes fixed on the coroner. "To tell you the truth, sir, I got such a fright when I saw him that everything afterwards is a bit of a blank. When I first came across him, I couldn't take it in for a few seconds, and then . . . then I realized." She wiped at her nose with a tissue. "I returned home. I didn't know what else to do. I'd only seen him for a moment and didn't know it was Michael. I only knew it was a young man and he was . . . gone, and the most awful feeling came over me, and I . . . I had to get away." Her throat made a deep sucking sound. "I knew there was nothing I could do for him and that the police and ambulance would have no trouble finding him, so I went home and left him to God. First thing, I lit a candle in my kitchen, got down on my knees, and prayed for him and all those he'd left behind."

Tricia cried into her hands. John made a strangled sound. Billy wrapped his arm around them both.

Feeney excused Kitty. Once she'd returned to her seat, he scanned the small group with sympathetic eyes. "That concludes today's proceedings, thank you." He removed several sheets of paper from a folder. "My findings, including autopsy and toxicology reports, are consistent with the testimonies offered and I declare the cause of the demise of Michael Liam Brennan to be suicide by hanging."

He walked to the front row and handed Billy a large brown envelope. Billy reluctantly removed his arm from around Tricia and John. Feeney pumped each of their arms, repeating his condolences. The brown envelope shook in Billy's hand. He didn't care if he ever opened it. The certificate might document the cause of death, but it didn't explain what had broken inside Michael. Didn't help them with how to go on.

Thirteen

BILLY HAD SPENT THE LAST COUPLE OF HOURS TRYING to write a catchy song for the march, a tune along the same lines as those drill songs soldiers used. So far, he'd only managed to pull one decent line of lyrics out of himself, *No more, no more, taking your life,* and was just circling a second, worthy line when Anna and Ivor clattered through the back doorway.

Ivor trailed his sister into the kitchen, dragging his back-pack after him. "Pick up that bag," Tricia said. "You'll rip the bottom out of it." Ivor looked as if something had been ripped out of him. He continued toward the hall.

"Not so fast," Billy said. He sat Ivor down. "What's going on?"

"Did something happen?" Tricia asked, standing over the boy.

"Come on, what is it?" Billy said, knowing he and Tricia were both wishing they could have this conversation with Michael.

"I hate school," Ivor said. "I'm never going back."

"Sorry, that's not an option," Tricia said, smiling.

"What's so bad about school?" Billy asked. He saw a flash of himself as a boy in the schoolyard, the other lads pointing and laughing because his supersized trousers were a lighter shade of navy than the official uniform. The same boys had also elbowed him and tripped him up during football training, saying he was fat and useless, and should quit.

Billy coaxed the story out of Ivor. During religion, Miss Cunningham had asked the students to imagine what they would do with God's powers. "When I said I'd talk to the people in heaven, Cormac Cullen laughed."

"What did Miss Cunningham do?" Tricia asked.

"She told him to be quiet, said what I said was lovely and that he shouldn't laugh. Then she patted me on the head like I was a baby or something and Cormac Cullen started sniggering behind his hands."

"Don't mind him," Tricia said. "There's obviously something wrong with him."

Billy remembered Cormac Cullen's father, Fintan, cornering him in the school bathroom, back when they were thirteen or fourteen. "You're so fat you can't see your own mickey." Billy felt sick, remembering. The taunt wasn't true back then, but he'd gone on to fulfill the prophecy.

Ivor moved around the table and dropped onto Billy's lap. "Everyone had way better ideas than me, too. They said they would use God's powers to stop hunger and for world peace and to bring the dead back to life." He slapped his forehead. "Why didn't I think of any of that?"

Tricia rubbed his back. "I'm with you, son. To be able to

talk to people in heaven, that's exactly what I'd use God's powers for."

"Me, too," Billy said.

Ivor sniffled. "At lunchtime, Cormac said I was a big fat dope and that a turkey had more brains."

Tricia eased Ivor to standing and wrapped her arms around him. "He's the dope, and a bloody bully."

Billy stood up. "I'll be right back."

In the yard, he phoned Ronin and made arrangements. When he returned, Ivor was sitting at the kitchen table, eating a slice of apple tart with a dollop of fresh cream. Tricia gave Billy a guilty look. *I couldn't say no.*

"Right," Billy said. "Let's go."

"Go where?" Ivor asked.

"It's a surprise."

"Don't go teaching him to fight," Tricia warned.

"I'm not going to teach him to fight," Billy said. He wished she hadn't brought that up. Years ago, when Michael was around eight or nine, he'd also had trouble with a bully. Billy and Tricia spoke with the principal. He chuckled and said, "I'm sure there's no harm meant." The day Michael arrived home with a burst lip, Billy brought him out to the garage. There, he instructed Michael on how to best beat up a bag of fertilizer. Michael's right uppercut proved impressive. The next time the bully picked on him, he broke the boy's nose. But, afterward, he'd only felt more miserable. "I can still hear the crunch of bone."

Billy had held Michael's head to the cushion of his stomach. "I'm sorry, son."

When Michael returned to school, he was given a hero's

welcome. No one else had ever been suspended for two whole weeks.

Ivor trailed Billy to the back door. "Come on, tell me," he pleaded.

Anna entered the kitchen. "Where are you two going?"

"I'm taking Ivor on a little adventure," Billy said, gathering himself.

She lit up. "Can I come, too?"

"No," Ivor said, fierce. "It's just Dad and me."

"Why can't I go?" Anna asked, disappointed.

"We need to go into town, Anna, remember?" Tricia said, rescuing Billy. "To get your new dance shoes." She smiled. "We'll have our own adventure."

Billy nodded at Tricia, grateful.

"Go on," Tricia said softly. "Enjoy yourselves."

Billy crossed the room and kissed her cheek, and the top of Anna's head.

The way Ronin had talked about his uncle's speedboat, Billy had expected it to be bigger, and sturdier, and with a bit more class. Not this small, gray-white two-seater with the algae stains on its body and the watery dirt on its floor. Even its off-white interior was stained with streaks of green. The white, peeling wheel looked like it belonged to a toy, and orange stuffing bulged from a gash on the driver's seat.

Billy cast another worried glance over the casket-like boat. The first night they'd brought Michael home in his white, silk-lined coffin, hundreds of mourners had tracked through the house. Over hours, they reached in to touch and kiss Michael, crying and praying. Their constant contact caused the gold edging on the coffin's net trim to flake and the glitter dotted Michael's dark hair, navy pin-striped suit, and bony, alabaster face. Specks of gold also got into his thick eyebrows, making them ever more striking. Billy and Tricia's first impulse was to remove the glitter and its whispers of mistake and wrongness, but then they decided to leave it.

Later, after all the mourners had gone home and the three remaining children had gone to bed, when it was just Billy and Tricia alone with Michael, as it was in the beginning, they had stood over their firstborn in the candlelight and watched him sparkle.

Ivor tugged on Billy's jacket sleeve. "Dad? Did you hear me?"

"What, son?"

"I said I don't think Mam would want me to go on a boat."

Billy forced a smile and winked at the boy. "That's why we're not going to tell her. This is just between you and me, man to man."

"I don't know." He was wavering.

"Just try," Billy said. "Think of school tomorrow and you telling everyone you got to race in a speedboat. Cormac Cullen will be dead jealous."

"But if I tell everyone, won't Mam find out?" Ivor said.

"You only tell the kids at school," Billy said. "And if it does get back to your mother, we'll tell her you and I made up the story, to trump that bully."

"I promise, Ivor," Ronin said. "The second you want to get out, I'll turn back to shore." He stepped inside the speedboat and reached out his arm to help Ivor aboard.

148

Ivor shook his head. "I don't know. I don't think I want to." The boy looked caged inside his life jacket. He tugged at its neck and scratched at the thick woolen hat on his head. He looked ready to tear both off him. As Ronin coaxed the boy, Billy's doubts grew. He'd hoped to join Ivor and Ronin on the water, but there wasn't room for a third. Not even a normal-sized man.

Ivor stepped onto the boat, Ronin holding on to one hand and Billy holding on to the other. The boat shook beneath the boy, making him wobble and cry out. "You're okay, son, we've got you. And Ronin will go nice and slow, won't you, Ronin?" Billy wished the weather was better. A gray, gloomy day, the river looked almost black.

"You're my captain, Ivor, I'm at your command," Ronin said. "You tell me what you want and it's done."

"Remember," Billy said, "he can't swim."

"Don't worry," Ronin said, suddenly solemn. "I'll take good care of him."

Billy could hear Tricia in his head. *What are you doing?*

"Go really slow," Billy said.

Ronin grinned. "How about I don't turn on the engine? We can float?"

Billy laughed. "What do you think, Ivor? Do you want to float or race?"

Ivor offered a shaky smile. "Race!"

"Okay, Captain Ivor," Ronin said. "Here we go." He used a wooden oar to turn the boat about inside the rushes and faced for the river. Then he allowed Ivor to turn on the ignition. The black engine on the back of the boat roared to life. Billy pushed down the urge to call the whole thing off. Ronin eased the boat to the right and glided over the water. Billy trained his eyes on them as they traveled farther away. If anything happened. If something went wrong.

Ronin turned the boat around and they passed in front of Billy. "All okay?" Billy shouted.

Ronin and Ivor gave a thumbs-up. Ivor still looked nervous, though.

Ronin ferried Ivor back and forth over the river, slowly gaining speed. "Looking good!" Billy shouted.

Fifteen minutes later, Ivor was waving his arms, elated. "Look, Dad. Look at me!"

"I see you! Well done, boy!"

"Faster!" Ivor shouted.

Ronin obliged. Maybe too much. He rode the boat hard, its front lifting high out of the churning water. Billy stopped himself from signaling to Ronin to slow down. He didn't want to ruin Ivor's big adventure. Whenever Ronin turned the boat, it leaned dangerously to the side. This latest turn, almost the boat's entire body rose out of the water, one corner plunging deep below the surface. They looked about to capsize. Billy almost couldn't stand to watch. Above the noise of the engine and water, he could hear Ivor cheering.

At last, it ended.

When the boat returned, Billy gripped Ivor's hand and pulled him back to shore. "You enjoyed that!"

Ivor grinned. "It was brilliant." He wrapped his arms around Billy's sides. "Thanks, Dad."

Billy shook Ronin's hand. "Thanks so much. He won't forget this, and neither will I."

"Anything for any of Michael's," Ronin said, a tremble in his voice.

Billy and Ivor walked up the grassy slope toward their car, Billy's arm around Ivor's shoulder. "I can't wait to tell everyone tomorrow, especially Cormac," Ivor said, suddenly sounding much older and more confident—that thickness to his voice barely noticeable.

"Make a right good story out of it," Billy said.

Ivor laughed. "Oh, I will." He stopped walking and looked up at Billy. "Do you really not think what I said today in class was stupid?"

"About using God's powers to talk to the people in heaven? No, not at all. I told you, I think that's an excellent use of God's powers." Billy rubbed the top of Ivor's curls, smiling mischievously. "I just wouldn't stop there. I'd also play the Lotto—"

Ivor slapped Billy's hand away, snorting, rolling his eyes. Then he turned serious again. "I talk to Michael every single day and I listen and I wait, but he never answers."

"I know, son, I know." They continued walking, Billy's arm around the boy's soft shoulders.

Days later, Billy asked John to carry the ladder upstairs. He trailed his son, breathing heavy. It felt good to have John's help, almost as if they were getting along, but it was also humiliating to not be fit enough to carry the ladder himself. He was getting there, though. Time was he couldn't get up these stairs without dragging himself along by the banister; now he was clearing the steps unaided. Someday, he would run up and down them, get Anna and Ivor to keep time and to count aloud the number of laps he completed.

John deposited the ladder on the landing, beneath the attic opening. Billy reached him, trying not to breathe so loud.

"What are you going up there for?" John asked.

Billy knew he didn't have to tell John it was to get to Michael's belongings. Tricia had cleared away all of Michael's things the day after his Month's Mind mass, except for some of the boy's clothes, his guitar, and a few well-chosen photographs. The rest she packed into boxes and stored deep in the attic. A longing had seized Billy to listen to some of the old vinyls Michael had collected.

"Can you climb up and lift off the panel?" he asked.

John glared at the square in the ceiling. "Are you even going to fit through there?"

Billy eyed the opening, fighting the feeling of defeat. "Just do it."

John scampered up the ladder, as if showing off.

"Easy, there," Billy said.

In moments, John had pushed up the panel and cleared the attic opening. He descended the ladder in record time, too, and moved toward the stairs. "Try not to kill yourself." He spun around, red-faced. "Sorry, I didn't mean that, it came out wrong."

Billy nodded, collecting himself. "That's all right."

As John moved downstairs, Billy braved the first rung. Then John reappeared, to hold the ladder steady.

"Thanks," Billy said, moved. He continued his slow, careful ascent.

He reached the top of the ladder, his head and shoulders inside the attic, lit upon by the swarm of dust. There was also a strong smell of stale, and a trapped, pulsating heat. His hands jumped from the ladder and onto the attic floor. He hauled himself up and forward, his chest landing on the pale raw wood, his legs dangling from the gap in the ceiling.

"Do you want a push?" John asked, sarcastic.

"What am I, Winnie-the-Pooh?" Billy said, making John laugh. He heaved and wriggled, forcing his way through the opening. Its hard rim scraped his flanks, breaking skin.

"All right," John called up. "I'll be in my room. Shout whenever you're ready to come down, I'll hold the ladder again."

"Okay, thanks." Billy considered ordering John to join him, and to show some gentler emotion for his brother at last, but he let the boy go.

Under the yellow light of the lone naked bulb, Billy found the vinyls and record player in the far corner. Slowly, gently, he sorted through the stacks of LPs, finding U2, the Beatles, Blondie, the Eurythmics, Queen, Michael Jackson, the Beach Boys, Culture Club, the Pogues, and even one of Billy's old favorites, Thin Lizzy.

He eased the *Jailbreak* album from its sleeve, struck in a horrible way by its title, and then by something much worse. There, on what should have been blank, ivory record paper, was Michael's handwriting, his cursive covering every inch of the album's inner sleeve. Billy read, his eyes filling and the bridge of his nose fizzing. Michael had penned what appeared to be his own lyrics in circles around the album sleeve, his handwriting staying within invisible lines that matched the spirals of the grooves on the record.

Billy grabbed at the other albums, pulling off their covers. He found a total of ten inner sleeves similarly filled with lyrics.

Won't somebody help me? Stars like fish in the sky. You are my beautiful forever, my perfect escape. How to get to another me? No one ever tells us we can drown in air, fall down so far inside ourselves. When you have it all, but feel so small. A head full of flames in the dark. Ribbons of love that tie us up, that can't be cut.

"Tricia," he shouted, shaking. "Tricia!"

Below him, John's footfalls rushed across the landing. "What is it? What's wrong?"

"Get your mother up here quick," Billy said.

Tricia's voice sounded on the stairs. She reached the landing. "What's going on?"

"Come up here," Billy said, trying to slow the thump of his heart.

Like John, Tricia climbed the ladder in record time. Billy took her hand, helping her inside. He led her to the vinyls, now scattered atop the cardboard boxes. "They're all songs he wrote."

Tricia, the last of the color in her face bleeding out, sifted through the inner sleeves, reading one, two, three of Michael's songs, each one faster than the last. Just as Billy thought she would break down and weep, she returned the vinyls to their covers, working fast and rough.

"What are you doing?" he asked.

"I've seen enough," she said.

"You don't want to read them all?" he asked, incredulous, angry.

"This is not how I want to remember him, not how I think he'd want any of us to remember him."

The hot attic air was cloying, choking. Billy had never felt further from Tricia, more opposite.

"What's going on?" John asked from below.

"Nothing, everything's fine." She disappeared down the ladder, her head bowed.

Despite the stifling air and the taint of must, Billy remained inside the small, low-ceilinged space, re-reading every word. There had to be clues, messages. *Won't somebody help me? My beautiful forever, my perfect escape.* He didn't only need to understand why Michael left them, but how he could have left them. Didn't Michael know they loved him? That they would have stood by him, no matter what? Would have done anything and everything to help him? In a whisper, Billy read aloud every last word his son had written, sending up Michael's songs, his finger tracing the spiral of lyrics like a record needle.

Fourteen

SATURDAY AFTERNOON, DENIS SAT NEXT TO BILLY at the kitchen table, a laptop and two steaming mugs of tea in front of them.

"I thought we'd have received a lot more pledges by now," Billy said.

"What's the latest number?" Denis asked.

Billy reached for his paperwork, double-checking the amounts. "One thousand two hundred and fifty-nine euro and seventy-five cent."

"Hey, that's great," Denis said. "Especially in this economy and what with all the other causes out there, too."

Billy wasn't convinced. He couldn't shake the worry, the shame, that if he wasn't fat and was doing any other kind of fund-raiser, like cycling around the country, he'd be getting a lot more support and pledges. He couldn't get Michael's lyrics out of his head, either. *Won't somebody help me? You are my beautiful forever, my perfect escape. Ribbons of love that tie us up, that can't be cut.* He rubbed his hand over his head. "I want to stuff my face."

"You don't mean that," Denis said.

"Yeah, I'm going to need a bit more coaching than that, sponsor."

Denis's finger scratched at his eyebrow and he looked suddenly uncomfortable. "The thing is, I shouldn't be sponsoring you. It's a slight against every honest addict out there. If you really want to succeed, you need to be part of an OA group."

Billy's agitation worsened. "Of course I really want to succeed, but not that way."

"That doesn't make sense." Denis insisted on searching online for local OA meetings. "Give it a go, can't you?"

Billy winced. Just that afternoon he'd searched the Internet for the fattest person in Ireland, terrified he would discover his own name. His search hadn't shown any specific findings for Ireland, but it did name a man in England. The poor fella weighed almost one thousand pounds.

Billy had studied the man's photograph—his arms, legs, torso, and stomach impossibly enormous and the hospital bed barely able to contain him. Billy looked almost good in comparison and had bordered on feeling smug. That was exactly the kind of response he didn't want to elicit in other, less obese addicts at an OA meeting.

"Here, there's an OA meeting in town tonight—"

"Stop! I said I'm not going, and that's the end of it."

Denis looked wounded. Billy sighed, remorseful. "Let's just get down to business, all right?"

With Denis's help, Billy pushed through his learning curve and purchased the domain name End Suicide Now! He then created a free website, and set up Twitter and Facebook accounts. The next crucial step was to find a filmmaker. He and Denis searched online, looking for every and any possible candidate in the country. Once the documentary was completed, Billy planned to get RTÉ and, ideally, BBC or one of the other big English networks to air it. From there, he hoped the documentary might go global.

The natural light fading, the men abandoned their online search and moved upstairs, to take "before" photographs for the new website. Billy pushed himself up the stairs. He was about to have his photo taken in his underwear. He was going to show all of himself, for all to see.

Inside the bedroom, he turned his back to Denis. He removed his shirt first, imagining his friend's horror at the rear view of his sweaty crevices, rolls of fat, and the angry purple stretch marks. "Well, this isn't awkward."

Denis chuckled. "No, not at all."

Billy dropped his trousers and stripped to his socks and underwear. He tried to suck in his stomach.

"Ready when you are," Denis said.

Billy pushed back his shoulders, straightened as best he could, and turned around. His eyes wanted to close, which he also fought. "Okay, how should we do this?" He looked about the room—for inspiration and a hiding spot.

"We should probably get a shot of you full-on from the front, and then maybe a couple of profiles, yeah?" Denis said.

"You really need me from all three angles?" Billy asked. Maybe he didn't have to put himself through all this. Maybe he was going overboard.

"Whatever you think," Denis said. "We could just post two images, a front shot and a profile?"

"Yeah, okay." Billy endured Denis ordering him to move about the room and pose ten, fifteen, twenty times, trying to get photos from his best angles and with the best light. He didn't know how Denis could say "best angles" with a straight face.

"Work it," Denis joked as the camera's flash went off like tiny explosions.

The ordeal ended. "We have a wrap," Denis said. "Well done."

"But I was just starting to get into it." Billy was only half joking. He'd dreaded Denis seeing him like this, and still dreaded putting his near-naked body on public display. But it was a little freeing, too. Like maybe now, because he'd revealed the worst of himself, he could stop hiding in plain sight. His naked, ugly self revealed, he was at last free of what he'd imagined to be this deep, dark secret he'd kept all these years, the secret of just how disgusting he was.

Denis scrolled through the photos he'd taken, looking pleased with himself. Billy struck a pose, gritting his teeth and flexing his arms. "Get me like this."

Denis laughed and clicked, shooting Billy in Incredible Hulk mode. Billy struck one powerful pose after another, all curved arms, planted legs, and bared teeth. He mimicked the Hulk's signature roar, making Denis laugh harder. Giddy, he climbed onto the bed and stood in its center, his arms curved at his head and a slight bend in his knees, as if he could barely contain the might of himself. He was an action figure. He could take on anyone, anything.

Denis raised the camera and captured more shots. "Brilliant! I love it!"

Billy roared again, louder and stronger than any war cry that had ever ripped through the Hulk's throat. He beat on his chest with his fists. "Don't make me angry. You wouldn't like me when I'm angry."

Denis was laughing so hard he couldn't stand straight. "That's exactly how Bill Bixby sounded."

Billy pounded on his chest again. "Fear the Hulk!"

They laughed hard. The bedroom hadn't heard such laughter in years. As if the very thought summoned her, Tricia opened the bedroom door. Startled, she looked from Denis and up to Billy standing on the middle of the mattress.

"Tricia." Billy scrambled to get down off the bed. Tricia retreated into the hall. "Wait," he said, but she was already gone.

Inside the garage, Billy set about making a tiny church for his miniature village. The six miniature Brennans watched from the edge of the workbench. The rows of defective dolls and soldiers peered down from their shelves on the wall. He glued the wooden church together, complete with a steeple and cross. Next, he inserted a pea-sized silver bell into the tower, and four stained-glass windows that he'd painstakingly cut from suncatcher ornaments. These were the only adornment he would allow, the church pointedly absent of confessional boxes, staring statues, and a bloodstained Jesus hanging from the crucifix.

Next, he lifted the cottage's thatched roof and placed his firstborn inside, the home for his tiny family replicated from the cottage inside the snow globe in the shop window—on that fateful day he'd tried to avoid Kitty Moore in town. Next to Michael, he placed tiny Billy, Tricia, John, Anna, and Ivor. He wished the toys had movable parts, so he could do more with them, so they would seem more lifelike. Beyond the cottage, the day is sunny, glorious. The six Brennans rush outside and play football next to the ice-blue tree, the black puppy darting among them, wagging his tail.

After, the family races on horseback on the beach, the puppy trailing, barking with delight. Michael breaks from the group and charges ahead on the chestnut stallion. Billy calls after him, alarmed. "Come back!" He kicks at his horse's flanks, giving chase. Billy catches up with Michael and grabs at the reins, pulling the chestnut to a stop.

Michael is laughing. "I'm all right, I just wanted to see how fast he could go." Billy tries to control his anger and panic, telling himself Michael is okay and that's all that matters. But this is Billy's kingdom and in his kingdom he cannot allow Michael to ever get away.

Michael frowns. "What's wrong?"

Billy forces a smile, struggling to calm himself. "Nothing, son. Everything's perfect." They circle around and rejoin the others.

Billy, Tricia, and the children gallop along the ocean's edge, their horses glistening with sweat as they race over the glittering sand toward the sun, the brightest light of all.

Billy pushed himself from bed and shuffled to the bathroom. He stepped onto the scale, his breath held. The number forced the breath right out of him. He stood off the scale and climbed back on. He had gained two pounds. He couldn't believe it.

He'd dieted and exercised so hard, had denied himself so much. This couldn't be happening.

He wouldn't go backward. He had to redouble his efforts. He would drop these two pounds in record time, and then some. He would do whatever it took. A week of nothing but shakes. An hour walk on the cove every day without fail, too, and wearing as many layers as possible, to sweat as much out of him as he could. Then he'd build up to an hour's jog every day. Hell, he'd run a marathon yet. He made his Hulk pose in the mirror. He wasn't going to let anything stop him. Least of all himself.

A short while later, long after Ivor should have appeared to breakfast, Billy found the boy in the bathroom, still in his pajamas and chewing on the bristles of his toothbrush, his mouth covered in white foam. Ivor scrunched his face and complained of a stomachache. "Nice try," Billy said. "Go get dressed right now, and then get downstairs. You'll enjoy the walkathon yet, wait till you see."

"No, I won't, I'll hate it. I always hate it."

"You don't mean that."

"How do you know? You don't know anything." Ivor pulled free of Billy and rushed out of the bathroom.

Billy let him go. The boy had remained mad with him ever since his spin on the speedboat. Billy's big plan hadn't worked. Ivor had returned to school with tall tales of his daring stunts on the river at breakneck speeds, but Cormac, everyone, couldn't seem to care less. "They hate me," Ivor had wailed.

Ivor and Tricia's argument carried up from the kitchen. He was still insisting he didn't want to do the walkathon. "You're going to school and that's the end of it," Tricia said. Billy looked in the mirror, finding little of the recent solace in his shrinking face. Ivor had looked ecstatic that day on the river, racing inside the speedboat. Billy could still hear his shrieks of delight. He'd felt sure the big brag would have infuriated Ivor's bully and impressed all the other kids no end, making Ivor feel like he'd won. But the grand adventure had failed. Billy had failed. Again.

The afternoon bore down warm and sunny. Perfect weather for the walkathon, perhaps, but it drew more talk on the car radio of climate change and the end of the world.

Inside Flynn's Field, a swell of adults and children. Several parents in orange vests stood out. One blasted encouragement and safety reminders through a bullhorn; a few handed out bottles of water and orange wedges; others wrote in black marker the number of laps completed on a page pinned to the children's backs. Those with first-aid skills stood by to administer to nosebleeds, twisted ankles, and asthma attacks. The rest, like Billy, had come out to cheer.

He lumbered toward the crowd, his hand checking for the outline of tiny Michael in his tracksuit pocket. A burst of roars and applause went up. Billy took heart from this great turnout for a school walkathon, picturing the show of force that would soon come out to support his landmark march against suicide. He found Tricia in the far corner of the field, working the fruit and water stand.

"You missed Anna," she said. "Sixth class was the first group out. She and her friends had a grand old time. They talked faster than they walked." Billy laughed tightly, aware she was only being pleasant for show. At home, ever since she'd walked in on him and Denis in the bedroom, she hadn't a civil word to say.

Thumbs Tom stood close by, here in support of his grandson. His eyes roved Billy. "You look like a man that's lost more weight."

"You better believe it," Billy said, pushing away a guilty stab over the two pounds he'd gained. That would be gone again soon enough.

He fixed his attention on Ivor, the boy dressed in light blue vest and shorts, a too-tight, shiny polyester number. The shorts looked especially sad, riding up the back of Ivor's thick thighs and catching between his buttocks. He struggled after his classmates.

"Come on, Ivor!" Billy shouted. The sign on Ivor's back read four laps, while most everyone else had cleared eight or nine. Aidan Burke, Nancy Burke's grandson, was tearing around the field. A missile, he'd already completed fourteen laps.

As Ivor started into his fifth lap, he looked to be in serious trouble, sweating, dragging his feet. Aidan Burke shot past, clipping Ivor hard on the shoulder and knocking him to the ground.

Billy moved across the field as fast as he could, pain stabbing his right ankle. He helped Ivor to standing. "You're all right, keep going, you can do it."

Ivor rubbed at his tears and shook his head hard.

"Come on," Billy said. "Look at everyone else, you're falling way behind. Let's go, let's do this." He grabbed Ivor by the wrist and pulled him along, following the path the children's feet had flattened in the grass.

"Stop, Dad, I can't."

"Yes, you can."

"I'm too tired, my legs hurt."

"Just one more lap, come on, you're almost there."

"I need to stop," Ivor said.

"Think about your school and everyone who sponsored you, you can't let them down." Billy pulled harder on Ivor's wrist.

Ivor pushed at Billy's hand, trying to free himself. "I need to stop."

"Come on, you're letting everyone get away."

Ivor cried harder. "Let me go, you're hurting me."

Billy picked up the pace, pushing through the pain in his right ankle and towing Ivor faster. The boy had several more laps in him, if he would only try.

"I need water," Ivor said, panting.

"You can get water when you're finished."

They cleared another hundred yards. Just as Billy was starting to taste success, he heard Ivor yelp and felt a hard tug on his arm. When he looked around, Ivor lay on the grass, pale and unmoving. Billy dropped next to the boy, his kneecaps hitting the dirt hard.

Tricia appeared and also knelt over Ivor. She touched her palm to Ivor's cheek. "He's out cold."

From behind them, Nancy Burke shouted, "Someone get some water quick."

Tricia glared at Billy, her expression crazed. "What have you done?" She lifted Ivor's right eyelid, and his left.

"Is he okay?" Billy croaked. He shook Ivor's shoulder. "Wake up, son. Come on, you're all right." He held the back of his hand to Ivor's nostrils.

Tricia slapped his hand away. "What are you doing?" She checked the pulse at Ivor's neck and his wrist.

An anguished cry gathered in Billy's chest, fighting to get out.

Thumbs Tom also appeared, his deformed hand reaching between Billy and Tricia, offering a dripping bottle of water. He waved his free hand, beckoning the first aid crew.

Tricia eased Ivor's head onto her lap and brought the water bottle to his pale lips. "Come on, son, wake up. You're all right. Take a little drink for me, now, good boy. Ivor?" Her voice climbed. "Ivor?"

Wake up, Billy silently screamed.

The crowd pressed closer, sending up anxious whispers. "Is he all right? What's going on?"

"Give us a sec," Billy growled. When he looked back down, Ivor's hand covered Tricia's on the water bottle, the boy drinking in deep gulps. The sense of relief almost knocked Billy off his knees, as did the sudden memory.

When Michael was a baby, he would clasp Billy's hand on his bottle of formula during feeds. The memory was so strong, Billy could almost feel Michael's fierce baby grasp and the sticky warmth of his tiny hand. Michael's eyes would also fasten on Billy, wide and inky blue then, and full of trust.

Ivor remained sprawled on the grass, his color returning. Billy reached to stroke the boy's head, but Ivor pulled away. Billy reached again, frowning. Ivor scrabbled backward on all fours, like a crab from a net.

"Come on, Ivor," Tricia said, hooking him under his arms and helping him to stand up. "Let's get you home."

After several sad attempts, Billy succeeded in getting up off his knees and onto his feet. Tricia held on to Ivor's arm, the boy still woozy. "Here, let me," Billy said, reaching again for Ivor.

"Don't," Tricia said through gritted teeth.

Billy scanned the onlookers, his shame mounting. "I was trying to help."

"Help?" she said, incredulous. "This is all your fault." Everyone started to move off, pretending at discretion and a return to the business of the walkathon. "Couldn't you have let the child alone and not always be pressuring him?"

"Me?" Billy said. When did he ever pressure Ivor? She was the one always nagging the boy about his weight. She pressured all the children, except John, her favorite. He wondered if she'd even admitted to herself how much she'd drilled Michael about going to UCD and getting that ag science degree. As for him? He hadn't wanted Ivor to look bad in front of everyone, that was all. Hadn't wanted the other children sneering and teasing.

Tricia's eyes cut to the parents and children still looking on while pretending not to. "There, you've made a show of us again, are you satisfied now?"

He whirled around and plodded toward his car, his knuckle in his mouth, his teeth biting hard. In his periphery, he spotted Aidan Burke, the boy bent over, his hands on his knees. Billy charged, hobbling on his right foot. "You!"

He wagged his finger in Aidan's face. "It was your fault. I saw that knock you gave Ivor." He looked around the field for Cormac Cullen. He had a few choice words for that lad as well. For his father, too, if he was here. Aidan started to walk away. Billy followed him. "You better say sorry to Ivor, you hear me?"

"For what?"

"Don't give me that."

Nancy Burke reached them, out of breath. "What's going on?"

"That lad needs to learn some manners," Billy said.

"I beg your pardon—"

Billy moved off, leaving her mouth hanging.

Billy couldn't shake the scene inside Flynn's Field. How the army of spectators had stared. He could imagine the talk.

Did you see him dragging the boy? Sure, you wouldn't do that to a donkey.

I'd say there's a lot more goes on there behind closed doors than any of us know.

It's pure neglect, the size they're letting the lad get to. And then what he said to Aidan Burke.

I thought Billy Brennan was a teddy bear, but now I'm starting to wonder.

Maybe Michael had more reason to do what he did than they're making out.

Billy needed fast food. Just this once. He would go to the pretty young cashier in Seanseppe's, the one with the black hair parted in the middle and flicked out like crow's wings. She always had a soft smile for him, and never reacted to his size, or the size of his order, not even his most outrageous pig-outs.

He phoned Denis. "I'm mad tempted, I need something hot and greasy and salty—"

"No, you don't. Now, calm down."

"Yeah, not working. I'd eat my own hand right now if it was deep-fried."

"Okay, okay, give me a few nice big breaths," Denis said.

Billy thought about hanging up, about the pretty, smiling cashier.

"I don't hear you," Denis said. "Come on, Billy," he said gently.

Billy drew a long, loud breath that felt slicing.

Fifteen

IN THE DAYS AFTER THE WALKATHON, BILLY TRIED to make amends with Ivor, but the boy wasn't having any of it. "Leave me alone."

Tricia continued to shut Billy out, too, doing and saying only the bare minimum to keep up some semblance of normalcy in front of the children. Billy retreated more and more to the garage and his other world.

"What are you at out there?" Tricia asked, but he brushed her off. No one needed to know about the kingdom he was creating. They would ruin that on him, too.

This particular evening, he lifted tiny Michael and tiny Billy from the cottage and placed them on the ledge of the clay bridge, above its middle portals. The two set about fishing, their legs dangling over the rushing river.

Billy, an excellent fisherman despite his missing arm, catches something large and fierce on the end of his line. He struggles to reel in the catch, gripping the pole with both his good arm and his stump. Using all his might, he raises the fishing rod straight, facing the tip skyward. The fight the fish is putting up, it has to be a record-sized carp.

Michael also grabs hold of the pole, helping to keep the tension on the line and stopping the carp from spitting out the hook. Both toys pull and pull, and just as the carp tires and they think they have him, the line snaps, sending Billy backward onto the bridge and plunging Michael into the churning water below. Billy roars, feeling kicking sensations in his chest, and dives into the river. He reaches Michael and hooks his good arm and stump under the boy's armpits. He drags his son to safety, the water ripping around them like dark cloth.

"It's all over," Billy says. "I've got you, Michael. I've got you."

Billy revisited the cove, hoping hard he wouldn't meet anyone he knew. Ever since the walkathon, he'd avoided people. He would have to face them eventually, and sooner rather than later—he wasn't going to get where he needed to be with his weight, the march, or his documentary if he stayed in hiding—but he'd gladly delay exposure for a little while longer.

He reached an imaginary starting line on the beach, the sound of the ocean loud in his ears. He readied himself, his arms hitched and his feet pawing at the sand like a bull in the ring. With a roar, he started to jog. As of that morning, he'd lost those two pounds he'd gained plus seven more, and was now at three hundred and sixty-five pounds. Never again would he allow the hand of the scale to move in the wrong direction. He'd subsisted mostly on the performance shakes, juiced wheatgrass, fruit and vegetables, and a high-protein, low-carbohydrate, no-sugar diet. All his dieting wasn't going to be enough, though. If he was going to shed half of himself as soon as possible, he would have to exercise every single day, and hard.

As he moved over the sand, he felt the need to hold out his hands in front of his barrel chest—afraid he would fall flat on his face. The pain in his knees and ankles snapped at him. His right leg hurt the most, the bones grinding. After only a few hundred yards, he had to force one foot in front of the other. With every stab of pain, he focused on all those who had sponsored him, and the naysayers he wanted to prove wrong.

Within minutes, he slowed to a limp, the pain in his right leg crippling. Every time his feet touched the sand, searing pain shot through his joints. He bit down on his lip and tried to continue, but the pain, the breathlessness, proved too much. At this rate, was he even going to be able to take part in the march himself? Tricia's voice filled his head. *You've made a show of us again.* If he became too banged up to lead his own march . . . It didn't bear thinking about. Defeated, he dropped onto the sand.

As the waves rose and fell, Michael's long-ago pleas niggled. *Don't let me go.* Then, when Billy had pulled Michael from beneath the water, how the boy had slapped and raged at him. *Get away from me.* Billy groaned out loud. His right knee and ankle felt as if someone were going at them with a knife. His breath came in short, tight streams. A cormorant dove into the glittering water, and then rose victorious, a blue-silver fish in its beak. Billy looked to the sky and out over the blanket of sea, at the almost impossible blues and greens, the world beating on, brilliant and glorious.

He struggled to remove his shoes and socks. After a messy effort, he got back up to standing. He removed tiny Michael from his trousers pocket and placed him inside his shoe, under the ball of his socks. He rolled his trousers legs up to his bumpy knees and limped to the water's edge, the broken shells and sharp stones nipping at the soles of his feet. His toes tested the water, its chill making him shudder and roll his shoulders to his ears.

He pushed on, till the freezing water climbed past his knees. His waist. His chest. Almost out of his depth, he flipped onto his back and floated, the salt water lapping at his ears and mouth. His arms and legs scissored the water as fast as they could, fighting the chill. Seaweed touched his face. He chased away images of the brown-green tendrils tightening around his neck and tried to relax. As his limbs cut the water, he marveled at the sudden absence of pain, at the laws of suspension. Even as his teeth chattered and the Atlantic snapped at him, he remained floating. He couldn't remember the last time he'd felt so light.

A couple of days later, Billy stood in front of the Sports Center in town. As awful as it had felt to attend the AA meeting a while back, it was nothing next to his walking into this place now, about to sign up for a swimming pool membership, and then strip almost naked in public. He'd decided to give up his torturous efforts at walking, and his sad aspirations to build to jogging and then running. Instead, he planned to swim in the pool every day—much kinder, gentler exercise. The downside was that he'd likely meet people he knew while he was letting it all hang out. He reminded himself how surprisingly freeing the photo shoot with Denis had proved. Maybe this wouldn't be so bad, either.

He stopped at the front desk to register, still unable to rein in his breathing. Then he plodded to the changing room—the space teeming with men and boys in various states of undress. He crossed the room, trying to ignore people's double takes and the wall-to-wall mirrors. He recognized a couple of faces, one lad from the factory and one older man from the chemist where Tricia worked, but he pretended not to know them.

He located an empty locker down the back, parked himself on the damp bench, and kicked off his shoes. After a struggle to reach his feet, he peeled off his socks. When he went to pull off his sweatshirt, though, he couldn't do it. Too many eyes. He moved across the wet, cold tiles in bare feet and entered the toilet stall, eying the wet patches on the floor with suspicion. He sidestepped the dubious spills and stripped down to his supersized navy boxer swim trunks. Then he waited.

As soon as the chatter and activity outside lulled, he lurched free of the small space. There in the corner, the weighing scale beckoned. Curiosity beat out mortification and he climbed aboard, this professional scale likely more accurate than his one at home. He waited for the numbers to settle, feeling watched. He stepped off and back on, to be sure. Three hundred and sixty-one pounds. He had lost a total of forty pounds. The number echoed inside him, biblical. He hiked up his arms and pumped the air.

The sense of triumph dissipated as soon as he emerged from the changing room and into the noisy, chemical-seeped pool area. Already the reek of chlorine annoyed his eyes and nostrils. He pushed on, his feet slapping over the sopping-wet tiles as fast as he could move. He would gladly take the cover of the poisonous pool over standing here in front of everyone, with so much of him showing.

At the water's edge, he hesitated, trying to decide how best to enter. The metal stairs didn't seem substantial enough to support his bulk. He held his breath and stepped off the wet, paved deck, dropping into the shallow end. He recovered from the chill shock of entry and the blindness of the gargantuan splash he'd made, only to hear the shrill sound of the lifeguard's whistle. "No jumping!" Everyone turned to look.

Worse, his big splash had caused a toddler to cry. The child's mother glared, the bawling, red-faced boy fastened to her hip. Billy raised his hand apologetically. "Sorry." The woman turned her back, an indignant swing to her water-beaded shoulders, and trudged to the other side of the pool, the boy still squawking and staring back at Billy. Billy brought his hands together and pushed down into the water.

He reached the deep end and burst through the surface, gasping. The chlorine burned his eyes. Next time he would wear goggles. His reflection in the rearview that sunny, blinding day came back, the fat of his face bubbling over the arms of his sunglasses and drawing ever more attention to his meaty head. The added humiliation of goggles hardly seemed to matter here, though, when he was already letting everyone see so much of his outsides. The two men he'd recognized in the changing room swam laps nearby, but he continued to ignore them. He touched the wall of the pool, turned around, and started back toward the opposite end, thinking, *Forty pounds*, thinking, *Michael*.

He tired after only three laps. He tried to continue, but his lungs felt as if they would burst, his rib cage as if it would collapse. *Get up*, he told himself, echoing his father's herding of the cows. If he could only make six laps today, and next time build from there. His arms sliced the water and his legs kicked. He told himself he would drown if he didn't go on, he would boil in a vat of oil, but he couldn't muster another stroke. He stopped mid-pool and grabbed the blue lane rope, struggling to tame his breathing. Earlier, on the drive into town, he'd noticed several crows on the telephone wires. The birds had swayed on first landing, as if they would fall, but they held on, their claws curled around the wire. His hand tightened on the lane rope, holding on until he'd recovered his breath and the painful tightness in his chest eased. Then he pushed off, finishing the lap.

The rest of the week, he returned to the swimming pool in the evenings, straight after work. He continued to see faces he recognized, but thankfully didn't run into anyone he knew well enough to have to stop and chat while standing in all his inglorious flesh. Every time he tired and thought he couldn't continue, he pressed on, squeezing the last possible lap out of himself. By Friday, he'd lost another three pounds. Forty-three pounds gone. It would never get old, this kind of ecstatic descent.

One night in bed, Billy jerked up from the pillow, and dropped back down. Tricia's face swam above him, concerned. She pressed her hand to his cheek, her first tenderness toward him in so long. "Relax, it's over."

His thumb and finger rubbed hard at his eyes. "Michael was a boy and he went missing. I couldn't find him—"

"Shush, it's okay." Her hand remained on his face.

He remembered the first time he'd seen her, in the village church, at their friends' wedding. She was wearing a short, floral dress and a little cerise cardigan, her hair so blond, her eyes so blue, and a smile that could heal wounds. It was love, and heartbreak, at first sight. *No way,* he'd thought, *a girl like that would have anything to do with a lump like me.*

She was still leaning over him on the bed. His fingers reached for her hair, its past luster gone. He lifted several dull locks, and moved his fingers down their shaft, letting each strand fall slowly away. Their eyes searched each other. His hand slid to the back of her neck and eased her face toward him. They kissed. He couldn't remember the last time he had kissed her full on the mouth. She pulled away.

Just as he thought she would turn on her side and get back to the business of sleep, she dipped her head again and kissed him. He struggled to rise up toward her, part lifting, part rolling himself, and fell against her. "Sorry." She was beneath him now and he rushed his lips back to hers. His hand slid from her neck and down her front to her small, soft breast. He caressed her, reverently, greedily, like rubbing a magic lamp. When he worked her erect nipple between his thumb and fingers, she made a little sound that he hoped was pleasure.

Oh, Tricia. He'd yearned for her for so long, this hardly seemed real. He'd thought they'd never get back here, never get back to the way they used to be together. He pushed aside the nightdress covering her soft skin and lowered his lips to her hard nipple. As he sucked, her hand rubbed the back of his head and her body arched against him. With a grunt, he drew up his knee as high as he could and straddled her thigh. His resurrected, burning flame of a penis humped against her, and in an unstoppable burst, he ejaculated.

With a soft cry, she pushed out from beneath the pin of his leg and torso and hurried to the bathroom.

He listened to the long run of water, imagined her wiping hard at herself.

When she returned to bed, she turned her back to him.

"I'm sorry, it's been so long," he said.

"It's okay."

He touched his hand to her shoulder, trying to turn her toward him. "We're not finished. I want to take care of you, too."

She scooted away, to the farthest edge of the bed. "It's okay, I said, go to sleep."

He rolled over. Quietly, secretly, he reached beneath the covers and touched his right knee, his fingers pressing the cap of bone. He waited for the flood of relief. As long as he could still reach through all his blubber and feel his bones, that always calmed him. He pressed harder, deeper, trying but failing to find the usual comfort in the solid knit of his skeleton.

Sixteen

ONE EVENING, BILLY FOUND JOHN OUT BACK, CLEAN-
ing cow shit off his Wellingtons. The boy, off school for the
summer, was spending most of his time up at the farm, fulfill-
ing Michael's role. Billy's stomach tightened. Had anyone
asked John if that was what he wanted?

"You were up at the milking?" Billy tried to sound casual.
John continued to drag his boots across the grass, leaving
smears of shit. Billy tried again. "You like the farming, yeah?"

"God, Dad, just 'cause you didn't."

"I'm only asking."

John started to walk toward the back door, holding his
Wellingtons by the neck.

"It didn't just happen to you, remember that," Billy said.
"The way you're carrying on, it's as though it's somehow worse
for you."

John turned around. "*I'm* the one making out it's worse for
me?" He shook his head. "You're classic, you are."

"What's that supposed to mean?"

"Oh, come on."

"If you've something to say, say it," Billy said.

"Forget it." John continued toward the house and then whirled around. "Fine. Okay. You want me to say it? You never cared about much of anything before you got all these big ideas of yours, and now there's nothing else for you *but* all that—"

"I cared about plenty—"

"No, you didn't," John said, his cheeks pulsating, his eyes full. "And why is it"—his voice shook—"I don't think you'd care this much if it was about anyone else but Michael?" Billy followed John and grabbed his arm, forcing the boy to face him. "Take that back. That's not true."

John shrugged free and disappeared into the house, leaving Billy heaving hard. Billy's hands curled into fists. The only thing he'd never cared enough about was himself. Jesus H. Christ. His now eldest son was a little shit. Nothing but a little shit. The cry Billy wanted to let out could cut the air. Why wouldn't the little shit just let Billy love him?

After dinner, Tricia returned to the kitchen dressed in her tawny-colored coat. She announced she was headed into town with their neighbor, Magda, and a few others to see a fashion show at the college. "Right so," Billy said, hiding his surprise, and his discomfort. It was hard to look at her straight ever since he'd spilled himself over her leg. It was hard, too, to see her trying to get on with things without him.

"Have fun," he added, trying to sound like he meant it. He should feel delighted for her, getting out for a few hours with friends, having a few drinks, a few laughs. Life goes on. Instead he felt resentment, and a pang of jealousy. When was the last time she'd gone out with him, just the two of them?

She held out her hand, her stud earrings on her palm. Ever since she'd gotten her ears pierced as a girl, on the day before her mother's death, she'd felt squeamish about her lobes and couldn't put in or take out her earrings. He eased her lobe between his finger and thumb and inserted an earring, then fastened it in place with the gold backing. The second earring done, he dropped his hands reluctantly, wondering if this was the only way he would ever again get to touch her with any intimacy.

As Tricia drove out of the yard, the blare from the living room grew—the TV yet again holding his three children captive. Billy thought to go join them, but doubted they would even know he was there. He moved to the radio. Found a classical station. In the center of the kitchen, as the sinking day pressed on the window and car headlights sliced the gray, he remembered his first dance with Tricia, on the night they met at the wedding.

He straightened his spine, raised his left hand, and curved his right arm around the memory of Tricia's thin, delicate back. To a waltz from the radio, he danced Tricia around the kitchen floor, one, two, three, one, two, three. He danced faster, leading Tricia, twirling her, dipping her, their faces feverish. He stopped, breathless, dizzy, his arms aching from all the emptiness he was holding.

Inside the tiny cottage, in their bedroom of golden walls, red silk curtains, and a bed linen patterned with black and white stripes, tiny Tricia undresses tiny Billy. Then he undresses her, peeling the last layers of satin from her skin with tender teeth. She presses the palms of her hands to his hard chest, her prints unlocking him like some secured doorway. He touches her face, his fingertips tracing her sharp cheek. She takes his hungry fingers into her wet, hot mouth. He kisses her, kisses his own fingers inside her—soft brushes with his lips, then tender kisses with tongue, then firmer, openmouthed gymnastics. He tugs with his teeth on her lower lip, his fingers slipping between her legs now. Their tongues flick and curl together, wet and slippery. He presses her down onto her back on the bed, falling on top of her, feeling the spill of her juice on his hand.

He kisses her neck, collarbone, and on down to her breasts. He sucks on her hard brown nipples. She rubs her hand over the top of his head, fingers his ears, twists his lobes. He enters her slick, tight insides and she wraps her thighs around his waist, demanding all of him. He glides his hard, lean body back and forth above her, the throb of his cock matching the thump of his fiery heart.

Billy hardened. He looked behind him to double-check that the garage door was locked. He stood up and leaned over his workbench, the flat of his hand pressed to the wood, to support him. With his free hand, he opened his zipper and satisfied himself fast and hard, his head turning every so often to check on the closed garage door.

At eleven o'clock, Tricia still hadn't returned home. Billy ordered Anna and Ivor to bed, and struggled up from his armchair to follow them. John remained on the couch, watching TV.

"Don't stay up too much longer," Billy said, looking at the clock on the mantelpiece. It was late for Tricia to still be out. "Do you hear me?"

"Yeah," John mumbled.

"Night, son."

Billy waited, but John didn't respond. "Are you all right?"

"Fine," John said.

"Did you want to talk?"

John looked up at him, his expression dark, confused. "About what?"

"What you said earlier. . . ."

John looked back at the TV. "It doesn't matter."

"It sure sounded like it mattered."

John's attention remained on the screen. "I'm trying to watch the telly."

Billy waited in the open doorway, hoping John would say more.

John's head turned like something about to bite. "Would you get out?"

Billy pushed back his anger. He was trying, damn it. "If you change your mind, you know where I am, okay?"

John bounced his leg, his hand a fist on his knee. Billy stepped into the hall and closed the door behind him. He climbed up the stairs, his mood as heavy as his tread.

After he'd tucked Anna and Ivor into bed, Billy stood on the landing, holding on to the railing. The TV sent up sounds of explosions and what appeared to be the collision of giant metal contraptions. John was all about warring these days, and especially with Billy. As Billy was about to enter his room, he caught some sound beyond the TV battle noises. He listened hard. There, behind the heavy gunfire, came the strum of Michael's guitar. He pictured John sitting downstairs, resurrecting Michael's music, alone and in secret. He moved to his bedroom. John would hate him to eavesdrop.

Billy took one look at his and Tricia's large, empty bed, and changed his mind. He entered the boys' room, finding Ivor already asleep on the bottom bunk. He could be looking at himself at age nine. He leaned down and kissed the side of Ivor's head. Ivor stirred, but didn't waken. Aside from those times in the days after Michael's death, it had been years since he'd kissed the boy. "I'm too big for kisses," Ivor had declared.

Billy checked his phone again. No text or missed call from Tricia. His thumb moved back and forth over the phone's screen. He pushed his pride aside and started typing. *Everything ok?* He waited.

Still waiting, he crossed the room, undressed, and climbed into Michael's single bed. He lay facing Ivor, trying to remember back to a time when his father had kissed him, even hugged him. He couldn't. Not once. His phone beeped. *All ok, home soon.* Relieved, he burrowed into Michael's mattress and pillow, trying to sink into the exact hollows made by his firstborn. The slim bed seemed fragile, something he could fall right through. He worried he would break it.

When Michael was small, and Billy wasn't so humongous, he had sat next to the boy on this bed many times, telling stories. Michael hadn't wanted tales from books or his father's imagination so much as real stories from Billy's childhood. Billy quickly ran out of any pleasant or interesting memories, though, and had to pass off made-up events as real.

Michael never tired of the stories and wanted to hear them over and over. "Tell me again about how you helped deliver the twin calves. Tell me about being Oisín in the school play. Tell me about the time Santa came to your house twice, on Christmas Eve and on Christmas morning."

Those stories had delighted and impressed Michael, but Billy had faked them all. He had wowed his son with tales of a Billy Brennan who didn't exist.

The week rolled on and Billy remained in Michael's bed at night. Sleeping there proved to be a form of torturous rapture, like getting to almost touch the horizon, and every night he found himself going back for more.

"Why put yourself through that?" Tricia asked. "Put John and Ivor through it, too?"

He shrugged. "I sleep better there."

Her face colored. Too late, he realized the unintended dig in his words, but before he could try to fix it, she spoke again. "We should get rid of that bed, and the bunk beds, too. Get two single beds in there for John and Ivor."

That cold feeling came over him. How hard she was. How quick to move on. "The room stays the way it is," he said.

Her eyes roved him, as if appraising his shrinking size, and she seemed to soften, seemed about to say something, but her expression hardened again. She grabbed her cigarettes and lighter and moved outside.

That night, Billy returned to Michael's bed. He would never allow Tricia to get rid of it. He felt closer to Michael here than he did anywhere else. He could still smell the boy on the pillow and mattress—that faint mix of soap, sweat, and the spicy, earthy deodorant Michael had favored.

Those fading traces also almost drove him out of his mind, though, adding fuel to the rabid energy inside him that railed to get back to Michael that final night. To stop the boy from leaving the house. From cutting down the clothesline. From tying the noose. From climbing the tree.

From jumping.

Seventeen

BILLY SAT AT THE LAPTOP, CHECKING HIS WEBSITE and social media accounts, his mood sinking. He didn't appear to be very good at this publicity business. The attention the march was getting remained underwhelming.

"What are you doing?" Ivor asked, entering the kitchen.

"Nothing." Billy lowered the lid of the laptop and turned around, forcing a smile.

"That's a lie," Ivor said darkly. He moved to the fridge, opened the door, and looked inside. He looked and looked. Something in Billy's chest broke open.

Minutes later, Billy returned from upstairs and found Ivor still in the kitchen. The boy was on his PlayStation, a hunk of red cheese in front of him on the table. "C'mon, son, come with me."

"Where are we going?" Ivor asked.

"It's a surprise," Billy said.

"Not another one," Ivor said, sarcastic.

"You're going to have fun, trust me."

"If it's something stupid . . ." Ivor warned.

In the yard, Billy dropped onto the driver's seat, making its broken back shake. Ivor followed him into the front of the car, scowling. Billy turned the key in the ignition and released the hand brake, not listening to the voice that told him this could be another disaster.

At the edge of the swimming pool, Ivor sat hunched over himself, his thick calves and swollen feet in the water, turning blue. Billy wasn't able to find the boy's swim trunks and had packed the same polyester shorts Ivor had worn for the walkathon. They fit worse than Billy had remembered and seemed to be trying to castrate the boy. Ivor, his teeth chattering, hugged the rolls of fat around his middle and again refused to get into the pool. Billy had bribed the boy five euro just to emerge from the changing rooms.

"You don't get a cent if you don't get in," he said, struggling to not let his frustration show.

"It's too cold," Ivor said.

"It's not cold once you get in and start moving." Billy loved the chill entry into the water, how its startle made him feel more alive.

"I can't swim," Ivor said.

"That's the whole point, I'm going to teach you."

"I won't be able to stay up, I'll sink."

Billy fought to keep his cool. "You won't sink, you pump your legs and move your arms, that's what keeps you up. It's like riding a bicycle. You took to riding a bicycle faster than Anna and both your brothers, remember? You were a superstar on your bicycle. You'll be a superstar swimmer, too, wait till you see."

Ten more minutes passed and still Ivor wouldn't get in the water. Billy raised the bribe to ten euro, then fifteen, then twenty. "And that's final." Christ, what was he doing? If Tricia knew.

"Fine." Ivor dropped into the water, setting off a spray. Billy's attention jumped to the lifeguard, afraid he'd shout or blow his whistle. The lifeguard, young, muscled, looked away from Ivor, as if making a pity call.

After more coercion, Ivor finally stretched out on his back in the water and allowed Billy to support his fleshy torso and thick legs.

"Don't let me go," Ivor pleaded.

"I won't let you go." Billy couldn't keep the shake out of his voice.

After several false starts, Ivor finally relaxed in Billy's arms and floated.

"You're doing it, Vor, you're doing it," Ivor told himself, elated. This was the first time Billy had heard the boy call himself by the nickname only Michael had used. That, and the smile on Ivor's face, thrilled Billy even more than seeing his weight on the scale earlier. In four months, he had lost a grand total of forty-nine pounds. He would never have believed.

Ivor, full of newfound bravado, tipped his head too far back, letting water cover his face. He panicked, flailing and spluttering. Billy pulled him to standing. "You're okay."

After Ivor recovered, Billy persuaded him to lie on his front and pretend-swim. Billy supported his stomach and thighs. "That's it, just like that. Your arms cut the water and your legs kick-kick-kick. Now, every time your right arm slices the water, you turn your head and take a big breath, and then put your face back in the water. That's it. Well done." Ivor swam on, pretending, going nowhere. It was wonderful. It was awful. Almost the greatest do-over of Billy's life.

Anna was in the kitchen when Billy and Ivor returned home. She sat staring at the laptop, watching those boy band videos.

"That rubbish again?" Billy said. It bewildered him, her having such interest in boys and music videos at only twelve. Tricia had insisted it was no big deal. "It's pure innocent," she'd said.

Of the remaining children, Anna seemed to be escaping them the fastest. If nothing else, the farm would tie John to home, and Ivor was the baby, but Billy could already feel Anna pulling away.

"Where were you two?" she asked in a voice that suggested she didn't care, but before Billy or Ivor could respond, she again asked, "What were you doing?"

"We went swimming," Ivor gushed, "and then we got ice cream—"

Billy laughed. "You got ice cream, I—"

"How come I wasn't invited?" Anna asked.

"Sorry," Billy said, "I didn't think. Next time, okay?"

"I hate the pool," Anna said. The red, angry expression on her face, she looked as though her head were burning something. "Chlorine turns my hair green." She moved toward the hall.

"Wait," Billy said, scrambling to think of a way to placate her. "How about we go down to Caroline's and get you an ice cream?" He didn't relish the thought of having to watch so soon again another of his children scoff a treat while he sat salivating and tormented, but if that's what it took.

"Forget it," she said, and left the room.

Ivor hitched his shoulders. *What's wrong with her?* "Thanks for today," he continued with feeling.

"You're welcome." A pleasant sensation stirred in Billy's chest, like the lap of warm water.

He found Anna in her room, lying on her bed with her back to the door, her body almost the length of the mattress. It didn't seem all that long ago since she'd taken up so little space on the bed. He felt an ache for when he would carry her, read her stories, and lie easily on the covers next to her.

She wiped at her eyes, sniffling. He sat down on the edge of her bed, picking at something to say. The pale yellow room sat tidy around them, everything in its place. She was like her mother in that. Her black dance shoes hung from a peg on the wall and her green dance dress—the expensive rig-out reserved for competitions and special appearances—hung from a pink velvet hanger. On her shelves, books and photographs, and pinned to her wall, shiny boy band posters. Her double bed was so much sturdier than Michael's single effort.

"You're lucky, having a room to yourself," he said. The silence ticked. "Do you not think so?" After a moment, two, he tried again. "Did you want to go for that ice cream now? We can go into town for it, if you prefer?"

She tightened the lock of her arms at her waist, unmoved by the bait.

"I'll leave you alone so." As he was about to move off the bed, she spoke, her voice ragged. "I used to wish for a sister to share my room, everything, with. And now Michael's gone and I feel so bad for ever having wished things could be different. I'd give anything for everything to go back to the way it was."

He lay down on the bed next to her, keeping an embarrassed, respectful space between them. Still, he wrapped his arm around her waist. He remembered those tiny, impossible knots he would try to get out of her necklace chains. Finding the right thing to say felt as hard as that.

"Listen," he said. "I don't ever want to hear you say you feel bad. What Michael did wasn't your fault. It wasn't anyone's fault." His voice wavered.

"But I wished for a different family," Anna said.

"We all wish for things. Nothing wrong with that when there's no harm meant. I'm telling you, Michael wouldn't want you lying here feeling miserable because of him. He'd want you to go on and be happy, to live your best life."

Billy heard how much he wanted to convince them both.

That night, at his workbench, Billy placed the tiny boat he'd made out of toothpicks onto the painted riverbank.

Tiny Billy and tiny Michael push out the boat and set sail on the gray-blue River Nore. They stretch out on their backs on the boat's aft, their army jackets off and their shirts open to their navels. They float under the middle portal of the bridge, its cover robbing them of the sun's golden warmth. "We're pirates in search of treasure," Michael says, his voice echoing inside the tunnel.

"Then so we are," Billy says.

As soon as they emerge from beneath the bridge, Billy jumps to his feet and looks through the paper telescope. Michael moves next to his father and studies the tattered map they'd found earlier in a blue glass bottle on the riverbank, washed up amid the rushes and next to the swans' nest. Billy looks back at the swans, one black and one white, both getting smaller in the distance. One mate for life, forever true.

Billy and Michael arrive at the castle ruins, make anchor, and disembark. Michael charges forward, following the map. Something about the boy's excitement and his open, hungry need disturbs Billy. He wants to change the course of the story, wants to undo Michael ever having found the blue glass bottle and its treasure map. His son should know that in his father's kingdom they already have everything they could ever want or need.

The next afternoon, Billy and Ivor again readied for the swimming pool. This time, Ivor didn't need to be bribed.

Anna insisted she wasn't interested. "I told you, chlorine doesn't like me."

Billy bit back a lecture. His daughter—his little girl—was wearing bright purple eye shadow and clumped mascara. He hadn't ever seen her wear makeup before, except when she was performing in dance shows and competitions. "Well, then, how about we do something together later?" he asked.

"Like what?" she asked.

"Whatever you want."

Tricia looked up from her phone. "You can't just tell her whatever she wants."

"She knows what I mean."

Anna's face crumpled. "Stop fighting. You two fight all the time now. That, or stone silence."

"No we don't," Tricia said.

"Yes you do," Ivor said.

"What do we fight about?" Billy asked, trying to make light.

"I don't know," Anna said. "I block it out."

"Yeah," Ivor said.

Billy and Tricia exchanged a guilty look. Tricia spoke to Anna. "Why don't we go into town while they're at the pool?"

Anna shrugged. "If we go shopping? I need new clothes."

"Yeah, of course, if you need them," Tricia said. Billy heard the hint of worry in her voice. Their money was stretching ever thinner in these recessionary times, especially after all the expense of the funeral. For the first time in twenty years, he was starting to think he would have to do better than the factory and his basic paycheck every two weeks. Otherwise, they were going to have to borrow money, and soon. He shivered. Wouldn't his father love it if Billy ended up having to go back to him after all this time, his head down and his hand out.

Billy checked his flyers on the Sports Center's bulletin board, hit again by that sinking feeling. He checked every visit, and every time the donations sheet remained blank. To make matters worse, someone had yet again pinned new material to the board, covering up his flyers. He unpinned the various cards and pages, noting the mad psychedelic colors on one chiropractor's ad, and moved his flyers back on top—dead center. It was the same with his flyers on display throughout the village and in town. Even at the factory. After the first rush of donations, the fresh flyers he'd posted had remained mostly blank, with little to no new monies coming in. He looked into Michael's gray-blue eyes on the bulletin board. He was not giving up.

A Sunday afternoon, the changing room was especially

busy. Billy and Ivor each entered a toilet stall to undress and put on swim trunks. It hurt Billy that Ivor was following his lead and was also too embarrassed to undress in front of everyone. *Monkey see, monkey do.*

They emerged, Ivor in navy trunks and Billy in black, their swimwear a similar style that fell to above their bumpy knees. They had both draped white gym towels over their meaty shoulders, their pudgy hands cinching the towel at their chests. They would enjoy the scrap of coverage the towel lent them until the last possible second before they entered the water. With their free hand, they both pulled on the end of their towels, trying and failing to make the short flaps cover their stomachs.

Billy plodded across the damp floor toward the weighing scale. He stepped on, telling himself not to get his hopes up. There was likely no change from yesterday's reading. The numbers jumped, and stopped. Three hundred and fifty-one pounds. He had dropped another pound overnight, bringing his total weight loss to the beautiful round number of fifty. Ecstatic, he turned to step off the scale. His delight fell away.

Ivor stood staring at him, that now-familiar rage back in the boy's face. He looked down at himself and then at Billy, his eyes filling. Billy reached for him, but Ivor turned around and toddled toward the pool.

Billy followed Ivor into the brilliant blue water, the chill giving him that unfailing rush despite his concern for the boy. "What's going on? What happened back there?"

"I don't want you to talk," Ivor said.

"Come on, something's bothering you—"

"Stop talking. I don't want you to say anything," Ivor said, almost wailing.

"Okay, okay," Billy said, anything to get the boy to calm down. "I won't say another word."

Ivor again allowed Billy to support his back and legs while he stretched out on the water. After several minutes of floating, Ivor flipped onto his front and Billy again put the boy through the paces of pretend-swimming. Next, Billy coaxed Ivor into trying to float on his back all alone.

After several failed attempts, during which Ivor panicked and refused to let Billy remove his hands, the boy finally managed to float solo. He made snuffling sounds, arrhythmic breathing that signaled both his delight and still the trace of fear. Billy clapped and cheered, making Ivor's face light up. Billy took a picture in his head. He never wanted to forget this moment. The pool teemed with people, and sounded too loud, but it was as if he and Ivor were the only two there.

Back in the changing room, as Billy and Ivor dressed, Ivor's words turned Billy's stomach cold. "Being fat is bad, isn't it?" His face was crimson.

Billy tried to think what to say, and then hoped to sound matter-of-fact. "Fat isn't bad, but it can be very unhealthy."

Ivor pushed past Billy and moved to the exit. "Ivor," Billy said.

"No!" Ivor said. "I said I don't want you to say anything."

Billy hurried after Ivor, feeling like that's all he did now, chase his children.

Eighteen

JULY 21. THE EVENING OF BILLY'S BIG MARCH. SIX months ago today, shortly before eight o'clock in the morning— right about when Billy and Tricia had learned that Michael hadn't shown up to milk the cows—Sergeant Deveney had arrived with his cap in his hands and the news that would shatter their world. Six months, and a part of Billy still couldn't believe, still expected to turn around and find Michael standing right there, smiling, waiting.

So much had happened in such a short time. In what sometimes felt like forever. He'd lost Michael, his firstborn, and it had prompted his goal to shed half of himself, and to try to stop suicide. Already, he'd dropped over fifty pounds. He saw a flash of himself sitting at a potter's wheel and sculpting those fifty-some pounds of fat into a boy. He squeezed his eyes closed, as if that could black out the strange-awful picture. Oh, to be a Dr. Frankenstein. To bring Michael back.

His resolve hardened. At least he could bring about change.

He could do good. And all in Michael's name. He'd never known he'd so much fight in him. Never known he could be capable of so much. His was no ordinary weight loss, no ordinary march, no ordinary documentary. He was going to change the world. A shiver passed over him, cooling the surge of bravado. He wished he'd more of an army around him. Wished he could believe that at the very least his wife and children would stand with him through it all. He swallowed hard. In a short while he would go downstairs and put his family to the test. It would wring out his heart if they failed him.

In the bathroom, Billy's face stared out of the mirror above the sink, his head and stomach in a spin. These past couple of weeks it had proven harder and harder to drop the weight and he'd hovered at a loss of fifty-three pounds for what felt like forever. To shift the scale again, he'd cut down to just the performance shakes and had increased his visits to the pool, swimming twenty laps every morning and twenty more in the evenings. But he couldn't keep that intensity up. It would kill him. Now that the scale was moving again—a total of fifty-seven pounds— he would revert to a more realistic diet and exercise routine, and hopefully rid himself of these awful, poorly sensations. His head and stomach were sick, too, from pure nerves.

He worried he might not be able to make it through the four miles of the very march he had masterminded. His body was pain-free in the pool—light, suspended, held. Walking, though, for any length was a whole different story. He had visions of collapsing on the road and getting carried off in a stretcher. That couldn't happen. He would do this. He had to.

At the mirror, he ran his free hand through his hair. He had always loved his thick, shiny mass of curls, their silky feel and healthy, blossoming look. Regardless of the sagging, bloated, blue-veined, purple-marked block of body below, no one could ever deny his lustrous crop of curls. He powered on the electric shaver and hesitated, wavering, but then took the blade to himself. The razor's buzz filled his ears, as if sounding a warning. It was only hair, though. Too much hair. As his curls fell away, he felt ever lighter. Felt surer of who he was becoming. He worked quickly, shearing down to his scalp, leaving only a shadow. Amazing how efficient and deadly the blade was, and yet how pleasant—a warm vibration along his head, a kind of caress.

Finished, he rubbed his coarse head with both hands, feeling its bumps and hollows, assessing its shorn, military look. He glanced down at the dark heap of curls around his bare feet. Tricia, his entire family, would be horrified. But he was a soldier now, waging a war. Another image flashed though him. He saw the village of seconds out in the garage, saw every last toy. The dolls and soldiers alike, they all raised their arms in unison and saluted him. He nodded at himself in the mirror, overcome. *Let's do this.*

After a quick shower, he hurried back into his bedroom and stood in front of the full-length mirror. His face and chins had definitely thinned out. He turned left and right, checking his profile. There was ever more give in the waistband of his trousers and tracksuit bottoms with each passing day, but he didn't see as much change in his body as he'd like, aside from his arms. Oddly, his forearms showed the most difference. They appeared thinner, almost delicate, as if they belonged to someone else.

He wrapped his right hand around his left wrist, liking how his thumb and middle finger almost met.

Fifty-seven pounds. He allowed the enormity of the loss to sink in. He was getting closer and closer to his goal. Just yesterday in the village, after he'd visited Michael's grave, he'd met Caroline outside the church. "Well, if you aren't meeting yourself backwards," she had said, admiring. Soon he would have sixty pounds off, and sixty-five, and seventy, and on and on. He would never again allow his weight to climb. He would never again let food control him. He was in charge now.

He strapped on the knee and ankle braces he'd purchased, and then pulled on his tracksuit bottoms. Topless, he moved into the boys' bedroom and struggled down onto all fours on the carpet. He reached beneath Michael's bed for the hidden cardboard box. It looked like a gift waiting to be wrapped. The idea disturbed him and he grabbed at the box flaps, removing with reverence the five awful-thrilling T-shirts.

He returned to his wardrobe mirror and pulled his supersized T-shirt over his head. He'd used the same photograph of himself and Michael on the T-shirts as he had for the flyers. His right hand moved to Michael's face on his chest. Above the photograph, a slogan in dark green ink read, *Suicide Is Not the Answer!* He moved his hand, allowing Michael to look out of the mirror. He studied Michael's pixilated face in the glass, again searching for any hint of the horror that was to come.

He pushed aside the ache and checked his wristwatch. He needed to hurry. He wanted to be down at the church a good hour before the march's official start time. The journalist from the local newspaper had promised he would arrive early, too, as had Sheila Russell from the Samaritans and the social worker

Kathleen Davey. It was hard to gauge how many in all would show. Local support seemed strong, but making a difference was going to require a lot more than just his friends and neighbors. He was hopeful of hundreds from all over, maybe even upward of a thousand—enough to cause a stir that would echo throughout the nation. He straightened in the mirror, his pose as rigid and proud as a soldier's.

He moved downstairs, his mind going over the checklist that had looped in his head over the past several days. He'd hardly slept for weeks, unable to silence his litany of hopes and fears, his list of all he had to do. He needed to double-check that he'd put everything into the car, including the song sheets. Earlier, he'd returned to Ajadi in the stationery shop, to make photocopies of his drill song. It was an easy song to learn, mostly just a case of calling the refrain back to him, so the song sheets were probably unnecessary. Still, they would be a nice touch, and a powerful keepsake.

He couldn't forget, either, to bring the bullhorn. He'd purchased the red loudspeaker versus the blue model that had first caught his eye, red more suited to the big effect. Denis would bring the video camera and extra batteries, to record the march and the meeting afterward, footage they would use in the documentary. Billy pictured himself and Tricia leading the marchers out of the village and onto the main road. They would hold high the supersized, double-sided banner between them, its signage reading in large green block letters, *Suicide Is Not the Answer!*

If today didn't sway Tricia, didn't move her to support him one hundred percent, then nothing would. She would see all he had put into his campaign and would, at last, be convinced. These past few weeks especially, he'd given the march everything he could. He'd knocked on doors, placed countless phone calls, distributed his flyers ever farther afield, and with Denis's help had done his best to get the word out on the Internet. Now all he could do was trust that his efforts would bear fruit.

He hesitated at the kitchen door, willing his family to like the T-shirts and to get the military look to his shaved head. He reached for the doorknob, his throat thumping, and pushed himself into the room.

Tricia's mouth dropped open, as if in a silent scream. She sank into her chair.

"Jesus Christ, Dad," John said. "What have you done?"

Billy held up the four T-shirts draped over his arm. "I got one for each of us." Tricia jerked backward, as if he were carrying venomous snakes.

"Don't you see?" he said. "It will be like Michael is right there, marching with us."

"Stop," Tricia said.

He held out a T-shirt to John, who also recoiled. "No way, I'm not wearing that."

Billy shook with temper. "Do you even care that your brother is gone?"

John lifted his square jaw, channeling his grandfather. "Did he care about any of us?"

"What class of a statement is that?" Billy said.

"It's the truth," John said.

"Your brother wasn't in his right mind when he did what he did—"

The veins in John's neck bulged. "Oh, for God's sake, say it. Why can't you ever say it?"

"You're one to talk," Billy said. "You've hardly mentioned your brother since—"

"Since he *committed suicide*."

"Michael didn't commit anything," Billy said. "Don't use that word about him, about anyone like him, do you hear me?"

Tricia stood between them. "Stop it, both of you!" She looked at Billy through the glint of tears. "Wear your T-shirt. Walk in your march. Do whatever it is you think you have to do, but leave us out of it." Her voice wavered. "I can't do this. I'm sorry, I thought I could, but I can't. I want to try to put all this behind us, but you, you want to keep . . . I don't even know what you want."

"I want to do something that counts."

"Just carrying on, that counts!" Tricia said.

"That's not enough!" Billy said. "My God, are you telling me you won't march in memory of your own son?" He glowered at John. "Your own brother?"

"Why should I march for him?" John said. "He's done nothing but march around my head these past six months. I want to forget about what he did, just like he forgot about us."

Billy drew out and slapped John hard across the face. Tricia gasped.

Anna and Ivor entered the kitchen. "What's going on?" Anna asked. John's hand dropped from his face, showing the angry red. Billy choked back an apology.

"Daddy, your hair," Anna said, shocked.

"You look like you have the cancer," Ivor said.

Billy faced Anna and Ivor, trying to steady his voice. "Come on, it's time to go."

"They're not going anywhere," Tricia said, moving between him and the children, as if guarding them. "They don't need to be put through all that."

Anna and Ivor both looked like they were about to cry. They looked frightened, too. Billy made himself as tall and collected as he could and walked out the back door, the four T-shirts still on his arm.

The churchyard was empty. Billy's eyes cut to his phone and back to the road. Forty minutes till seven o'clock and the start of the march. He moved through the graveyard, down to the back wall, and to Michael. The brass plaque on the temporary wooden cross gleamed, thanks to all the polish Tricia gave it. *Aged 17 years.* His throat felt as if it had a trapped bird inside.

On the afternoon of Michael's removal from the house and transfer to the church, the hearse had rolled slow, slow over the five hundred yards of road. The six pallbearers and three-hundred-plus mourners followed on foot, Michael held high in his dark coffin. Billy rode next to the funeral director in the front of the hearse, too fat and unfit to carry his own son the short distance to the village and the beginning of his end.

Inside the church, Billy had insisted on swapping places with Tricia's brother. He needed to at least carry Michael up the aisle and to the altar. He struggled along, his arm on his father's shoulders, his father's arm on Billy's massive, sweat-soaked back. No one had wanted him to risk trying to carry the coffin even that short distance. But he'd shown them.

The next day, he carried Michael back down the aisle and out to the hearse. At the graveyard, he carried Michael to the open grave. It had taken all his strength, but he'd done it. Six months later, and Billy could still feel the weight of his son's coffin on his shoulder. He stayed with the heavy sensation for several long seconds, a sob about to tear out of him. The coffin had left a red line, right at the point that connected Billy's neck and shoulder. He had wanted that hot, tender mark to stay, but it had faded within days.

He plucked the dead leaves from the purple geranium on Michael's grave. "We're going to be all right, son. Your mother and me, your brothers and sister, all of us. You don't worry about a thing, okay? You just rest in peace now, like you wanted."

He returned to his car on shaky legs and stood waiting— the banner, bullhorn, stack of battery-operated tea lights, and photocopies of the drill song all inside the open boot of the car. He watched the road, his panic feeling bigger than the church behind him. Where was everyone? Just as he thought something inside him might burst, Denis drove up.

As Denis approached, Billy petted his buzz cut. "Don't say anything."

"I'll try not," Denis said, making light. He accepted the T-shirt intended for John and pulled it on over his denim jacket. He asked after Tricia and the children.

"They're not coming," Billy said.

"What? I don't understand."

"It doesn't matter," Billy said.

"Of course it matters."

"Drop it, okay?" Billy watched the road, praying for the throngs.

The journalist, Jimmy, arrived. He'd sounded young on the phone, and looked even younger in person. Billy greeted him, trying to hide his dismay at the lad's boyish pink skin, gelled hair, and lip piercing. Jimmy admitted the best he could promise was a short article in the online version of the local newspaper. Billy cursed himself. He should have held out for a journalist with more seniority to write up the event on a grand scale, not jumped at the first fella who agreed to cover it. Jimmy looked about, pulling a face. "Where is everyone?"

Just then, the director of the Samaritans, Sheila, showed up. Minutes later Kathleen appeared, the pretty social worker with that single blond curl at the front of her dark hair. After greeting both women, Billy's attention returned to the direction of his house, willing Tricia to have a change of heart. He didn't dare hope that Lisa would defy their parents and drive down from Dublin to join him.

His nearest neighbors, Magda and Peter, appeared with their daughter, Sorcha, a good friend of Anna's and the oldest of their four children—four children, something the two families no longer had in common.

"Look at you, and your T-shirt," Magda said, her tone tender but also unsure.

"Thanks for being here, it means a lot." He looked behind her to Peter and Sorcha. "Thank you."

"Of course," the three chorused.

Magda scanned the small group. "Where's Tricia and—"

"They're all still up at the house. They won't be joining us." Before she could quiz him, Billy moved back to his car, busying himself.

At twenty minutes to seven, the football trainer, Molloy, appeared in his white van, followed by a short convoy of cars that carried the rest of the football team. Moments later, Ronin

Nevin roared up on his motorbike. He and Billy exchanged nods. The boy's visits to the house had dwindled in recent weeks. Truth be told, that was easier all around. Billy and Tricia would never get used to seeing him without Michael.

Billy handed Molloy a wad of song sheets to distribute to his team. Molloy looked from Billy's buzz cut and down to the song. "I see you went all-out."

"That's right," Billy said, trying not to sound slapped down. "I wrote it myself."

The cold, hard feeling in his stomach worsened when Sergeant Deveney arrived in full uniform. For a heart-squeezing second Billy thought maybe Deveney was going to put a stop to the march. It crossed his mind that perhaps he needed a permit. Deveney merely nodded in greeting, though, and slinked over to Molloy. He and Molloy fell to mutters, both men looking from Billy's shaved head and down to the song sheet. Billy pressed on, handing out more copies of the drill song and trying to ignore more skeptical and embarrassed looks from some.

Three more cars parked in the ditch. Billy's chest contracted. Sarah, Michael's ex, emerged from the middle car, wearing that same black coat covered in dog hairs. Again, he held back on his usual firm handshake, afraid to damage her, and because yet again she'd weakened him. Michael's long, full life replayed in Billy's head, with Sarah, or someone like her. More of Michael's friends rose up from the three cars and joined Sarah. One of the drivers clapped Billy's shoulder. Billy missed the man's name, but caught that he was Michael's guitar teacher, the one who had told the boy he was talented enough to pursue a professional music career. *He thinks I could really be someone.* Tears coated Billy's eyes.

A car with Westmeath registration plates parked on the grass verge in front of the church. Two middle-aged couples got out, stone-faced. Billy hurried toward them, his hand held out. Both couples had lost children to suicide.

"Tell me about them," Billy said.

One of the men, his left eye turned in, seemed to talk to the empty space next to Billy. "Our daughter, Rachel, was only fifteen." His wife, short but with a strong stance, added, "We still can't put into words how much we miss her."

The second mother nodded. "The same. Finn was nineteen, our second of three. It's been five years and I still can't tell people we've only two children." Her husband wrapped his thin arm around her shoulders.

"Rachel and Finn," Billy said. "I'll keep them in my thoughts tonight."

Moments later, Kitty Moore appeared on her bicycle. Billy rushed toward her, overcome. "Are you sure you're up for this?"

"If you can, then I sure as hell can." Her cheeks colored. "I don't mean physically, I mean . . . well, you know what I mean, I hope."

"I do," he said, filling with thanks and admiration.

With only five minutes to spare, Vera and a couple of other women from the factory arrived. Next, Bald Art pulled up in his maroon Škoda, along with four other lads from the factory. Billy shook their hands hard, repeating, "Fair play to you, thanks." He stared out the road. Where were the others? He'd thought Tony might show, and Lucy for sure. Caroline and Thumbs Tom, too. Where, especially, were all the rest of the families and friends left behind after suicide the whole country over?

Denis appeared next to him. "It's after seven. Did you want to wait another bit or should we get going?"

"Let's give it a few more minutes," Billy said. At a quick head count, they were a mere group of forty-plus. Over the next several minutes, two more cars appeared—one carrying a couple from Navan. Their son, Frank, had taken his own life at twenty-six, leaving behind two small children. The other car carried an elderly widow up from Dublin. Her husband, Diarmuid, had killed himself last year, at age sixty-seven. Billy thanked them over and over.

At seven-thirty, Billy accepted he could wait no longer. He powered on the battery-operated tea lights and, with leaden movements, passed the candles around. Still daylight, the almost invisible flames didn't deliver nearly the effect he'd imagined.

Just as the group was headed out, Lisa's BMW sped into view. She parked and hurried toward Billy. "Sorry, I had to stop on the way down and put oil in the car." She smiled. "If Mam and Dad disown me, it's on your conscience." Her smile widened. "Look at you, you've lost even more weight!"

"Yeah, thanks, and thanks for being here, I needed that," he said.

Her eyes turned damp, and then she took in his shaved head. "Whoa, I'm not sure about that new look, though."

"Not now, sister."

She grinned. "Whatever you say, William."

Billy and Ronin moved to the front of the group and raised the banner high. *Suicide Is Not the Answer!* More tears pressed Billy's eyes. It should be Tricia by his side. He blinked hard and nodded at Ronin. They walked in unison, leading the small group from the gates of the graveyard and out onto the road. Billy couldn't stop trembling. This was the moment, the event, he would remember for the rest of his days.

He marched toward the village proper, struggling to keep himself together. The banner obstructed part of Ronin's profile, and whenever Billy looked over, all he could see was Michael. He came over all loose, jangly bones and worried he'd drop the banner. It both helped and hurt to think of Michael marching by his side. He tightened his grip on the banner pole and tried to steel himself. He needed to make the most of tonight. This was his big stand against a merciless killer and the indifference of too many. With his free hand, he lifted the bullhorn to his mouth, about to begin his drill song. Only the banner dipped horribly to one side and looked broken. He adjusted his grip till the banner leveled and, satisfied, he raised the bullhorn again.

No more, no more, taking your life.

There are better ways to beat the strife.

The response from the group behind him sounded faint and embarrassed. He sang louder and urged the others to do the same. "Come on," he roared. "Lives depend on us!" They marched past Caroline standing outside her shop, her face crumpled and her arms laced tight across her ribs. The posture reminded him of Tricia. Caroline turned around, flipped the shop sign to closed, and joined the procession.

Several punters, including Thumbs Tom, stood gathered outside Kennedy's, drinks in hand and all looking somber. Billy's breath caught. Were they not going to join him? Were they just going to stand and gawk? Right as he reached them, they downed the last of their drinks and fell into rank behind him.

More men and women spilled from the pub and joined the marchers. Billy's chest swelled.

He led the growing, gallant group out onto the main road toward town and the major roundabout. Vera, Bald Art, and a few others from the factory bore signs reading *Beep If You Care*. A blast of horns sounded, gladdening Billy ever more. He felt sure they would meet more marchers along the way and that by the time they returned to the village hall their group would have amassed to a more impressive number.

Deveney jogged up next to Billy. "Let's march off to the side, in single file. There's cars backed up big time."

"Yeah, that'll make a statement, all right." Billy had no intention of clearing out of the way or apologizing for taking up too much space. He'd spent his whole life doing that. Before Deveney could respond, Billy roared into the bullhorn.

Trouble comes to everyone.
Please talk with someone.

After, the group filed into the village hall, Billy still in the lead but without any of his earlier bravado. His elation as he'd exited the village had soon left him. He and the group had marched for almost two hours, covering the four miles to the roundabout and back at Billy's sad pace. No one else had joined them along the way and the entire experience had proved uneventful. He felt heartsick.

He trooped down the center aisle, flanked on both sides by rows of empty seats. His inner thighs smarted and the soles of his feet felt on fire. His knees and right ankle stabbed at him. His throat was raw from shouting. All of that was nothing, though, next to his humiliation. It wasn't just the awful turnout. Several times as they had walked, he'd struggled with his breathing, light-headedness, and the sharp pain in his joints. It had taken every ounce of his everything to force one foot in front of the other and not give up.

He pushed himself to the front of the room and struggled onto the stage. He hadn't felt such gloom in a space since the funeral home. The dim and dusty chapel-like hall required all the lights to be turned on to make the place feel habitable. The yellow cast to the bulbs recalled his fridge back at home and the sense of disappointment it delivered. A ravenous hunger battered his stomach. His fingers morphed into sausages. He licked his lips, his appetite further whetted by their salt taste. He felt mad to eat. To eat and eat.

No one braved the front rows. The young journalist, Jimmy, remained at the back of the hall, texting. Then he turned around and walked out. Sweat stung Billy's eyes and the room started to spin. He bit down hard on his lower lip, tasting more salt. Maybe Jimmy had stepped out to take a call and would return. Billy saw a flash of John, the hateful look on the boy's face after he'd hit him and the anger of the hot, red mark. The fearful, furious way Tricia had looked at him, too, as she'd stood between him and the children. A sour squirt of vomit burned the back of his throat.

Lisa stared up at him. She looked distressed, as if expecting him to fail, as if knowing he could never pull this off. Just as he thought he might faint, Denis appeared by his side with a dripping-wet bottle of water from the ice cooler. "You've got this," Denis whispered. Billy drank, his eyes closed in thanks.

He powered on the microphone and scanned the small

gathering. Their numbers might be in the tens, but they were here. Friends, neighbors, colleagues, strangers, his sister, they had all shown up. He opened his mouth, unsure of how to fill up the silence. Thankfully, words came. "I want to thank each and every one of you for coming here tonight." He managed a smile and pushed a note of humor into his voice. "I know the march and the drill song, and, yeah, okay"—he pointed to his head—"this buzz cut"—the group gave a nervous little laugh— "might all have seemed unusual and maybe even a bit much, but some, if not most of us here, have all been thrown into the unusual and the awful, and now all we can do is deal with that as best we can. My son Michael's final act on this earth is still something I can't get my head around, something I don't think I'll ever be able to get my head around, and in its aftermath I've made a few choices of my own.

"Those choices all come down to the same thing. I'm choosing to try to save lives, including my own, and to try to make the world even a little better. That's why we're all here tonight. To save lives. To make the world even a little better." A small burst of applause sounded and the elderly widow from Dublin held her hand to her contorted, red-splotched face. Billy gave her a sympathetic smile.

"We're here tonight especially," he continued, "to give meaning to those lives already lost and to help those who feel they can't go on to believe they *can* go on. Our goal is to get the suicidal to believe they can and *must* go on. Suicide can no longer be an option, end of story." Louder, longer applause sounded.

Denis circulated a clipboard with contact sheets along the rows. Billy asked surviving family and friends to please sign up to take part in his documentary on the devastation of suicide, a film he hoped would air nationally and, ideally, internationally. He also passed around the pledge sheets, asking people to dig deep and sponsor his weight loss. "Go big," he said. "Not like I did, but with your money." More laughter.

He invited Sheila from the Samaritans and Kathleen from Social Welfare to the stage. They moved toward him, both looking apprehensive. Before turning the podium over to them, he again thanked everyone for coming out to march. To think he had imagined thousands. Christ. He tried to gather himself, his voice hoarse. "I didn't get the numbers I'd hoped"—he could no longer control the shake in his voice—"but I got each one of you, and together we're going to make a difference." More applause.

He welcomed Kathleen to the podium. She stepped toward him, her expression growing ever more uneasy. "I think I'll just . . ." Her voice trailed away and she moved off the stage. She stood at the top of the room to address the crowd, not needing to raise her voice to get heard among so few. Billy felt ever more foolish, having used the stage and microphone himself. As Kathleen spoke, listing the warning signs of suicide, Billy held on to the sides of the podium, his attention fixed on the hall doors, as if his family, the hordes, might still come.

Nineteen

BILLY AGAIN PHONED IN SICK TO WORK—HIS THIRD
sick day, now. He didn't care. He didn't care about much of
anything. The march had been nothing like he'd hoped. To
his surprise, Tricia didn't rage. Maybe she felt guilty about
abandoning him. And so she should.

Anna visited him on Michael's bed. "Are you okay, Dad?
Can I get you anything?"

"It's just a cold," he said. She didn't look convinced.

Later, Ivor also appeared. "When are we going swimming
again?"

"Soon, I promise." Billy knew he was disappointing the boy,
but he hadn't the energy to do or say any more.

Tricia didn't go near him. He tried not to care.

Hunger, and a full bladder, forced him out of bed. He weighed
himself. Three hundred and forty-seven pounds. He'd gained
three pounds. He wanted to punch the bathroom wall. He

didn't understand. He might not have exercised since the march, but he'd consumed nothing more than the performance shakes. Surely he should have lost weight? Why was everything going against him? Why couldn't the world let him win, just once?

His stomach dragged him downstairs. He realized he was alone in the house. Ever since Michael, he didn't like to be alone in the house. It was a whole new kind of empty.

He opened the fridge. It seemed to pull him inside. He saw himself crawling into the appliance and closing the door. All hands and teeth, he would clear every shelf, stuff everything inside him. He was shaking. *Give it up,* he thought. *Stop struggling. Stop fighting.* He knew how to make the pain, the misery, go away. How to get soothed and sated. Food had never failed him.

He eyed the wrapped meats, cheese, bread, fizzy drinks, and leftover pasta. He pulled open the bottom tray and spotted the bars of chocolate hidden at the back. The shaky feeling worsened. His stomach growled. If he started, he wouldn't be able to stop. He rushed the door closed and pressed his back to it.

It felt like his heart was banging on the appliance. His panic and agitation climbed. His heartbeat pulsed in his palms. A sharp pain squeezed his chest. He couldn't breathe. His right arm weakened. Numbed. He was having a heart attack. He was going to drop dead. Another sharp pain cut across his chest.

Dr. Shaw removed the stethoscope's earpieces. "You'll live to fight another day."

Billy exhaled, sharp, dismissive. He wasn't sure he'd any fight left.

"A panic attack," Shaw continued, echoing the 999 emergency operator. Billy was almost disappointed. If his heart was giving out, he could stay in bed for as long as he liked, and to hell with the factory and everything else.

"You've lost weight," Shaw said.

Billy nodded, not wanting to go there. He could see himself putting back on all his weight, and then some. He'd have gone off the deep end already, if it weren't for Denis.

"How much?" Shaw asked.

Billy shrugged, needled by the three pounds he'd regained. "Over fifty pounds."

"How have you been losing it?" Shaw asked.

Billy wouldn't meet the doctor's beady eyes. "Exercise, dieting. The usual."

"Over fifty pounds, in . . ." He checked his chart. "In less than five months. That's significant. You really should have come back to see me before now. It's important to do this under medical supervision. If you go too hard and too fast, you could very well give yourself a heart attack."

Billy pretended to listen. Now that he knew he was all right, at least physically, he wanted to just get a sick cert to keep the factory off his back, and to get out of there as fast as possible.

Shaw's voice turned graver. "Your mother was in with me, too, Billy. She told me about your fund-raising efforts, said the stress was getting to everyone. It's really taken its toll on her, and clearly on you, too. I think it's best to slow down. Take a step back from everything for a while."

Billy struggled off the exam table and marched out. Slammed the door after him for good measure. Why the hell was Shaw telling him about his mother? What about supposed doctor-patient confidentiality? Billy didn't need Shaw, anyone, to make him feel any worse than he already did.

The following week, Billy returned to work. He didn't want to, but he had to. First thing, Bald Art was lying in wait. "Welcome back," he said.

Billy grunted, and moved around the man, took his place at the conveyor belt. He didn't want to see or talk to anyone, least of all Bald Art.

"You feeling better?" Bald Art asked.

"I'm here, aren't I?"

"I'll get straight to the point. I don't mean to play hardball, but there's clearly an issue with you and the seconds," Bald Art said.

"What?"

"The seconds," Bald Art said, his scalp slick and shiny under the fluorescent lights. "You've started taking them again."

"So what?" Billy said. "Please, go away."

"Like I said, I'm not trying to play hardball. I know you've been through a lot—"

"I'm serious," Billy said, feeling at breaking point. "I can't do this right now."

"I'm going to have to ask you to cooperate, Billy, and to give me your word that the seconds will be disposed of in the manner mandated by factory policy."

Billy shook his head. "Are you for real?"

"This is very real, Billy. We have policies for a reason—"

"What reason?" Billy asked.

"There has to be order—"

"Don't talk to me about order—"

"I'll thank you not to raise your voice or take that tone. I'm your supervisor, Billy. I'm also the one who could report you to management—"

"And tell them what?"

"Tell them you've been stealing factory property."

Billy almost pushed Bald Art away. He would have, too, if the man hadn't participated in the march. "Please," he said, waving Bald Art away. "Go on about your business and leave me alone."

"I'm trying to be understanding here, Billy, but I'll have to insist you treat me with respect and that you toe the line."

"I'm warning you, Art."

"Are you threatening me?"

"Oh, get lost, would you?"

"I'm not going anywhere until I get your word you'll stop taking the seconds and will place them in the bin each day, as per your job description. Otherwise, I'll have no choice but to take this further."

Billy reached up and turned on his machine. He saw himself hauling Bald Art onto the conveyor belt and ferrying him on up to packaging.

"Do I have your word?" Bald Art asked.

"Yes," Billy said through gritted teeth. He didn't need any more trouble, or stress.

Throughout the rest of the day, anytime he dropped a damaged toy into the black bin, it felt like the nick of a knife at his insides. He wasn't saving anything anymore.

That night on Michael's bed, Billy couldn't drift off, his body vexed by energy that demanded to be spilled. There was nothing for doing at this hour, except eating. He would knock out his own teeth, though, before he'd go back to secret pig-outs in the night. Secret pig-outs at any time. The march had changed the tide of things. Had made him feel like a loser. He needed to get back to feeling like he was in charge and in control.

Across the room, John's snores climbed. Every so often, Ivor spoke in his sleep, mumbles Billy couldn't make out. Tricia was on the other side of the wall. It sounded like she was pacing their bedroom, that floorboard that creaked going off every few seconds. Billy longed for her. For the way things used to be. For all the things gone from them. He shot up on the narrow bed, remembering the clothesline he'd cut down and had yet to dispose of. He rose in the dark and went outside.

He walked through the fields, toward the band of trees behind the football pitch. The same path Michael had taken that terrible night. Billy dragged the end of the rope along the ground like a snake, similar to how he imagined the previous clothesline had trailed Michael.

He stopped in front of Michael's tree. Pitch-black, he couldn't see Michael's initials. He reached out, his fingers feeling the tree trunk for the letters, like reading Braille.

He uncoiled the clothesline, letting in a stampede of feelings. He knelt on the ground and took the gas lighter from his coat pocket. The rope caught, and burned and twisted. He watched it blaze. Liked how it lit up the dark.

When he returned home, the world still in deep black, he

went straight to the bathroom. He weighed himself. Three hundred and forty-eight pounds. Jesus. He'd put on another pound, making a total gain of four pounds since the march. His resolve faltered, but only for a moment. He was done with wallowing. He opened the medicine cabinet and removed the electric shaver. He took the razor to his head, shaving the sprout of fresh curls to oblivion.

Billy easily spotted the journalist among the scatter of locals and visitors down by the quays. Tall, lean, and well dressed in beige khaki trousers and a starched white shirt, he was pacing up and down, talking on his phone. Billy remained inside the safety of his car, watching the sun again make the gray-blue river glisten.

Jack Dineen had responded favorably to Billy's e-mail and wanted to profile him for the *Independent*, in their coveted Sunday edition. The news should have delighted Billy, but ever since he'd found out he felt riddled with fear and confusion, his need for publicity always pitted against this urge to lie low and hide.

He was vexed with himself for not doing more with the media before the march. Then he would surely have drawn a much bigger crowd. The truth circled him. Maybe he hadn't sought more publicity because he knew people rarely took him, or anyone of his size, seriously. Worse, deep down he'd feared he would fail and that the more public he made his diet and the march, the more public he would make his disgrace.

But what of it, these small-minded notions of success and failure? What did they matter? He saw the elderly Dublin widow in the meeting after the march, her damp blue eyes. He also saw the parents of Rachel, unable to put their pain into words, and the parents of Finn, unable to say they now had only two children. Billy needed to push his fear and shame aside. He knew what really mattered. From here on out, he would rev everything up. He would circulate his pledge sheets ever wider and make phone calls to friends, neighbors, businesses, politicians, and the greater community. Everyone and anyone he could think of.

Jack Dineen finished his call and looked up and down the quays, his air impatient. Billy hauled himself and his dread out of the broken driver's seat. He plodded toward the thirty-something, pulling down on the cling of his T-shirt and wishing Jack didn't look quite so young, lean, and attractive. They shook hands, Jack's grip strong, his smile wide. His eyes, though, held a hint of contempt. "Nice to meet you." Before Billy could respond, Jack looked him up and down and, frowning, said, "Perhaps we should sit someplace?" He charged toward the row of benches painted that signature dark green.

When they were both seated, Jack placed a recording device on the bench between them. "Do you mind?"

Billy, still winded from his best attempt at a quick-march and trying not to breathe so loud and fast, stared at the machine. The device, not much bigger than a mobile phone, sported a dimpled silver ball at its top, like the decapitated head of a microphone.

"It also has video capability," Jack continued. "Maybe we can—"

Billy's hands shot up. "No, no, audio is fine."

Something like glee flashed in Jack's eyes. "So! Yours is quite the story, thanks for giving us an exclusive."

Billy balked. "'Quite the story.' You said that with a bit too much enthusiasm."

Something close to contrition crossed Jack's face. "Sorry, I didn't mean to sound insensitive."

Two young women, loud, laughing, walked past in heels, blouses, and dark, tight skirts. Jack glanced at them, admiring. The auburn-haired girl, the prettier of the two despite the heavy makeup, spotted Billy and immediately sobered, casting him a look of utter pity. Billy turned his attention back to Jack, the blood rising in his cheeks. "What do you want to know?" he asked sharply.

Jack tucked his chin, taken aback. He recovered. "Let's start with your fund-raiser for suicide prevention. How and why?"

The two women sat down on the next bench. They pulled sandwiches out of white paper bags, still laughing too loud. The brunette sat with her back to Billy. The auburn-haired girl sat facing him. He watched her stretch her mouth around a fat baguette. As she chewed, her finger moved to the corner of her brown-red-painted lips and pushed an errant shred of lettuce into her mouth. Billy's stomach growled.

"Billy? Are you okay?" Jack asked.

Billy took a deep breath. "'How and why?' I'm not sure where to start."

Jack pushed the recorder closer to Billy on the bench. "Wherever feels right."

Fear seized Billy. This journalist would try to get inside him, to see what made him tick. He could paint whatever kind of picture he liked of Big Billy Brennan, and of Michael, too. He would also try to get some sob story around why Big Billy was so enormous. He might also insist Billy explain how he could possibly have had no clue Michael felt such depths of despair.

Another burst of laughter erupted from the other bench. Billy winced. Jack glanced at the two women and back at Billy. "Would you like to go someplace more private?"

Billy stole a longing glance at the gray-blue river. He had thought this would be the perfect place. Reluctantly, he led Jack to his car.

Inside the car, Jack's dark eyes strayed to the large gap between Billy's shoulder and the broken driver's seat, its defeated slope betraying the burden of him. Billy continued to talk, willing Jack to focus on him. He was trying to get across how special Michael was, how utterly senseless his death. "I don't know," he finished. "I suppose we have to accept something in him snapped—" The recording device on the dashboard buzzed, startling him.

"Sorry." Jack grabbed at the recorder and changed its batteries. The recorder's light burning bright red again, Jack asked Billy to talk about his own childhood.

Billy shook his head. "We don't need to bring my past into this. This is about Michael and the here and now. About how I'm trying to help people like him, before it's too late."

Jack pressed him. "I think readers would really like to get a sense of you—"

Billy shook his head, his irritation returning. "This isn't about me."

"I beg to differ—"

"It's about getting the word out on my sponsored diet and the documentary I plan to make, so I can help save lives in my son's memory."

Jack stabbed the point of his pen into his notepad, leaving dots of ink on the page like a dark blue rash. "Okay, then, if you insist. Why don't you tell me the one story you think best captures Michael?"

"Only one story? That's hard." Billy thought for several moments, his hand rubbing at his mouth. "I remember Michael's first day of school. He walked around the kitchen in front of his mother and me, marveling at how his uniform trousers, these navy cords, made this noise when he moved. The legs swished together, you know? I can still hear it. The delight on Michael's little face, you'd think he'd just discovered the most wonderful thing ever." Billy laughed softly. "Then there was the way he'd sing around the house. He was always singing. Right up to the end he was singing." Billy's voice broke. "It used to drive us mad, by times, to tell you the truth. Now, though . . ."

"Can you give me something more?" Jack asked gently. "Something that will really help readers know Michael?"

"Well, they can't, can they?" Billy said severely.

"I'm sorry, I—"

"No, it's okay," Billy said. "I'm the one who's sorry."

"Please, take your time."

Billy raked his memories. It made him feel a little sick that he wasn't flooded with stories. It was scary how much he'd forgotten. How much he didn't keep account. There were so many little things he could share about Michael, but to have to tell one story that was big and interesting enough for the newspaper?

He remembered the dog Michael brought home. Michael was eleven, maybe twelve. He found the half-dead animal in a field and carried it in his arms for more than a mile. It looked to be poisoned and Billy doubted it would live. Tricia and

Michael nursed the dog, little more than a pup, really, around the clock for days. At last, its whimpers stopped, and when he fully recovered, he proved to be lively and lovable. Michael, a U2 fanatic, named the dog Bono. He, all the children, doted on that dog. Billy's voice trailed off.

"Do you want to take a break?" Jack asked.

"We must have had Bono for a month, maybe more, when the vet phoned. The dog's family arrived at our house that evening. Michael, John, Anna, and Ivor, they all cried. It turned out the dog's real name was Duke. His family, the two little girls especially, were shrieking, and hugging and kissing him. They fed him chunks of roast chicken right out of their hands. When they put Bono, Duke, into their car, Ivor let out a wail. Michael wrapped his arm around Ivor's shoulders. 'Look how happy they are,' he said. 'Look how happy Duke is. We should be celebrating for them.' That was the sort of lad he was. Kind. Very, very kind."

Billy wondered if Michael could possibly have imagined that taking his own life was some form of kindness to himself.

Jack reached for the recorder on the dashboard. "We can leave it there for now, if you like, do the rest over e-mail?"

Billy shifted on the broken seat, rousing himself, and agreed to keep going. Outside, the two young women remained on the bench, their laughter piercing.

Twenty

THEIR NEIGHBOR MAGDA APPEARED THROUGH THE back door, clips in her caramel hair, her face its usual color of bone. She spoke to Billy and Tricia in a rush. "I need to get to work, but come out to the car for a sec, I've something for you." Billy pulled himself away from the Internet, still trying to find a filmmaker for his documentary—a search that was proving near-impossible.

Inside the boot of Magda's car, a stone birdbath finished with shiny, colorful tiles. "I decorated it myself," Magda said. "I thought you might like to put it right here in front of the window." Billy and Tricia glanced at each other. Magda intended the gift and its songful visitors to distract them from the band of beech trees beyond the football pitch. Tricia hugged her. Billy nodded his thanks, not trusting himself to speak.

Back at the laptop, Billy received an e-mail from Jack Dineen. He'd given the paper an exclusive, and until his profile was published, they had him in a publicity chokehold and he couldn't allow other media outlets to pick up the story and spread the good word. He speed-read Jack's e-mail. His profile would run in two weeks. His pulse throbbed at his right temple. Jack could have written anything about him—and Michael. What if Billy came across as a sad, fat fool? If the article dishonored Michael somehow? Billy went over every moment of the interview again. There was nothing bad Jack Dineen could have taken away from their conversation. Was there?

Billy had also asked Jack for any leads on a filmmaker. Jack recommended Adam Simon. He didn't know Adam personally, Jack explained, but the filmmaker had some nice credits, and also a special interest in suicide. Billy, his breath held, clicked through to Adam Simon's website. The thirty-eight-year-old hailed from Dublin and boasted a couple of independent films and a Special Mention at the Cannes Film Festival. His website didn't reveal any special interest in suicide, but a quick search of the Internet did.

Five years ago, Adam's twelve-year-old nephew, Rory, took his own life. The story was all over the news for weeks and had sparked a nationwide debate on both suicide and guns in the home. *Why would someone so young do such a thing?* the papers had asked. Billy's palms turned damp. He remembered the poor boy, all right. One of the youngest suicide victims on record.

Newspaper reports revealed Rory had written a note before putting the barrel of his father's handgun into his mouth. Billy couldn't decide if it would be any easier or harder if Michael had left a note. Nor could he think about the gun between Rory's lips and his small finger on the trigger.

He e-mailed Adam Simon, his fingers never having typed so fast. Everything would work out, he told himself, the profile, the documentary, his entire campaign. It had to.

———

Three days later, Billy approached the Granary Restaurant, feeling pure class inside his new suit and purple tie. He couldn't remember the last time he could close his shirt collar or cinch his tie. The fancy gray pin-striped suit fit like a dream. No one need ever know he'd bought it secondhand in the charity shop. He'd entered the musty, cluttered space in search of a plus-sized cardigan and couldn't believe his luck when he'd not only found a suit that fit, but one he liked. His finding such a suit in his size and in excellent condition was as good as miraculous. It had to be a sign. This lunch was going to go great.

Yet, as he neared the restaurant's entrance, fresh anxiety set in. This Michelin-starred restaurant was one of the best in the country and he might not survive it. He was going to want to eat everything in the place. The last time he was here, a couple of years back for his parents' fiftieth wedding anniversary, he'd enjoyed one of the best meals of his life—filet mignon with béarnaise sauce, buttered carrots, and potatoes au gratin. He'd fantasized about the meal for months afterward, and could almost taste it now.

Denis had worked hard earlier to convince Billy he wouldn't buckle beneath the towering temptation. "You've got this."

"What if I don't?" Billy said. "What if I cave?"

"You won't, trust me. Trust yourself," Denis said.

Billy pulled open the restaurant door. *It's not food I need to fill me.* He entered, greeted by the waft of fresh herbs, roasted meats, and butter-rich sauces. His stomach cried out, keening. The restaurant host, dressed in a black suit and a white shirt with gold cuff links, led Billy to his table.

Billy scanned the fixed-price menu, three courses for fifty-five euro. His stomach tightened. It was an obscene amount for lunch, but he had to win this Adam Simon over. He checked the time on his phone again. Two minutes after the hour. What if Adam didn't show? If he'd changed his mind?

The waiter appeared, to take Billy's drink order. The twenty-something looked dapper in a starched white shirt and black dress pants, his dark, gelled hair parted dead center. Billy, still keeping his hair shorn tight, experienced a moment's regret for his former head of curls.

"Sir?" the waiter asked.

Billy ordered water with fresh lemon and refused, in a weak voice, the basket of French bread. His eyes returned to the entrance, and then to his phone, checking for a text or missed call.

Despite the recession, customers packed the restaurant—mostly tourists and businesspeople. Their animated chatter, and the glitter of crystal glasses and sparkling jewelry, all made for a lively ambience. The luxurious mood was further heightened by the flickering candle and single white rose on each table. Large oil paintings in yellow and orange hues covered the walls. Several crystal chandeliers dropped low from the high ceiling, lavish and glittering.

Billy read through the tormenting fare on offer, his stomach crying out, *Feed me!* He snapped the leather-bound menu closed and fixed his attention on the candle flame on his table, trying to distract himself from the dishes the waiters were carrying back and forth, their colorful look and mouthwatering smells enough to send his stomach out of his body to go foraging.

Billy raised his hand, about to wave down his waiter. He

could no longer resist a basket of warm French bread with those rounds of butter rolled in sea salt. Right then, Adam Simon arrived, saving Billy from himself. Another good omen. Billy breathed a sigh of relief.

Simon's face dripped apology. "Bad accident on the M50," he said, his voice deep, gravelly. "So sorry."

"No problem," Billy said. "Glad you could make it." They shook hands. Simon easily scooted into the red leather booth.

"Fatal, too, I bet," he continued. "A truck smacked into the back of a mini. I don't have to tell you who won." His voice held an odd note of humor.

Billy waited for him to say something more, but the filmmaker merely scanned his menu.

The waiter returned. "Ready to order, sirs?"

They ordered. Filet mignon with gorgonzola sauce and all the trimmings for Adam, and for Billy the grilled salmon with green salad and light, very light, dressing.

"Just salad with the salmon, sir?" the waiter asked.

Billy nodded, his teeth on edge. Adam Simon asked for a bread basket. Billy wiped the sweat from his face with his napkin. He was a mess of tattered nerves, anxious he'd mess up his spiel, mess up his diet. How would he contain himself while watching the filmmaker put away steak, buttered carrots, and potatoes baked in garlic, cheese, and fresh cream? It would be hell. After a struggle to free himself from the booth, he hurried to the men's room.

He entered the end stall and phoned Denis, his hunger practically a force outside of him, snapping at the air. Denis was just about able to talk him down. "I'm telling you, Billy, you need to go to OA. You need an OA sponsor."

"I can't do this now." Billy ended the call, his thumb almost going through his phone. He remained inside the stall for as long as he dared, pushing back his temper, and his panic. He took long breaths in and out. *It's not food I need to fill me.*

He returned to the table and squeezed back inside the red leather booth. Thankfully, the food hadn't arrived. Adam wore an expression of mild curiosity. "You all right?"

"Fine." Billy steered the conversation to his End Suicide Now! crusade. "I want to help save as many lives as I can, and that's where the documentary comes in. I've already gotten the names of families interested in taking part, those who have lost someone in the same way, and I plan to get more. I'm hoping their stories will really move people, make them realize that suicide is everyone's problem—"

Adam pointed his finger at Billy. "I like you." He lifted a ball of butter and picked at the salt granules with the nail of his trigger finger, the one he'd just trained on Billy. Over several long seconds, he went at the butter, seeming intent on stripping it of every last speck of salt.

Billy pressed on. "There's so many people affected—we're talking almost six hundred suicides last year alone, and those are just the reported cases—but all those families, friends, and communities left behind, they aren't getting on board, at least not with anything like the numbers and enthusiasm I'd hoped. The *Indo*'s profile I mentioned—it's coming out the weekend after next and I think that'll really help to get the epidemic and my efforts the attention they deserve. At least, I hope so."

Adam at last looked up from the greasy mess he'd made of the salt and butter on his hands. "Christ. People. It's the whole Catholic guilt thing, and the stigma around mental illness. The anger and blame, too. People think suicides are selfish, that they abandoned them."

Patrick Keogh's angry face filled Billy's head.

"Everyone thinks, too," Adam continued, "that it can't happen to them or theirs—" The food arrived, the succulent aromas from Adam's steak snagging Billy's breath. Before Billy could stop himself, he smacked his lips together.

"You're absolutely on to something," Adam continued, acting as if the food hadn't appeared.

Ravenous, Billy couldn't wait. He started in on his salmon and colorful salad. He ate slowly at first, wanting to appear polite and in control. Also, he was never much of a fan of seafood, and especially not salad. After just a few bites, though, he plowed in with pleasure and abandon. The entire meal tasted delicious—the seafood juicy, flaky, and topped with a sweet salsa; the salad a mound of arugula, tomatoes, cucumber, almonds, and all drizzled with a mouthwatering lemon-basil vinaigrette. Never would he have imagined such foods could satisfy him, let alone excite.

"You've got to make the kind of film that's so harrowing, so compelling," Adam said, "it won't let your audience look away. Know what I'm saying?" He didn't allow Billy time to respond. "See, most people won't take a stand on things. Me? I cleaned my twelve-year-old nephew's head off his bedroom walls. I can still see that wallpaper and its pattern of bright airplanes, a fleet of gray and green and yellow aircraft all splattered . . . It was like scraping at my own insides. As if I had also turned to pulp. After that, I'm up for anything, you get me? I only wish I'd caught his bedroom on camera, before the cleanup. That would make people think."

Billy's stomach lurched. "I'm sorry, how horrific."

Adam reached out his hand and extinguished the candle burning in the center of the table. The flame out, he looked closely at his thumb and finger, as if checking for burns. Billy's knife and fork remained poised over the last of his food, his appetite deserting him. Then Adam snapped out of his trance and started to eat with gusto.

Billy felt queasy. A high-pitched buzzing built in his ears. When he spoke, his voice sounded distorted. "The film I have in mind, I want it to be hard-hitting, of course, but I wouldn't want to traumatize viewers—"

"Oh, I know, I know," Adam interrupted, waving his bloodied knife in the air. "We have to spoon-feed viewers, I get it. Remember, though, you want people to stop looking away and to start taking action. Trust me, that's going to require some harsh treatment."

"I understand, but I want to emphasize, I intend the film to be inspirational and hopeful. It's about raising awareness, yes, but it's also about convincing the suicidal to seek help—"

"Yes, yes, that, too," Adam said, sounding ever more irritated.

Billy, his stomach clenched, turned the conversation to their timeline. He hoped to complete the documentary as soon as possible.

"Suits me," Adam said.

"And cost?" Billy asked, the ball in his stomach getting bigger.

"Leave the financial backing to me, for now at least. I've got some contacts I can work. Meanwhile, you need to do everything you can to get the word out, that'll go a long way. Your profile in the *Independent* is a start, but it's not nearly enough, you get me?"

"Yes, for sure, but I think once that runs, there'll be a domino effect."

"Okay, good." Adam flashed his bright white teeth. "We're going to make one mother of a film."

Billy's unease climbed. Adam certainly seemed to have the credentials and the hunger for the job, but he was strange, and maybe even crazy. Billy might never find another filmmaker with Adam's expertise, though, or his passion and financial contacts. He reached across the table and shook Adam's hand, catching grease and salt granules from the mauled butter ball. He moved his hand down to his lap, slyly wiping it on his napkin. Overall, things had gone well. Very, very well.

In the canteen, during the tea break, Billy filled Denis in on the lunch. "I tell you that salmon and salad tasted delicious. What's more, I refused to take as much as a sliver of dessert. Adam Simon was all, 'Come on, we're celebrating!'"

Denis clapped his back. "Good for you, that's brilliant. But I don't like the sounds of this Adam Simon. Why would he try to sabotage you?"

"Ah, no, it wasn't like that. He just got caught up in the moment. Speaking of which"—Billy was full, himself, of urgency and excitement over what needed to happen next—"it's critical we find more subjects for the film."

"Subjects?" Denis said, sounding a rare note of annoyance.

"Sorry, that's the lingo Adam used."

"I definitely don't like him," Denis said.

"He's on our team now, so you better like him. He paid for lunch, too. That was a big relief."

"Hmmm."

"Stop that. You and Adam will be spending a lot of time together. You're going to be a big part of this film, too."

"I am?" Denis asked, brightening.

"Of course you are."

"You're my rock," Billy added, feeling bad for his anger during the call from the restaurant toilet.

"I think there was something quare in that meal," Denis said, making Billy chuckle. "So what's next?" he asked.

"We need to put out a major call for sub—" Billy corrected himself. "For film participants. We'll spread the word online and on the radio, really jump on this. It'll be an opportunity to plug my weight-loss campaign, too, and appeal for more donations."

"I can actually see a nerve jump in your cheek," Denis said.

Billy felt it, too, right above his ever-sharpening jawline. The pulse of his own electricity. Never before had he felt so fired up. So fierce.

Twenty-one

NOW THAT IVOR HAD MASTERED FLOATING IN THE pool, it was time for him to try treading water.

"You ready?" Billy asked. Ivor nodded, looking nervous. Billy eased his left hand from beneath Ivor's armpit. "How's that? You want to keep going?"

Ivor nodded again, his teeth snagging his lower lip. Billy slowly removed his right hand, ready to catch the boy if needed. Ivor's arms and legs moved madly inside the water, keeping him afloat.

"Look at you," Billy said.

Ivor's face lit up. "I'm doing it."

They treaded water together, their arms and legs synchronized. "Wait till everyone hears about this," Billy said. Ivor's heartwarming expression deepened, a cross between how he looked when he beat Billy these evenings at chess, something else they'd taken to doing together, and how he looked whenever he saw baby animals.

After, as soon as Ivor disappeared into the toilet stall to dry off and get dressed, Billy stepped onto the scale. Three hundred and thirty-four pounds. He could hug the scale. Kiss it, too. He had lost a total of sixty-seven pounds. Seventy pounds was now within sight, as was seventy-five, and eighty, and on and on. He stepped off, smiling to himself, and moved into the toilet stall next to Ivor, to dry and dress himself.

Minutes later, as he left the stall, he saw Ivor step off the scale with a thud, his head down. Billy wrapped his arm around the boy's fleshy shoulders. "What's going on?"

Ivor's head remained bowed. "I'm fat."

Billy couldn't tell the boy he wasn't.

He couldn't think of anything to say until they were on the way home. "So you're fat," he said. "That's just one part of you. There's a lot more to you, too. Besides, fat isn't bad, son. It's just a word. Like thin, tall, short. It shouldn't be a put-down. Problem is, at my size, and with the way I need food, it's not healthy." He was talking to himself as much as Ivor.

Ivor didn't respond. "Hey," Billy said. "Are you listening to me?"

Ivor drew a deep breath. "Yeah."

Billy's thoughts jumped to their chess games, and his tiny kingdom in the garage. "We're the king of ourselves, you and me. We're not going to let anyone put us down, least of all ourselves, am I right?"

"Yeah," Ivor said, nodding, smiling.

"Let me hear you say it," Billy said.

"I'm the king of me," Ivor said, his voice booming inside the car.

Billy laughed. "Now," he said. "While we're on important subjects, how are we going to celebrate your big birthday?"

Ivor grinned. "I don't know."

"Ten," Billy said, shaking his head. "Double digits."

"Yeah, I know," Ivor said, giddy.

The day the *Irish Independent* published Billy's profile, he drove to town first thing. He felt so frantic, he almost went to Caroline's shop, to get the paper into his hands soonest, but he didn't want to face her or anyone else he knew. Not yet. With a pang, he wondered how people would react. Word of the interview would spread like the bird flu, he knew that much. He caught himself. Here he was, worrying about what was being said about him, the very thing he had condemned Tricia and his parents for fretting about. He shouldn't care. He didn't care. Still, he shivered.

In town, inside the newsagent's, he scanned the *Indo*'s front page, his scalp prickling when he saw his head shot in the bottom index. The paper had used the photo from his End Suicide Now! website—his thick neck and naked, bloated shoulders on display in all their fleshy glory. Worse, the headline read "Massive Man Hopes to Halve Himself in Son's Memory." He turned to page twenty-two, almost ripping the paper in his impatience.

After the first manic scan, he read the article again. Jack Dineen hadn't included the story about Michael rescuing the dog and then returning it with such grace. That story showed who Michael was. Jack had mentioned the quays, weather, seagulls, and the two women eating lunch on the bench, everything but the story about Michael and the dog. *The women's youthful, care-free laughter carried, striking a chilling contrast with the weight, both literal and figurative, that shrouds Billy Brennan.*

He paid, eying the shelves of brightly colored sweets and chocolate, the shiny foil bags of crisps in various cheese flavors. The impulse to grab at his favorites and shove them into him was overwhelming. He abandoned his change and rushed out onto the street. When he looked up, his lungs too tight to work, the sun had climbed higher, but even its budding brilliance seemed like a stain in the sky.

Billy arrived home, queasiness stirring up his empty stomach. Why had he done the bloody interview? Why had he put himself out there like that for everyone to see? For everyone to tear down? Tricia sat at the kitchen table, the *Independent* spread wide. John stood next to her, also reading Billy's profile. Tricia would have bought the newspaper in the shop after mass as usual, and likely had to withstand commentary from Caroline and everyone else in the place. He considered continuing past her and John, wary of what they would say, but remained rooted to the spot, unable to move. "I'm not happy with it, just so you know. He didn't write what I wanted."

Tricia didn't look up. John's attention also remained on the newspaper. On the counter next to the sink, Billy's phone buzzed, signaling a text. "That's been going off for the last half hour," Tricia said. "Texts and calls."

Billy had left in such a rush earlier, he'd forgotten his phone. He rubbed his eyes with his thumb and finger, as if that could make all this go away.

"My phone's been going off, too," she continued, "calls from your mother, Lisa, Magda—"

"Christ." On top of the empty, hollow feeling, his stomach cramped. He was going to be sick.

"What are you so upset about?" she asked. "I thought this was what you wanted."

"I wanted the article to be about Michael and the great loss he is, and about doing something that matters in his memory. Not about the shriek of seagulls and those women, complete strangers, and waxing fancy about my size."

"At least it's well written and sympathetic," Tricia said. "It's not like he paints you in a bad light or anything."

"Why would he paint me in a bad light?" Billy's voice held a dare—a warning.

"This should at least bring in more donations," she said. "And it'll get way more people to pay attention to what you're doing. That's what you wanted, isn't it?"

Adrenaline surged through his chest and up into his head, buzzing. He started to sweat, and to feel sicker. "I said, why would he paint me in a bad light?"

"Leave it." She lifted her eyes to John.

"Don't let me stop you, have at yourselves." John marched toward the kitchen door.

Tricia made to go after him. Billy's hand shot out, covering hers on the table. "No, I'll go."

She looked down, furious, but didn't pull her hand away. To his horror, he spotted salt and grease on his thick fingers and a thin line of chocolate in the bed of his nails. He stared, disbelieving. Had he gorged himself on bars and crisps at the newsagent's after all? Only imagined that he'd walked away?

He blinked, and the stains disappeared. His relief only lasted a second. His family did nothing but make him doubt himself.

"If you're not going to go after him, I will," Tricia said, again making to get up from the table.

He pressed down on her hand, wanting to hurt her a little, to get all the ugly out. "Say it."

She remained seated, her eyes glittering with tears and rage. "Fine. You couldn't have made all these changes long ago, when it might have made all the difference?"

"What difference?"

She pulled her hand free and looked into her lap.

"Say it!" he said, making her flinch.

"If you had been stronger all these years, had acted the way you're acting now, maybe Michael would never have done what he did."

He felt folded over the electric fences on his father's farm, the voltage zapping and burning him. He'd known this whole time she'd blamed him. He'd known, and yet he'd hoped. Tears stung his eyes. He wanted to rip out their ducts. See if he'd stand here in front of her crying. "Do you not think for the rest of my days I won't be wondering that same thing?" His breath seemed as knocked about as the rest of him, unable to enter and leave him straight. He thought to go out to the garage and the other world he was making. Instead, he felt pulled to the empty living room. There, he closed the door behind him and settled on his armchair, Michael's walnut guitar on his lap.

He strummed, thinking Michael's fingers had worked these chords, had pressed these very strings in the guitar's neck. Michael had been here before him, his body curved around the shiny, sturdy instrument, his right hand here, his left hand there. For a long time, Billy sat with the feel of the guitar, of Michael.

Over the following days, the regional newspapers picked up Billy's story and his local paper gave him front-page coverage. To his great relief, the response was overwhelmingly positive. At last people were making a fuss about his efforts. Several strangers recognized him on the street, too, and called out praises. One middle-aged woman went so far as to ask to take her photo with him.

Despite this welcome turn of events, the rush of attention and approval was also unsettling, as if his popularity in the newspapers suddenly gave people permission to support and like him. *Hey presto.* He couldn't help but think that without the public fanfare, people would still feel largely indifferent and dismissive of him and what he was doing.

"You're famous," Denis gushed.

Great momentum, Adam Simon e-mailed, *keep it going.*

Lisa phoned, saying she wanted him to know how proud she was. "It's just a pity what it's doing to Mam and Dad."

He didn't say what it was doing to him that his parents, his own wife, and his now oldest son still couldn't give him anything close to the support he needed. He also didn't say how Tricia had admitted she resented the change in him, and the cost of it not coming much sooner. That she blamed him for Michael's death.

A little more than a week after the *Independent* published his profile, Billy drove alone to Dublin to take part in a radio interview, on *All the Talk* with Frank Galvin. The show was the nation's most popular call-in broadcast, every episode drawing upward of four hundred thousand listeners a day. That number alone turned Billy's legs to rubber, making it almost impossible to work the car pedals. He'd slept badly, too, terrified he would sound stupid on air, or that panic would strike him dumb, or that someone, maybe many, would phone in and hurl abuse. There had been those couple of horrible tweets, calling him opportunistic, and a fat bastard. If only Tricia had offered to go with him, for moral support. But she hadn't as much as wished him good luck.

He was so nervous he hadn't eaten breakfast. That was a first. Over the miles, it seemed every ad on the radio conjured nothing but food—jingles and promos about porridge, sausages, chocolates, scones, cheese, and more. His favorite sandwich swam in front of him—ground chicken mixed with mayonnaise, celery, and pepper and salt, till it formed a creamy, tangy spread. Then he'd pile the lot onto a French baguette with butter, lettuce, tomatoes, and Edam cheese. Bliss.

He killed the radio and its ads, and inserted a CD. As the Corolla traveled closer to Dublin, he blared Christy Moore, tapping his hands in time on the steering wheel. He sang along at the top of his voice, not a note on key, but he didn't care. When the songs got to be too much, lyrics about not being able to go with those who leave us, he turned the radio back on, to the classical station.

The contents of the radio producer's office looked like they'd been spilled out of boxes rather than set down with any care.

Black-and-white photographs of celebrity guests littered the walls, every mismatched frame hanging crooked. His desk was an explosion of papers, pens, snacks, mugs with dribbled tea stains, and at least three pairs of reading glasses. Tall plants, in various stages of dying, crowded a corner. Yellowed leaves and rounds of dust littered the floor. Billy's unease soared.

"Nothing to be nervous about," Matt or Mick said. The fiftyish producer was short and portly, with a tweed cap that likely hid his bald spot. That was the second time he had tried to reassure Billy, and it made Billy feel ever worse. Yet again, Billy's heart amazed and scared him with how fast it could go.

"Now," the producer continued. "No bad language, that's number one, and number two, try to remember listeners won't see gestures, nods, facial expressions, you get it. And you want to avoid long pauses as best you can." He gave a small chuckle. "You want to keep talking, that's actually number one. No yes-or-no answers, either, you check me? Be yourself, yeah? You'll be great."

Billy's stomach gurgled like water going down the drain. The producer's unruly eyebrows shot up. "Sorry," Billy said, mortified. "It always wants in on the act." The producer threw back his head and laughed. Billy smiled tightly and clenched his stomach, afraid it would pipe up again.

The producer led Billy into the recording studio proper, and introduced him to the famous Frank Galvin. Frank pumped Billy's hand, the presenter's face round and red, jolly. His tie boasted more colors than a rainbow. "A pleasure. Please, take a seat." Billy sat into the black bucket chair, grateful of its size and comfort. "Just be yourself," Frank said, echoing his producer.

Matt or Mick pushed his cap back on his head, revealing a

high, wrinkled forehead, and brought the large desk micro-phone close to Billy's face. Next, he showed Billy the button to press if he needed to silence his microphone, should he have to sneeze or cough.

Frank pointed to the green light on the wall behind him, and the identical light behind Billy. "When they turn red, we're live."

"You'd think it would be the other way around," Billy said, his voice coming out high and thin.

"Remember, in here, red is go," the producer said.

"Thanks, Mick," Frank said.

"Thanks, Mick," Billy said.

Mick gave Billy a thumbs-up before he disappeared behind the closed door.

"Here we go," Frank said softly, three fingers in the air. "One." His first finger dropped. "Two." With his free hand, Frank reached for the switchboard, killing the music. "Good afternoon, and welcome to *All the Talk*."

As Frank Galvin introduced him, Billy experienced that floating sensation, as though he were rising out of himself and drifting toward the ceiling, leaving his massive body behind. Frank's voice grew fainter in Billy's head. Billy fixed on the mute button, about to hit it and admit he couldn't do this.

Then he was talking, answering Frank's questions and tell-ing listeners about his morbid obesity, sponsored diet, village march, and planned documentary. He rushed to tell them about Michael, the boy's smile, his love of music and football, and the story about the stray dog.

He also shared how much he looked forward to losing all two hundred pounds, half of himself, and to one day getting to wear Michael's favorite sweatshirt. How he especially longed for the time when someone would come up to him and say, *Because of you, because of your son, Michael, I didn't kill myself.*

The switchboard lit up. Caller after caller shared how they'd lost a loved one to suicide. How they, too, never saw it coming. *Thank you,* they told him, *something major needs to be done.*

On his way home, Lisa phoned. "You were brilliant, well done."

"Thanks, that means a lot."

"Seriously, I can't say it enough. You were amazing." Her voice cracked. "I'm sorry I ever doubted any of it."

It took him a moment to be able to speak. "That's okay, don't worry about it."

"I'm so proud of you, well, well done."

"Thanks, sis."

"You're welcome, Will." They laughed.

Denis also phoned. "You're doing it, man, you're really affecting people. You're making all the difference."

"Thanks. Thanks so much." Billy felt he would burst. He knew that feeling well. But never in a good way. Until now.

Tricia was sitting at the kitchen table when Billy arrived home, drinking coffee and kicking her crossed leg in time to the caffeinated beat of her heart. She pushed aside her coffee-stained mug and reached for a fresh stick of nicotine gum. She'd taken to rolling the silver foil wrappers into tiny balls and dropping them all over. He and the children would find them littered throughout the house, like a trail she was leaving.

"Well?" he said.

"Well, what?"

"Did you listen?"

"Yeah." She rolled the silver ball of foil faster between her finger and thumb.

He felt a flash of irritation. If he had to pull it out of her, forget it. But he couldn't stop himself. "What did you think?"

She looked up, the tears in her eyes making his chest constrict. "What you're doing is great, it is." Tears spilled onto her cheeks and she wiped at them hard. "But I hate it. I just hate it."

He stepped toward her.

She raised her hands in a yield sign. "Please, I really want to be left alone right now."

He hesitated, thinking maybe she wanted, needed, exactly the opposite.

Her hand pressed her chest. "Jesus, when I think back. I was hell-bent on getting married, couldn't wait to get away from my family and start over." She gave a small, harsh laugh, like glass cracking. "I had this crazy idea that everything would have to go better the second time around, that I'd never be that unlucky to wind up in another broken family, especially not with you. You never said it, but I knew you wanted the same things I did, another family, another chance." She rubbed at her nose and eyes. "And you made me believe we would have that together. You lost all that weight and said I'd filled the empty feeling, said you were a changed man. But it didn't last. We didn't last. And now Michael is gone and I'm right back where I started, stuck with a wreck of a family."

His throat felt glutted, full of words he wanted to say, but couldn't. She thought their family was a wreck. Thought she was stuck. As he walked out the back door, she spoke again.

"Just so you know, I'll always be asking myself, too, what I should have done better."

He continued out to the garage and into his other world, where he could right everything that needed fixing. Could let out the wail gathering in his chest.

Twenty-two

WHEN BILLY ENTERED THE BEDROOM, TRICIA WHIRLED around. "Jesus, you scared me. For a second there I thought . . ." With so much weight lost, seventy-nine pounds and counting, his and Michael's resemblance was now striking.

"Sorry." He felt oddly like a trespasser, still not back in their room, still pulled to Michael's bed every night. A big part of him was waiting for Tricia to invite him back, unsure if she wanted him there.

"I wish we weren't doing this today," she said, moving to the wardrobe mirror and pulling her brittle hair into a bun.

He spoke to her gaunt face in the glass. "I tried, but there was no talking him out of it. I even said he could have his party at the pool and invite a few friends, but he wouldn't give in." Billy wondered if Ivor remembered Michael had celebrated his tenth birthday at Dublin Zoo and that's why he was so insistent.

In a couple of months, on November 19, they would have to endure what would have been Michael's eighteenth birthday.

Already, the boy was gone eight months. It didn't seem possible. Time had warped and sometimes it seemed they had lost him just yesterday. Other times it seemed so long ago. They'd already survived the first day without him, the first week, first month, and the first football championship final, but they had yet to endure his first birthday with him gone, the first Christmas and New Year's, and his first anniversary. Everyone said things would get easier with time, especially after they'd survived all the firsts, but that brought up another kind of pain.

"Maybe it won't be as bad as we think," Tricia said. She crossed the room, lifted her handbag off the bed, and walked out, leaving Billy alone.

The afternoon was overcast, but at least the rain was holding off. Tricia had traveled up to Dublin with Billy's mother, while he had driven the three children. Billy's mother never failed to join them for the children's birthdays, which was more than his father or Lisa ever did. He had to give her that much. The two women stood at the zoo's entrance, amid the colorful mill of people and the convoy of baby strollers all rushing inside. Tricia and his mother searched the crowd of oncomers, looking impatient. They had obviously made better time on the road and had found easier parking than Billy.

Anna called out and raced toward her mother and grandmother. Billy reached the women, flanked by John and Ivor. He'd managed to avoid his mother ever since his profile was published, and she looked his shrinking body up and down, unable to hide her surprise. His hand flew to his stomach, realizing it didn't hurt the way it normally would after a long drive. He fit so much better in the car, in everything, now. Yet he had almost missed the hard press of the steering wheel during the journey, a constant for years.

"Sorry, hope you weren't waiting long," he said. The shock remained on his mother's face, but she made no comment. He knew she wouldn't remark, either, on the growing media attention he was getting. Unless it was to criticize. Hundreds of donations were flooding in online and in the post, bringing the running tally of promised funds to eleven thousand five hundred and ninety-eight euro. Billy's followers on Twitter and friends on Facebook also continued to climb, as did the visitors to his website. All this from strangers, and nothing from his own parents. His temper pressed on the back of his face, as if trying to get at his mother.

One by one, the six Brennans moved through the entrance turnstile, John looking livid. He hadn't wanted to come, but Billy and Tricia had insisted, stopping short of reminding him that Ivor was now his one and only brother. As if by silent agreement, the six walked straight to the lion exhibit. There, Billy read the dull brass plaques, searching for the name of the male cub born shortly before Michael's tenth birthday. Tricia appeared next to him, also reading, also searching. There was no mention of an eight-year-old male. Billy studied the five lions lazing about the dirt, wondering.

"Remember the time we were here for Michael's birthday and the zoo ran that contest to name the newborn cub? What names did we come up with at all?" She gave a little laugh. "They didn't use any of them anyway."

John walked away. When he didn't return, Billy followed him. John's face looked achy and the edges of his eyes were red.

"Michael wanted to name the cub Mikewali and I wanted to call him Johnwali." His face crumpled. Billy squeezed John's shoulder, unsure if the boy would want any contact. John suddenly laughed through the glint of tears. "Mikewali and Johnwali." Billy also sad-laughed.

When they turned around to rejoin the others, Billy reluctantly let go of John's shoulder. Tricia watched, her expression tender.

They studied the zoo's map, trying to decide which exhibit to visit next.

"Let's go see the gorillas," Ivor said.

"Sounds like a plan." Billy curled the map into a cylinder. Memories of paper telescopes cut at him. He had to stop his thoughts from going to Michael. This was Ivor's day. A happy occasion.

They arrived at the gorilla habitat, all the Brennans but Billy licking ice-cream cones. The giant silverback, eating on a leafy dark-green stalk, seemed to stare right at Billy. Two smaller, female gorillas sat close by the silverback, each chewing on a blade of straw.

The silverback stirred, and started on the prowl, moving toward the two females. He grunted and trembled, his entire body vibrating. Billy studied the animal's massiveness, marveling at the enormity of his head, shoulders, arms, stomach, and behind. Billy was almost as big, but without any of the grandeur. One of the females moved off, looking back over her shoulder every few seconds as the male gave chase.

"There's going to be a fight," Ivor said, nervously.

"Awful-looking things," Billy's mother said. "Let's find something nicer to look at."

John protested, saying he wanted to watch the gorillas fight.

Anna's fist rubbed at her eye, her blond hair limp and dampened with sweat, her upper lip marked with an ice-cream mustache. "I don't want to see another fight," she said, quietly. "I've seen enough of those."

Billy's mother looked from him to Tricia, her brow furrowed. He kept looking at the gorillas, his expression blank. In his periphery he checked Tricia, wondering if she'd felt a similar dart of guilt. She remained intent on the gorillas, her face not giving anything away.

The female gorilla stopped on the rocks and hunkered in submission beneath the silverback. He mounted her from behind and thumped his bulk against her. People pointed and laughed. The silverback pumped faster, harder. The female turned her head to look at the massive male, seeming distressed.

Billy's scalp crawled. Back when he and Tricia were still physical, whenever he'd reached for her during those last months of intimacy, she'd worn a similar look and often refused him. Whenever she had tolerated him near her, she insisted he not mount her, saying she couldn't breathe. Instead, she'd straddled him, her hand working his penis into her, a disturbed look on her face.

The silverback pulled out of the female. Billy's mother made some outraged sound.

"Okay, let's go," Tricia said, hurrying off. She tossed her half-eaten ice cream into the green litter bin, looking repulsed. Billy stared after the ice cream, wanting it back. Wanting everything back.

Minutes later, they stood watching the elephants. When one of the four deadened-looking creatures raised its trunk, it seemed like a silent cry for help. Billy searched Ivor's backpack, finding shortbread biscuits, the plainest treat in the boy's stash. He fired four biscuits into the enclosure, hoping each of the elephants would get one, not knowing how else to make them feel better, if only for a few seconds. Anna and Ivor also clamored to feed them, laughing at how the giant animals hoovered the treat from the ground. "That's enough for them," Billy said. "We don't want to harm them."

Billy's mother sat down on a bench. "Are you all right, Maura?" Tricia asked.

"I just need to sit for a minute." His mother didn't sound well. Billy glanced over. She looked tired and pale.

"Come on, let's keep going," Tricia said. "Before we're thrown out." She jutted her chin toward the *Do Not Feed* signs.

After a tour of the African Plains, Tricia again consulted the map. If they hurried, she announced, they would catch the keepers feeding the seals and then they could go get lunch. Hands sprouted in Billy's stomach, slow-clapping. Just as quickly, his anticipation died. He was pretty much the same size now as he was on his last visit to the zoo almost eight years ago, when they were celebrating Michael's tenth birthday and taking for granted all the life and goodness the boy still had ahead.

It would stay with Billy forever how the newborn lion cub on that visit had opened its mouth so many times in so many minutes while the seven Brennans watched, their breaths fogging the Plexiglas.

"Look, Dad," Michael had said. "He's hungry."

It had bothered Billy that Michael assumed the cub felt hungry, just as Billy always felt hungry. But it bothered him much more now that it was obvious the cub was mimicking his parents and trying to roar. *Monkey see, monkey do.*

As they reached the seals, Billy's mother complained of a sharp pain at her right temple. Moments later, she collapsed. Billy and Tricia dropped to their knees next to her. His mother groaned and held her hand to the side of her head.

Billy gripped her free hand, rushing her with questions. "Do you want water? Have you pain anywhere else? Are you able to sit up?"

A crowd pressed around them, and several called out for medical assistance. "You're all right, Maura," Tricia said. "You're going to be okay."

Someone spoke up behind them, saying an ambulance was on the way. His mother moaned again, her face pinched with pain and much too pale. Dr. Shaw had tried to tell Billy she wasn't well. He should have listened.

"You hear that, Mammy?" he said. "Help is on the way. You're going to be grand." He had tried to make his voice match Tricia's calm reassurance, but he heard his panic. Heard how he'd called her Mammy, something he hadn't said since he was a boy.

The male paramedic pressed the flat of his blue-gloved hand against Billy's chest, stopping him from entering the ambulance. "Whoa, there, big fella. You can't travel with us."

The female paramedic, much younger than her partner, must have seen the panic in Billy's face, and the humiliation. "Let him try." She looked at Billy. "You'll have to stay in the back, though, and keep out of the way." After several attempts solo, and then with the aid of both paramedics pulling on his arms, Billy managed to climb inside the vehicle, hot with shame. He sidestepped into the corner and made himself as small as he could. Outside, a female zookeeper urged the large crowd of onlookers to disperse.

As the ambulance sped toward the hospital, Billy's mother went unconscious. Billy's heart beat in time to the siren's wail. Tricia had remained at the zoo with the children, trying to save the birthday celebrations. He had promised to phone her from the hospital once he knew more. On the street, people of a certain age blessed themselves as the ambulance passed.

Billy remained crouched over his mother's feet, the only pose that made sense in the cramped space. His hand clasped her nylon-clad foot, just as he had clasped the ankle of the bronze sculpture of Michael's Wellingtons. The female paramedic struggled to tap a vein in his mother's arm. The repeated in-and-out of the needle made Billy squeamish. When the paramedic wiggled the needle inside his mother, still trying to stab a vein, he thought he would vomit. She then resorted to the back of his mother's hand. The needle hit its target on the first try, but made his mother's papery skin bulge like a stalk.

"It could just be dehydration," the paramedic said in her lilting Northern accent. "We're giving her some fluids right now, that should help."

Billy watched his mother, trying not to think that this could be all his fault.

As the ambulance arrived at the hospital, his mother came to, her hand rushing to the side of her head. She moaned, and complained of pain at her temple and pressure behind her eye. Billy's thoughts jumped to a tumor, or a stroke. He searched her face for signs of palsy. She appeared normal, aside from the scrunch of pain and the now-gray hue to her complexion. He asked the paramedics, his voice too loud, too sharp, if they could give her something for the pain.

In the emergency room, amid the acrid smell of disinfectant, Billy waited on a comfortless plastic chair next to his mother on her bed, both of them hidden behind an orange curtain. He studied the outline of her feet under the pink blanket, a part of her he had no recollection of ever having touched prior to the ambulance, and which he would likely never touch again. He found himself missing the heat of her foot and its solid, smooth feel. In his head, he continued to call her Mammy.

A young male doctor appeared, thin and tanned. He shone a light in Billy's mother's eyes, and asked her question after question. The pain and pressure had eased, she told him. She said she thought she might be all right. Said she needed to get back to the zoo and the business of celebrating her grandson's tenth birthday. "He's my last grandchild."

Billy needed a moment before he could speak. "Ivor will be fine, it's you we need to worry about right now." He tried to make light. "I'll make sure Tricia keeps us some cake."

The doctor looked Billy up and down. *Like you need cake.* Billy's face burned. He might sometimes miss his size and how it wrapped and hid him, but he would never miss moments like this.

"Did you phone Lisa?" his mother asked. "Is she on her way?"

"I've no phone coverage in here," Billy lied, hoping the doctor wouldn't say otherwise. Lisa would fuss and cause a scene, give orders to him and everyone else. "I'll phone her and Dad later, when we know more. No point in worrying them."

The doctor ordered a brain scan. "Just to rule out anything sinister." *Sinister* sent a shiver through Billy. Minutes into the wait for an orderly to wheel his mother to radiology, she dozed off. Billy escaped to the hospital canteen and returned with the *Independent* and the *Times*, a cup of too-weak tea, and several bars of chocolate, a reward for the day he was putting in.

The tea scalded his mouth and the chocolate didn't taste right. He checked the date on the wrapper, and then realized there was nothing off or different about the treat, but with him. He could taste the amount of sugar in the bar and how it coated his mouth with an aftertaste, and not in a good way. He found himself craving a shiny red juicy apple with crunch. He threw away the tea and chocolate, and walked outside, to stretch and get some air.

As he walked, he phoned Tricia. "They're worried she may have had a stroke," he said, surprising himself with the exaggeration. It was just that Tricia hadn't sounded this kind, this concerned, since those early days after Michael. And his mother's condition could be serious. The results of the brain scan could be sinister.

"Oh, no," Tricia said.

"Well, we don't know anything yet for sure."

"Have you phoned your dad and Lisa? Do you want me to call them?"

"No, no." He hoped he didn't sound cagey. "There's no point in worrying them just yet. I should know more in an hour or so."

"I don't know, I think they'd want to be with her."

"She's still sleeping, wouldn't even know they're here."

"Poor Maura."

"I'll phone again as soon as I know more. I'll phone Dad and Lisa then, too."

"Do you want me to drive over there and wait with you?"

"No, I'll be okay. You stay with the children. How's Ivor? Is he having a good time?"

"Yeah, yeah, great. He's a bit worried, of course, they all are, but we're keeping ourselves well distracted. Don't worry about us, you just take care of yourself."

"I will, thanks." His scalp tightened. Why did it take tragedy to bring out the best in us? And why was that state of grace so fleeting?

After he rang off, he tapped his phone to his lips, considering a call to Denis, to also play on his friend's sympathies. He pushed his phone into his trousers pocket, telling himself not to be pathetic.

When he returned to his mother, she was still sleeping. A short, squat nurse appeared, wearing large, black-framed glasses that Billy could swear didn't contain lenses. She checked his mother's vitals and assured Billy they wouldn't have to wait much longer for her to be taken to radiology. "She's sleeping peacefully, must have needed a good rest." Her eyes stayed on him. "You're the father from the newspapers, aren't you, the one doing the suicide prevention fund-raiser? I heard you on the radio, too. Well done, you're an absolute inspiration."

He thanked her, too overcome to know what else to say. After she left, he returned to the end of the bed and looked at his mother's thin, pale face, seeing how old she'd gotten, how fragile. She could never say anything even close to what that nurse had said. She just didn't have it in her.

As soon as Billy's mother awoke, she insisted he find a landline and phone his father and Lisa. When she went on about it, he pretended to fiddle with his mobile and then feigned surprise at his sudden ability to get coverage. "Isn't that convenient," his mother said, as if wise to him.

Thankfully, Lisa was in London for work and could only execute her reign of terror by text and calls. "Make sure they don't leave her to rot on that bed," she said.

"Yes, Lisa."

"And write down every single medication they give her, and every test they run."

"Yes, Lisa."

"Get the names of all the doctors and nurses who go near her."

"Yes, Lisa."

Lisa's voice caught. "Is she going to be all right?"

"I think she's going to be fine. Try not to worry," Billy said, earnest now.

"Thanks for being with her," Lisa said.

"Of course. Go on, I'll call you again just as soon as I know more."

Billy phoned his father then, picking at the words to cause the least alarm. He needn't have worried. "Is that right?" his father said. "Well, be sure and call again when you know the results."

"Right, yeah, okay." Billy looked at his dead phone, disbelieving. He'd seen his father get more worked up over a calf having scours.

Over three hours after Billy's mother returned from radiology, the doctor finally reappeared. He was smiling, his tan making his teeth look white-white. "Good news, the scan is clean." *Clean,* Billy thought. Like illness and damage were dirty. The doctor suspected Billy's mother had suffered dehydration, exertion, and something he called "age-appropriate vertigo." In short, she'd overdone it.

Billy's mother looked at him hard. "You hear that? That's because you left me standing in front of the zoo for so long today."

"Looks like she's feeling better already," the doctor said with a smirk, and disappeared behind the orange curtain.

Billy phoned his father. "Yeah, the doctor was just with her, she's going to be grand."

"Oh, very good," his father said, still deadpan.

"Tell him the doctor said I overdid it," Billy's mother said.

"Yeah, we should be out of here within the hour," Billy said into the phone.

"Tell him I've overdone it and I've a touch of that vertigo," his mother said.

Billy tucked the phone below his chin. "You can tell him yourself when you get home."

"I'll see you whenever so," Billy's father said.

"Yeah, okay, 'bye."

"I suppose he's frantic now," his mother said.

Billy was about to say something harsh, but stopped himself. His mother had tried to sound scornful, but he heard longing there, too. "He is of course frantic, but sure don't you know him, he'd never let on."

"He's the worst," she said, still with that attempt at disdain, but he could tell she was pleased. It had never occurred to him he wasn't the only one in the family starved of the right kinds of attention.

Later that night, he and his mother finally left the hospital. They took a taxi back to the zoo and his mother's car. On the drive home, Billy's mother complained about the long hours on the bed. "They never gave me as much as a cup of tea." She also decried the thick accents of the foreign nurses and doctors. "They're impossible to understand."

She sniffed. "You're not to tell people about this. I wouldn't want anyone to think I'd taken a turn, have them talking about me, saying I'm getting on."

Billy drove faster, imagining he could get ahead, could leave his mother and the other half of the Fiat sitting on the road, spewing their fumes into the night.

Twenty-three

IVOR WANTED TO JUMP OFF THE DIVING BOARD.
Billy was adamant. "You need to wait until you learn to swim,
it's not safe yet."

"But I can almost swim."

"Almost isn't close enough." Guilt poked at Billy. Ivor would
learn to swim much faster and better with proper lessons, but
Billy wanted to be the one to teach him.

Ivor stretched out on his front in the water, supported by
Billy. The boy went through his paces, all synchronized legs,
arms, head, and breath. "That's it, well done," Billy said.

Later, Ivor messed about with a few boys in the shallow
end while Billy completed his laps. All the practice Billy had
put in, all the progress he'd made, and still he didn't feel fit
enough, didn't feel he could ever catch enough breath or gen-
erate enough power. He pushed through his eighteenth lap,
his chest tight and his breathing ragged. Dr. Shaw's warnings

nagged. Billy often experienced dizziness and pressure on his chest, and it wasn't because of another panic attack, either.

He still had a long way to go with his weight loss, more than one hundred and fifteen pounds till he reached his goal. Maybe it was time he called in the professionals and stopped going it alone. Stopped making Denis carry the mother lode as his sole sponsor and lead champion. He wouldn't please Shaw by going back to him, though. Instead, he would phone Shaw's secretary and get a referral to a nutritionist at the hospital, see what they could do for him.

"Dad! Dad!" Ivor shouted. Billy scanned the pool. "Up here! Look!" Billy found Ivor at the diving board, on the top rung of the ladder.

"Get down out of there," Billy shouted, trudging through the water.

Ivor rushed along the diving board. At its end, he stretched out his arms and tucked his head.

"No, Ivor, don't!" Billy shouted.

Ivor dropped through the air.

Billy dipped under the surface and powered through the water. On reaching Ivor, he wrapped his arms around the boy's legs, pinning Ivor to his shoulder, and lunged at the pool wall. They surfaced and hooked their elbows to the edge of the pool, both breathing hard. Fresh grief cut at Billy. So many times he had imagined wrapping his arms around Michael's legs and raising the boy, slackening the rope and saving him.

Ivor pumped his free arm in the air. "I did it."

Billy smiled, hiding the state he was in. "Well done, son, well done."

Billy quick-stepped to the garage. He had resumed taking the seconds from the factory, pocketing one for every two he threw away. Even if Bald Art realized the numbers in the bin weren't what they should be, what was he going to do, strip-search Billy? Billy snorted, picturing the scene. Then just as quickly the pall returned. Too many people always wanted to keep things the same. They didn't want change. Even if it was change for the better. Bald Art wanted to keep throwing away the seconds just because that was the way things had always been done. What a spectacular lack of imagination. And that problem wasn't particular to the seconds, either. All the toys needed to be recast.

The factory needed to do more with the dolls and soldiers to get children more interested and excited—to get the toys to transport them. Right now the toys were nameless and storyless, and didn't have movable parts. Aside from the great craftsmanship that went into creating them, there was nothing to make the toys stand out, nothing to make children or adults hanker to bring them home. As Billy brooded, the toys in his miniature village seemed to look up at him, impatient to be brought to life.

Sometimes he had the urge to visit the real village of Inistioge. He imagined sitting on the scenic bridge and looking down on the rushing River Nore. Saw himself visit the ancient castle and sacred priory, and walk among the various clusters of trees and the period cottages and stately homes—the place more magical and picturesque in person than he could ever have conjured in his head, or in this replica. He couldn't bring himself to visit, though. To go to Inistioge itself would only drive home the pretense of everything he'd created here in his garage.

The seconds continued to stare, waiting. "All right."

Inside the cottage, tiny Michael calls out. Tiny Billy and tiny Tricia abandon their game of chess and rush to his bedroom. Michael stands at the window and points at something in the night. On the other side of the room, his brothers remain asleep, the moon a spotlight on their faces. Billy and Tricia look, but cannot see. "It's a light," Michael insists, shining amid the trees on the distant hill.

Tricia coaxes him back to bed. "It's just the full moon reflecting off of something."

He insists it's not the moon. "Can't you see it?"

Billy fights his panic. It's his kingdom and yet he cannot see it. He tells Tricia to return to the warmth of the fire, promising to rejoin her shortly to finish their game of chess.

Michael tugs on the sleeve of his father's shirt. "There!"

Billy leans in close to the window, his breath blurring the glass, and pretends to see the light.

"Do you think it's a fallen star?" Michael asks.

Billy continues to play along, his unease growing. "Could be."

Michael wants to find the star and bring it home. Billy marvels at the mind of a child, able to think of rescuing a stray star and having it live among them.

Outside, they walk through the village, across the bridge, and into the woods, the air tinged with the silence of sleep and the thick and heady, almost rotting, smell of hawthorn. With the glow from the full moon and a flashlight, and the supposed fallen star that only Michael can see, they creep through the woods.

Every now and then the boy startles at the scurry of unseen creatures in the branches and foliage—birds, mice, and rabbits that sound impossibly large. The boy turns his head left and right, his shoulders pulled up to his ears, and asks in a frightened voice if there are foxes, or worse.

Billy forces a laugh. "Don't worry, I brought only friends here." He, too, finds himself unnerved, though. The scuttle in the trees and shrubbery sounds too loud and menacing. His worry builds. How can there be anything in his kingdom he didn't bring here?

Moments later, Michael covers his eyes and holds on to the tail of his father's coat, blindly following. He claims they are almost at the fallen star and its bright light is too much. "How can you stand it?" he asks, sounding ever more afraid.

Billy's fear also pitches. Something is wrong in his kingdom, his wonderful world.

"Daddy?"

Billy collects himself. He is the ruler here. Nothing bad can happen. The trick, he tells his son, is to not look straight at the light, but at its edges.

Michael risks a peek, and smiles. "It works."

Billy feels he can breathe again, feels everything might be all right again.

When they arrive, Billy scales a tree and pretends to place the stray star inside the breast of his coat. He lowers himself to the ground and orders Michael to keep his eyes closed. He eases open the boy's coat and nestles the star next to his heart. Michael opens his eyes and gushes at the light pouring through the wool. Billy doubts even the imaginary star is shining as bright as the boy's face.

"Thanks, Daddy. You're the best daddy."

The boy's words make Billy feel like a giant. "My pleasure, son."

"You're the best daddy," Michael says.

"All right, let's get you and that star home."

"You're the best daddy," Michael repeats.

"Stop, that's enough," Billy says, his delight turning to a sick feeling.

"You're the best daddy."

At his workbench, Billy staggered backward, away from the village and the seconds, and hurried out of the garage.

Days passed. Billy found himself avoiding the garage and his tiny kingdom, still not recovered from what had happened there. Just as he was considering another visit—of course he was in full control of it, for Christ's sake, how could he not be?—the phone call came. At first Billy thought it was a prank. The caller introduced herself as a TV producer for RTÉ and invited him to fill a cancellation spot during the weekend, on *Matters with Maeve*.

Convinced, flabbergasted, Billy could hardly form the words to accept. He hung up, the shock wearing off and elation setting in. Just as quickly fresh anxiety sank its claws. He saw a flash of his mother on Ivor's birthday, on that hospital bed. This was really going to catapult him into the public eye, and might just send his mother and father to their graves.

He walked across the yard and around the side of the house, finding Tricia on her hands and knees in her vegetable garden. He stood over her, bubbling again with excitement, willing her not to take it away again. She pulled a head of butter lettuce from the dirt and placed it in the empty basket next to her.

"You're not going to believe it," he said.

When he told her, she looked off into the distance, maybe at the imaginary line where the green hills met the empty white sky. "You can never know, can you, the turns a life will take?" Her deadened words doused his delight and he experienced a moment's anger, and then great sadness.

Much too clumsily, he made it down onto his knees in front of her. She gave a little start of surprise, and then some hardness seemed to crack and her expression softened. "Help me," she said, reaching to pluck scallions. "Grab a few beets there."

He tugged on the large green leaves, pulling the round beets from the dirt, like a cluster of small, soiled hearts. She took them from him, their hands meeting for a moment. *Help me,* he wanted to say. *I'm trying my best. What's it going to take?* But she was already walking away, cradling the basket of vegetables in her arm like a baby.

The next day at the factory, Billy scheduled another meeting with Tony. Lucy gushed when he appeared at her desk. She'd read the newspaper articles and had heard him on *All the Talk,* said she couldn't believe he was the same man. She chortled. "You're going to nothing, too." He touched his shrinking stomach, unable to stop a grin. He had lost eighty-five pounds and counting.

When he entered Tony's office, Tony rushed forward, his arm outstretched. "Well, well, would you look at you." Tony's praise felt entirely different from Lucy's and Billy ignored the supposed compliment, hating how Tony, and too many like him, suddenly found Billy more agreeable because of his weight loss.

Once they were seated, Tony asked, "What can I do you for?"

Billy took a moment to savor how much better he fit in the metal chair this time around, its arms no longer scraping him, and then laid in. "You never got back to me about the factory matching donations for my fund-raiser and I'd like you to reconsider that. You're aware, I'm sure, that I've gotten quite a lot of press of late. What I'm doing is finally capturing people's imaginations. It's inspiring them and giving them hope. And this weekend I'll be on RTÉ, on *Matters with Maeve*—"

"*Matters with Maeve?* Are you serious?"

"I am, and I thought maybe you didn't want me to go on air in front of sixty-thousand-plus people and tell them you wouldn't honor my request?"

"But with this recession—"

"With this recession this kind of publicity and goodwill is exactly what you need."

Tony's thumb and finger petted the sides of his mouth, as if trying to tame an invisible mustache. "Where are you now with donations? How much have people already pledged?"

Billy did a quick count in his head.

"Goodness. Thirteen thousand. Okay." Tony tugged on his lower lip, making wet sounds. "How about this? I'll match donations up to fifteen thousand *and* you go on national television tomorrow night and mention the factory every chance you get, sell the toys hard. Mention, too, that we're going to have a big sale before the Christmas."

Billy winced, dreading their first Christmas without Michael.

Tony continued, "We could reach a whole new customer base—"

"What if," Billy said, seizing on Tony's flush of excitement, "in addition to the regulars, we also sell the seconds? Children could conjure great stories around the toys' lacks and differences."

Tony held up his palms. "Whoa, there, now, I think you might be getting a bit carried away."

"I think, Tony, you might need to get a bit more carried away yourself, otherwise I doubt you'll ever again see an upswing in company sales." He told Tony about the stories he and Michael had made up about the damaged soldiers, and the stories Billy was still making up for them. He stopped, realizing he'd admitted to taking home the seconds.

Tony didn't seem bothered. His thumb and finger went again at the sides of his mouth.

Billy kept after him. "You could sell the seconds, too, at this big Christmas sale. I can talk them up on the show. I'll bring a few with me and tie it all in, say how just because something is different or broken it doesn't mean it still can't have value." He thought of Tricia, of what she'd said about their family being broken and her being stuck, like it was something they could never fix, never come back from.

"That's good," Tony said, bucking now in his chair. "That's really good."

Billy smirked. "Looks like I'm not the only one getting carried away."

Tony shook his head, his smile embarrassed. "Touché."

"While we're on the subject," Billy said, "I was thinking you could do with making the toys more relevant and appealing."

Tony's expression dulled to defensive. "What do you mean?"

Billy mentioned the packed tour buses on the roads carrying schoolchildren and tourists, all chasing a bygone Ireland that was once heroic and great. "Right now our toys, as beautifully crafted as they are, are just toys, but what if we made them something special? If we had a whole line of heroes from Irish history and mythology, like Fionn MacCumhaill, Oisín, and Cú Chulainn, and the queens Medb and Niamh, and Grace O'Malley, and on and on. We make those kinds of toys and print storybooks to go along with them, and get all those tourists and schoolchildren to stop here and not just above at Newgrange."

Tony performed a complete spin in his swivel chair and grinned at Billy. "I think you're really on to something. You better say all that on the show, too, talk up this whole new line of Irish heroes we're creating." His hand swatted the air. "To hell with the board, I'm making an executive decision on this."

"Great. And another thing, the toys have to have movable parts, their arms, legs, and heads."

Tony pushed back on his chair, almost to the point of tipping over. "I don't know about that, now, the costs—"

"I'm telling you, you'll be well rewarded for the investment."

Tony nodded. "Maybe. I'll have to think about that." He looked at Billy hard. "These new toys and the books, is this something you'd be interested in taking the lead on?"

Fear rushed in. Billy was no leader, no manager. To see his ideas to completion, though, and to make more money, that would be something. He inhaled, thinking, to hell with fear. Where had it ever gotten him? He nodded. "Yeah, all right, I would."

Tony smiled, wolfish.

"That is, of course," Billy said, "if there's a raise involved, and royalties."

Tony rubbed at the back of his head. "My God, man, you're really pushing me into a corner now."

A short while later, Billy strode out of Tony's office, triumphant. It struck him he hadn't once reached for tiny Michael in his pocket.

At home, Billy took a long, hot shower, taking pleasure in lathering and rinsing his shrinking body. His elation over his growing successes fizzed inside him. Successes that now included a huge promotion and besting Bald Art. He chuckled to himself.

He moved downstairs and into the living room. He knew straightaway something new was wrong. Tricia and the children sat staring at the TV, their expressions pained. A photograph of a young girl filled the screen, her hair blond and curly, her eyes bright blue. "Another one," Tricia said, her voice as thin as the rest of her.

The girl was only fifteen, the sister of the nineteen-year-old down in Cork who had killed himself just three months ago.

"God, those poor parents," Tricia said.

Billy could not come to grips with having to go through the shock and horror a second time.

The TV screen shifted back to the familiar face of the reporter. He was especially somber, saying suicide was now the leading cause of death of young people in the country, and young men in particular, even surpassing the record numbers of those killed in road accidents nationwide.

Billy and Tricia looked at each other, fresh waves of alarm coming off them. *The number one killer* went off in Billy's head like a firecracker. Tricia powered off the TV. "Everyone, go wash your hands before dinner."

That's it? he wanted to shout. *Go wash your hands?* He rushed out of the house and into the garage, where he paced back and forth, fighting a frantic, sick feeling. He stopped, his hands squeezing the back of his head and his eyes fastening on the tiny world he was struggling to keep wonderful. Tricia, his parents, everyone, had better pay attention now. Had better completely and utterly support him in his takedown of the nation's number one killer.

Twenty-four

A MESS OF NERVES AND HOPE, BILLY LAID THE ARMY uniform out on the bed, readying for his grand appearance on national television. He had a huge opportunity tonight to make people wake up and take a historic stand against suicide, a national killer and crisis. And he had to give it everything he could. He scanned the army gear again, drawing a deep breath. He'd found the uniform after a frenzied search of the garage, a Halloween costume from years back that he'd never worn because it hadn't fit. It looked like it might now.

Before he could change his mind, he stepped into the camouflage pants. His stomach sucked in, he tugged the waistband and managed to make the button close. He pulled on the matching jacket and moved to the wardrobe mirror. He fussed with the front of the jacket, trying to let as much of his T-shirt show as possible, with its photograph of him and Michael and its slogan, *Suicide Is Not the Answer!* He rubbed his hand over the harsh feel of his fresh buzz cut and pushed his army cap down onto his shorn head.

A wave of grief came over him. Not only for Michael, and the brother and sister in Cork, and everyone like them. But for himself, too. He would never be able to explain to anyone how a part of him missed his ever-diminishing massiveness and its protective padding. Its hiding space. His shedding that cushion was like losing a childhood friend, a faithful shield that had wrapped itself around him for decades. It was terrifying to let all that go. To unbury himself and let himself be seen. It was the second-hardest thing he had ever done. Yet he was somehow surviving without Michael. He would survive this strange loss, too. Trembling with fresh determination, he drew himself up tall and saluted his reflection.

When he entered the kitchen, Tricia shook her head, her look of horror bringing back the evening of the march. "You can't go dressed like that."

"I'm sorry, I have to do this my way. If that news story last night hasn't persuaded you—"

Her expression hardened. "It persuaded me, all right. Of the importance of keeping everything as normal as possible around here. Of not going on about suicide and copycats and mental illness, making all of us think on it all the time."

He started to speak, but she pushed past him. "The children are waiting. I'll let you decide if you really want them to see you like this." She marched up the hall, her shoulder blades two sharp points in the back of her black coat.

He followed her into the living room. The children were sitting on the couch, also dressed in their best.

John shot to standing. "You're not seriously going on TV like that?"

"Are you, Dad?" Ivor asked.

Anna looked miserable. "Please change, Daddy."

Billy didn't say that he already had.

In the kitchen, John, Anna, and Ivor trooped out to the car. "Last chance," Tricia said. "Are you going to get out of that rig-out or do you want the whole country to think you're an absolute head case?"

He strode out past her. The children stood waiting at the locked car. He continued across the yard, telling them to follow.

"What are you at now?" Tricia asked, furious.

He led them down the back of the garage and lifted the covers off the miniature village and its inhabitants.

"Wow," Anna said. "It's beautiful."

"So this is what you've been at all this time," Tricia said, a note of wonder in her voice.

Billy asked Anna to put the toys into the vinyl carrier and bring them out to the car. Ivor helped him to lift the village by its base and they carried the tiny world outside.

"Where are you bringing all that?" Tricia asked.

"It's going on the telly with me," Billy said.

"You've lost your fucking mind," John said.

"John!" Tricia said.

Billy faced John. "I'm trying to do some good in the world, in your brother's memory. For Christ's sake, if you can't get that by now—"

"What's wrong with everyone?" Ivor asked, panicked. "Why's everyone fighting? I thought this was supposed to be exciting, Dad going on TV?"

"No one's fighting," Tricia said.

Billy dropped onto the driver's seat and slammed his car door closed. Anna also sat in. He found her in the rearview as the other three joined them, and gave her a look that he hoped said everything was going to be okay. She nodded, her lips pressed together. He could tell how brave she was trying to be. How much she wanted to believe him.

As the Corolla crossed the miles, hardly anyone spoke. Anna kept her attention on her phone and Ivor lost himself in his PlayStation. Next to Anna, John's eyes had closed and his head bopped in time to the music thumping through his earphones.

Billy paced the "green room," a term he'd learned from the show's producer, in circles. At first he'd thought she was making a joke, but, no, it was the actual showbiz jargon. With his hand, he wiped the sweat from his forehead. Stage fright had resurrected his old cravings with a vengeance, and the tantalizing, spring-green walls inspired fantasies of chocolate-mint ice cream. Worse, the colorful array of food on offer tugged. His stomach bucked to get at the platters of strawberries, nuts, sausage rolls, chicken skewers, iced cakes, and countless chocolates. He reminded himself how little he'd enjoyed the bar of chocolate in the hospital and made a mental note to phone Shaw's office on Monday, get that referral to a nutritionist.

He wondered who would watch the show. He knew Denis, Tony, and likely everyone else from the factory would. Lisa, too, from London. She'd had to travel again for her job, otherwise, she'd assured him, she'd be in the front row, cheering him on. Yet again his parents had opted to keep their distance. He had to believe they would watch the show from the secrecy of their sagging couch, if only out of curiosity. He'd also told Adam Simon and Jack Dineen he was on tonight. He wondered how many other families in the same post-suicide situation would watch. If the Hallorans would, the family of the double suicide down in Cork.

He followed the production assistant with the big, clownish feet to the edge of the set and waited for her to give the signal. He couldn't stop sweating, couldn't regulate his breathing. The too-tight waistband of the army pants bit into him something savage. He resisted the urge to open its button, the assistant looking him up and down again, her continued shock at his fatigues on full display.

Billy was parched, his tongue sticking to his teeth, but he didn't dare drink anything in case he would need to relieve himself during the show. The show. God. He didn't know what he would say on camera, in front of the nation. His mind clouded, the thoughts not forming. He didn't think he could speak. His words seemed to have left him right along with his saliva. The assistant touched his elbow. "You're on."

An awful sensation came over him, as if hands were tugging on his heart, trying to drag it out of him. Maybe he shouldn't have worn the uniform. Maybe he'd gone too far. If he went on this show tonight and sixty-thousand-plus people thought he was crazy, *an absolute head case,* then everything would be ruined.

The assistant, frowning, urgent, repeated, "You're on. Go. Go."

Billy lumbered across the set, his heart beating out of kilter. Maeve stood up and shook his hand, invited him to sit down. He could smell her floral perfume, and that, along with his nerves, made him dizzy. She introduced him to the audience. The cameras panned from him to Tricia and the children in the front row. They nodded and smiled, even John. The camera returned to center stage and zeroed in on Billy.

"You and Tricia lost your son, Michael, to suicide earlier this year?" Maeve said.

"Yes. January twenty-first, a Wednesday." He gestured with his hand toward his family. "The worst day of our lives."

"Tell us about him?"

Billy exhaled hard. "He was great. And I'm not just saying that because he's gone. He really was a wonderful son and big brother, and a fantastic lad all round, you know? Everyone said the same things about him. He was a gentleman, good and kind and funny. He'd do anything for anyone. He was a brilliant footballer, too, and we had high hopes he'd play for the county someday and bring home the Sam Maguire. He had a great love of singing and music as well, and was mad about the guitar in particular." He inhaled with a sharp hiss, hoping to say the next sentence with a clear conscience. "He was also passionate about the farming." He paused, feeling he had spoken the truth to the best of his knowledge. He struggled to go on. "No one could believe he did what he did. We still can't believe it. He had it all ahead of him."

"The whys, and the sense of waste, have to be so hard?"

"Yeah, they are. It's all hard."

Maeve gestured to the miniature village and its inhabitants arranged on the coffee table between them. "Tell us what you have here."

"I built everything myself. I really liked the idea of making a tiny world for the damaged dolls and soldiers from the factory—I work in a toy factory, Duffy's Delights—and we specialize in hand-crafted wooden dolls and soldiers. When Michael was a boy I would bring home the damaged toys, the seconds as we say, and he and I would make up these stories about the soldiers and their various flaws, and how they had turned their lacks into advantages. We made heroes out of them."

"How lovely. Can you tell us some of those stories?"

He laughed self-consciously. "Yeah, well, we imagined for this one soldier with damaged hands that a grenade had detonated right as he'd unpinned it, and then despite his terrible injuries he went on to become a superstar drummer."

"I like that so much," Maeve said. "The idea of the broken living bigger and better lives than they might have otherwise."

"That's it exactly." Billy then plugged his plan to make the seconds a featured product in the factory shop, right along with the best of the toys, because they had value, too. The audience clapped long and hard. He waxed, also, about the forthcoming dolls and soldiers modeled after heroes from Irish history, culture, and mythology, drawing more applause.

Maeve congratulated him on his weight loss of ninety-one pounds and counting. Almost halfway to his goal. More lively applause.

"Your plan is to lose two hundred pounds, half of yourself, in an effort to save lives?"

"That's right, yeah."

"That's great. *You're* great."

He felt his face and insides warm, until her next question, about his hopes to prevent suicide. "Do you think you're taking on the impossible?"

He reached for the right words. "I feel I have to at least try. The crisis is so much bigger than Michael and me and my family. In the past decade alone there have been more than five thousand suicides in this country, and that's just the ones we know about." The feeling of hands pulling on his heart worsened. He pictured the frantic organ being dragged into his stomach, where it would be eaten. "And of course, just yesterday, there was that terrible tragedy down in Cork."

"Yes, heartbreaking," Maeve said.

"Horrific," Billy said.

"Our thoughts and prayers are with the Halloran family and everyone affected." She went on to mention Billy's website, with its detailed information on suicide prevention resources, and also gave out the number for the Samaritans' hotline. She urged those in trouble to seek help. Then, an apologetic smile on her face, she broached the subject of his army uniform. "Your whole approach to this fight on suicide . . . you go so far as to say you're waging a war . . . some could see it as too incendiary?"

He struggled to come up with a response. The silence ticked. His attention jumped to his family. He could see the anguish in their faces, willing him to end the awful pause, but to not say anything crazy-sounding. He looked straight at Tricia. Her eyes urged him on. Anna, too. *You promised, Dad.*

He faced Maeve. "I'm just doing my best, you know? Trying to make something good come out of Michael's great loss. It's such a senseless waste." He drew a breath, struggling to keep his voice steady. "In fighting to keep others alive, I'm also trying to keep Michael's memory alive and to give his too-short life the most meaning possible."

"This has become your life's work," Maeve said.

"Exactly," he said, struggling not to break down. "In Michael's name."

Applause erupted. As soon as the audience quieted, he continued. "I'm wearing this uniform tonight to show people how serious I am and how hard I'm willing to fight to save lives, raise awareness, and bring about positive change. I'm on a mission and I intend to succeed."

The audience broke into more loud and long applause. In closing, Maeve thanked him for his passion and plugged the making of his documentary. "Best of luck with the film, Billy, and with your sponsored weight loss. With all of it. You're terrific." She turned to Tricia and the children and again offered her condolences. They smiled bravely. Billy looked down at the coffee table and the miniature village. There, outside the cottage, stood his tiny family of six, the center of his kingdom.

There was high chatter on the drive home. "You were brilliant," Anna said.

"Yeah, everyone kept clapping and clapping," Ivor said.

John remained quiet on the backseat. Just as his silence

threatened to sour the mood, his hand reached out and curled around the top of Billy's shoulder, pressing his collarbone. "Well done, Dad."

"Thanks, son." Billy put all the feeling in his every fiber into those two words.

True to form, Lisa and Denis phoned and both gushed into Billy's earpiece. Meanwhile, Tricia and the others fielded messages and posts on their phones. "You've like a thousand new Twitter followers," Anna said.

Tricia's hand covered Billy's on the gear stick. "You did great," she said, softly. Euphoric, he gripped her fingers in his. Was it possible? Was she finally on his side? She pulled her hand free and reached into her bag for nicotine gum. He shifted on his broken seat, fighting the plunge of disappointment. He'd wanted the spark between them to have flared for much longer.

They traveled for miles. Anna, and then Ivor, fell asleep. Only the radio filled the silence. Tricia stared out the passenger window, chomping on nicotine gum and making wet, smacking sounds. Billy glanced at her profile every so often, trying to gauge her expression. She seemed far away, unreadable. He tried to recapture the surge from her hand on his earlier. Behind her, John hitched his elbow on the thin window ledge, his hand under his chin. Like Tricia, he was staring into the darkness, a look of concentration on his face, as if trying to make out something amid the blur of passing shadows.

As they turned into the village, a familiar car drove toward them. Billy strained to see, to be sure, wondering what had brought Patrick Keogh out this far. Keogh tapped his car horn in a salute. At least he was being civil this time around.

At home, when they entered the kitchen, John spoke up. "If

it's okay, I'd like to sleep in Michael's bed tonight, from now on, actually."

Billy and Tricia exchanged a look of surprise. "Up to your dad," she said.

Billy nodded. "Yeah, of course, son, no problem." Maybe he only imagined a look of relief cross Tricia's face.

The five moved up the hallway, Tricia steering Anna by the shoulders and Billy steering Ivor, both children still half asleep. As they neared the stairs, Tricia spotted the brown envelope on the carpet beneath the letter flap.

Billy brought the envelope to the dim light of the hall lamp. On its front, in thin, small black handwriting, *For To Save Lives.* He counted the money inside. Three hundred euro.

"Who's it from?" Tricia asked.

Billy blinked back tears. There was no note or name, but he knew. "Patrick Keogh."

"God love them," Tricia said. Three hundred euro was big money for the Keoghs.

Billy eased the folded envelope into the breast pocket of his army jacket, next to tiny Michael.

Upstairs, as John climbed into Michael's bed, Billy kissed the top of Ivor's head. "Night, night." He crossed the room and turned off the light. "Night, John."

"Night, Dad."

Billy moved into the hall. It had been a long time since John had called him Dad and now he'd said it twice in one night. Tricia was putting Anna to bed and he called good night through the door.

Minutes later, Tricia entered their room. Billy tensed on the bed, hoping he had understood her correctly and that she hadn't expected him to sleep in John's bunk. She moved in front of the wardrobe mirror and fiddled at her right ear. He realized with surprise, and then a needle of irritation, that she was removing her earrings. Since when could she bear to touch her lobes? She must have asked one of the children to put the earrings in earlier, demoting him ever further.

"Who put those in?" he asked, trying to sound casual, annoyed with himself for needing to know.

"I did."

"You did?"

She shrugged. "It was stupid all these years. I think I got it into my little-girl head that my getting my ears pierced against my parents' wishes and my mother dying the very next day was somehow connected, like my being bad was to blame, and then I could never let the holes close up, even though they made me feel sick." She shrugged again. "Maybe I wanted to keep punishing myself."

Of late, she'd confided in him more than she ever had. "Fair play to you," he said, even while wishing she hadn't taken the intimacy away from him. "On giving up the cigarettes, too." He hadn't made nearly enough of her beating the killers, either. Hard to, given her reaction to all his changes. It hit him again the cost, to her mind, of his changes coming so late.

"Me?" she said with a rasp. "Look at all you've done." She turned off the light. While he tried not to watch, she undressed, and pulled her nightdress over her head. She slipped between the sheets. He tried to suck himself in, hoping to make himself ever smaller and less objectionable. They lay together in the dark in silence.

Just as he was about to give in and say good night—she

never said good night first—she spoke. "You did great tonight, really."

"Thanks." He was afraid to say any more, in case he ruined something.

"Where did all those ideas come from, to sell the seconds and make a whole new line of toys?"

"All mine. Actually, Tony wants me to head up the entire project."

"Are you going to?"

He hesitated, unsure where this was going. "Yeah, I am."

"You're full of surprises these days," she said kindly.

"Yeah, well." A deep sadness settled over him. He would always be trying to make up for the past.

Her hand covered his under the blankets and squeezed. "Good night." She rolled over, turning her back to him.

"Good night." Long after she appeared to have fallen asleep, he stayed awake, marveling at how good something so small had felt—John clasping his shoulder, Tricia squeezing his hand.

Twenty-five

THE NEXT MORNING, BILLY SAT AT HIS KITCHEN table enjoying a wedge of grapefruit, a small heap of scrambled eggs, and a feeling of satisfaction unlike anything he'd ever known. He'd appeared on national TV, on *Matters with Maeve*, and he'd done well. Better than well. The house phone rang, shrill and surprising. So few people used that number now, not since they'd all gotten mobiles.

Tricia answered. "Howaya, Maura." She swung around to face Billy. "No, of course not," she said, sharper. "Okay, fine, yeah."

She ended the call. "She and your dad are on the way. She wanted to know if you were still wearing the army uniform."

If the comment had come from anyone else, Billy might have chuckled. Instead, he felt heat in his face and a hardness in his stomach.

Minutes later, his parents arrived, both bundled in dark coats. While Tricia made tea, they sat at the table, shifting on the wooden chairs.

"Hard to believe, seeing you on the telly last night." His father sounded almost admiring.

His mother sniffed. "Hard to believe that uniform."

"Do you know?" his father said. "You've surprised me, so you have. I didn't think you'd do as well as you've done, never thought you'd get the response you're getting."

All his life Billy had craved this kind of praise from his father, but now that it was here, he felt unbearably uncomfortable, as if his nerve endings were exposed.

His mother gave her shoulders a little shake and nodded at his father. "Give it to him, can't you?"

"I'm getting to it," his father snapped, reaching inside his coat.

Tricia set two steaming mugs of tea in front of his parents and a small plate of biscuits glittering with sugar. Billy's stomach sighed. The truth annoyed his head. He would always struggle with food, with his parents.

His father handed Billy the folded check.

"Before you take that," his mother said. "We want your word there'll be no more of that awful uniform or shaving your hair. I thought my eyes were going to fall out of my head when I saw you in that getup on national TV."

Billy glanced at the check. Eleven hundred euro. An amount no doubt chosen to exceed Lisa's donation. "You needn't worry, I'm not planning on wearing the uniform again. It did its work."

"And the hair?" she said.

He rubbed his hand over the top of his head, a part of him missing his curls, curls just like those on his three sons. "We'll see."

His mother clapped her hands together, years seeming to

fall away from her face and shoulders. "Thank God for that much at least."

She and his father left a short time later, seeming pleased with themselves. Billy remained pinned to his chair. Outside, from Magda's decorated birdbath, the chirp of birds that sounded part song and part whistle. Tricia leaned back against the sink, her arms folded over her scant stomach. She spoke, a faraway quality to her voice. "Just once, after my mother died, I broke down crying in front of my father. He kept going about his business, saying nothing and polishing his shoes faster, blacker. The more he ignored me, the harder I cried. I couldn't stop.

"Then, out of nowhere, he started going on about Bertie Murphy, the local vet, and how he was the best yodeler anyone had ever heard. 'That man could yodel for the country, so he could, could win an All-Ireland medal if he was let.' Then Dad got up, put on his shoes, and walked out the back door. Left me sitting at the table, a crying, snottering mess." She paused, red blotches breaking out on her neck. "Sometimes we don't know what to do with people, maybe especially those closest to us." Her eyes filled and her face creased with pain. "I'm sorry, I've tried, but I just can't stop thinking that it took what Michael did to bring out all this in you. I keep thinking if only you'd cared enough about the children and me from the get-go, if you'd cared enough about yourself, we wouldn't be here right now."

He bowed his head, a ball of thorns in his throat. He'd disappeared inside the hulk of himself a long time ago, and Tricia had resurrected him for a while during those early years, but eventually he'd sunk back inside himself, where it didn't hurt so much that he wasn't the right kind of son and husband and father.

"Can't you say something?" she said.

He shook his head, unable to lift it. "I thought I had time. I was always going to stop bingeing and get fit the next Monday, and the next Monday, and the next. Then Michael, and . . . and, I don't know . . . I couldn't let it be for nothing. I had to make some kind of sense, some good, come of it. He died and I couldn't save him, so I wanted to save myself, save what remained of this family. Then I realized I could save others, too, while I was at it." His head jerked up. "Michael saved me. My own son saved me, and believe me, if I could have it any other way, if I could bring him back and trade my life for his, I would in a heartbeat." He pressed his fist to his mouth, afraid he would get sick, would cry and not be able to stop.

She crossed the floor and hugged him, pressed his head to her rib cage. Astonished, he wrapped his arms around her waist. She was all loose bones against him. He tightened his hold.

Days later, amid the gray and drizzle, Billy hurried toward the Red Café, reminding himself again of the woman's name. Nell Riordan. She had phoned him at the factory, asking to meet, saying she'd seen him on *Matters with Maeve*. "Your courage, the way you just told out everything and how much it all means to you, it inspired me, so it did," she'd said. He'd felt a rush of pleasure, but also a small disturbance. He'd been able to talk freely about the hard things in public, in front of tens of thousands of viewers, and yet there was so much he couldn't bear to tell himself, or those around him.

He entered the café, wondering again why exactly this Nell Riordan wanted to meet. His heart surged. A part of him couldn't help but hope she was here to tell him she'd felt suicidal and his appearance on the show had swayed her. If he could just know with certainty that what he was doing mattered. That he was making a difference. That he'd saved even one life in Michael's name.

A woman waved from a table by the sunny yellow wall and stood up to greet him. Middle-aged, she wore her beige coat cinched tight at the waist and her face bloomed round and pretty. He pulled down on his tracksuit top—still in the habit of trying to cover himself.

They shook hands. "I hope I didn't keep you waiting?" Billy asked.

"Not at all. I just got here."

After some small talk about the traffic and her drive up from Glendalough, they studied their menus. Despite the wonderful waft of deep-fried, home-baked, vanilla, almond, and sweet, sweet cinnamon, Billy wasn't all that hungry. Dessert, all his old favorites, no longer held the same power over him. These days, his hankerings were more for foods like the delicious salad and salmon he'd enjoyed at the Granary Restaurant. The nutritionist up at the hospital had assured him his taste buds and cravings would continue to change for the better.

She also said it wouldn't take much to reignite his bad habits and send him right back to where he started, or worse. He couldn't risk that, so now he avoided sugar whenever possible and had cut out everything deep-fried. Anytime he felt tempted, he reminded himself how those minutes of release and rapture felt like nothing next to the awfulness he experienced once he came off that high, stuffed and sickened.

Nell seemed in no hurry to break the silence. Unable to

stand it, he lowered his menu to the table. "So, you wanted to chat?"

"Yes," she said. "I wanted to thank you so much for what you're doing, all the people you're inspiring and the lives you're trying to save. You've shown me the importance of coming out of hiding and breaking the silence." Her round cheeks turned scarlet. "I wondered, for your documentary, if you have anyone on board who tried . . ." Her eyes filled. "Who tried and survived."

"No," he said, barely breathing. She was exactly what the documentary needed. Wait till he told Adam Simon.

The waitress appeared. Nell licked her lips, her eyes darting over the menu. Billy ordered a pot of tea. "The same for me, please," Nell said.

He felt she wanted more. "Feel free to order whatever you want, don't hold back on account of me."

"That's okay," she said. The waitress moved off and they smiled uneasily at each other. Impossible as it seemed, Nell's cheeks burned harder. "I'd like to take part in your documentary, if that's okay? I'm hoping it will help others to hear how I tried, and how I'm glad I survived."

"It will, absolutely."

Her hand tugged at her hair. "An overdose, that's what I did. We had painkillers lying around the house for years, from the dentist as well as the doctors. I put the whole lot into me, washed them down with vodka. If my husband hadn't found me when he did . . ."

"Can I ask why?" he croaked.

"I was depressed for years. It didn't make any sense and I hated myself for it. I had great friends, a lovely house, a grand husband, two fabulous kids, and yet every morning I didn't want to get out of bed. I had to force myself to go through the motions of each day, still trying to be a good mother, a good everything. I hid it all from everyone, my tears, my panic attacks, and my constant urge to throw myself down on the ground and admit I couldn't go on.

"Everything kept getting worse, day after day. I was frantic and chronically exhausted. I knew I wouldn't be able to go on putting up a face and pretending. Everyone was going to find out, and the shame and mortification tore into me. No one would understand, I told myself. No one would care. They'd all look at me and think I had everything I could ever want. They'd say I needed a right kick up the arse."

Billy wondered if it was possible Michael had also suffered a devastating depression in the midst of what everyone believed to be a good and full life, and if that had similarly added to his anguish, driving him to do what he did. Nell continued. "It got to the point where I believed I was never going to get better, that I was going to go completely mad. The rest of my life stretched out before me like an endless prison sentence. I thought of all I had, my home and family and friends, and if that couldn't make me happy, then nothing would ever make me happy. I couldn't get the terrible thoughts to stop. I wanted the misery and agony to end. I convinced myself I was so wretched, so out of my mind, everyone would be better off without me."

"I'm so sorry you had to go through all that," Billy said.

She wiped at her tears with her paper napkin. "I read all these books, and all these Internet articles, trying to find myself—this woman who was so miserable she wanted to kill herself, but who could still go on day after day, somehow managing to hide it all from everyone, even her own husband and best friends." Her brow and chin puckered. "I couldn't find myself anywhere in the literature and it made me feel even more alone, and ever more convinced that no one would understand and, worse, that no one would be able to fix me."

"What changed?" he asked gently.

She cried harder. "When I woke up in the hospital, this one counselor, Roslyn, she kept promising me I would feel peace again. Hope and happiness again. She told me, while I was still lying on my hospital bed, all pumped out and not long conscious, to think of just one thing to feel grateful for.

"I kept crying, kept shaking my head, kept telling her to go away and leave me alone. She wouldn't leave, though. Said she was staying right there by my bed till I cooperated. 'I'll be grateful when you leave,' I told her. She spun around, walked out of the ward, and then reappeared moments later. 'Well?' she asked. 'Did it work? Did you feel grateful?'

"I stared at her, gobsmacked. I *had* felt glad she'd left, and a little disappointed, too. That's when I first thought maybe, just maybe, there was still hope. Then, after, when I saw the effects of what I'd almost done on my family and friends, my two children especially . . . after that, I kept giving whatever thanks I could, for even the tiniest of things. And now, well, now I thank God every day I'm alive. Thank Him for that incredible gift. Back then, I'd never, ever have believed that was possible."

Billy could already see her on the big screen, saying everything she'd just said and getting through to people, letting everyone like her, like Michael, know they weren't alone, or beyond saving. That they could find hope. And peace. And even happiness.

Twenty-six

ONE SUNDAY MORNING, ADAM SIMON PHONED. THE
filmmaker sounded euphoric, urgent. "Lights, camera, action,
Billy boy. We need to head to Cork right away, you beautiful
man, you."

"Cork? What? Why?" Billy, yanked from sleep, felt mud-
dled. Had Adam Simon really called him a beautiful man?

"That family of the brother-sister suicide? They're going to
take part in our documentary."

Billy scrambled from bed, grabbing at his trousers, and a
fresh shirt. "Are you serious?"

"What's going on?" Tricia asked, also bleary-eyed.

"You better believe it, Billy boy. I'm almost at yours, be
ready in fifteen." Adam rang off.

"Billy?" Tricia asked.

"I've to head out, with Adam Simon, the filmmaker. I'll be
gone most of the day." Something told him not to tell her about
Cork, at least not until after they'd shot the interviews.

"Ivor will be disappointed to miss the swimming," she said.

"I'll make it up to him." He hurried onto the landing, then turned back to her. "I'll get home as early as I can this evening, maybe we can all go into town, go see a film or something?"

"Yeah," she said. "Sounds good."

"We need to do more together," he said.

"Yeah, for sure," she said.

Ever since that morning after his TV appearance, when they'd held on to each other in the kitchen, they'd enjoyed a truce. More than that, they were getting back to something like they used to be together before Michael left them. On good days, he could even hope they would get back to how it was in those early years.

"All right, then, see you later." He turned to go.

"Wait!" Tricia's outburst seemed to embarrass her, and when next she spoke, she sounded hesitant. "I'll explain to Ivor about the swimming. He'll understand. It's not about when you do it, just that you do it."

He broke out in goose bumps. "Yeah, great, thanks."

She nodded, as if they'd settled something. "See ya."

He moved downstairs, tapping Denis's number on his phone. Despite what had just happened with Tricia, he felt a knot in his chest. He wanted Denis by his side today, to help him withstand what lay ahead.

The three traveled to Cork in Adam's white HiAce, all wedged together on the bench seat—Adam driving, Denis in the middle, and Billy pressed against the passenger door. Behind them, piled in the stomach of the van, was a bunch of camera equipment, battery packs, various stands and reflectors, and Billy didn't know what else. Despite the ropes and bungee cords, some of the contents shifted every time the vehicle stopped and turned corners. The sliding sounds only added to the climbing tension in the crowded space.

Ever since they'd picked up Denis, he'd remained silent and sour, brushing off Adam's repeated attempts at conversation. The filmmaker talked about the weather, sports, film, and Billy's "spectacular" TV appearance, but Denis wouldn't engage. Billy's face pulsated with embarrassment and temper. Like Denis, he also felt nervous about meeting with what remained of the Halloran family, especially so soon after the daughter's passing, but if the Hallorans were able to go through with it, then so should they. It was all for the greater good. The Hallorans, and the woman he'd met at the Red Café, Nell Riordan, they would be the makings of the documentary.

It didn't help Billy's mood any, either, that he was squashed up against the passenger door and couldn't shake the fear he would fall out. He double-checked the lock, picturing the door bursting open and the traffic plowing over him. Almost noon, his stomach punched at its lining. He wished he'd thought to bring a protein shake. He'd also forgotten to bring tiny Michael. His fretful hand repeatedly checked for the toy's solid outline against his thigh, as though it would miraculously appear.

The stilted conversation dried up and the only voices in the van came from the radio. Billy experienced a pang for Ivor and their missed outing today to the pool. He pictured Ivor finally swimming—the boy was close, oh, so close—saw father and son glide together through the water, their arms, legs, heads, and breaths synchronized, the pool opening for them like a magic pathway. Tricia's parting words came back. It had seemed something like forgiveness.

The news headlines crackled from the radio, three teenage boys killed last night when their car hit a wall. No indication, the newscaster intoned, of the involvement of drugs or alcohol. Billy thought of the boys' families and the shock and horror they were going through. He felt pinpricks of guilt and shame whenever there was talk of the tragic deaths of the young, it hanging in the air that those victims would have given anything to live, while Michael, and others like him, had ended it all.

Adam again tried to draw Denis into conversation, this time asking about his beginnings in Dublin, their mother city. Denis uttered only one-word responses. Billy smoldered. Why was Denis acting so rude? He knew how much Billy needed Adam to make this documentary, a film that could save lives and memorialize Michael. Billy wanted to elbow Denis hard in the ribs and say, *Answer him, can't you?*

Denis's uncharacteristic behavior added to Billy's growing unease about his miniature village and its inhabitants, how he seemed to be losing control of them and his fantasies there. *You're the best daddy.* Billy shuddered. Denis, the best friend he'd ever known, besides Tricia, besides his children, seemed to be turning against him, too. That voice niggled, saying it knew he would ruin things with Denis. Saying he would end up alone. He shifted on the cramped seat, agitated and restless.

"Are you all right?" Adam asked.

Billy startled, not realizing he'd groaned aloud. "Just getting a little hungry."

"Me, too," Adam said.

They stopped at the next decent-looking restaurant. When

they parked, Denis shot Billy a pointed look. "We should let Adam go ahead, we'll follow in a few."

"That's all right," Billy said with an edge. "We can all go eat now." He didn't feel like listening to one of Denis's sermons, or going over the Twelve Steps. It was lunchtime. He was only human and had his needs and wants just like everyone else. And he was going to need to fortify himself. They had a big afternoon ahead, about to poke around the remains of hearts destroyed.

The small, busy restaurant required patrons to order and pay, and then sit down. Billy stood in wait, tormented by delicious-looking platefuls of meat and potatoes, and fish and chips, and fruit tarts with fresh cream. Christ, those juicy burgers, greasy fries, and creamy coleslaw. That oozing tart thick with apples, its crust thin and golden. They served fresh whipped cream, too, and not that fake stuff. Billy's heart raced. He was one customer away from the cash register. It was his turn to order next. The stress of what lay ahead at the Hallorans threatened to make him crack all over again. He could scream with how much he wanted everything he couldn't have.

It was going to be killing to face the Halloran family and see double his pain and horror mirrored back to him. The thought made him ravenous. He would eat big just this one more time, to dislodge the maw of dread in his gut. Even as he tried to rationalize, guilt blazed across his chest. If he caved now, he'd let himself, everyone, down. He cringed, imagining the other customers' horror if they saw him stuffing himself. From the glances he was getting, it was clear most everyone recognized him. Some were openly staring. Others nodded and smiled. A few fell to whispers. He couldn't stop trembling. Even his head was shaking. He'd gone so long being invisible, this starting to be seen, this starting to be held so very accountable, sometimes felt too hard.

So much good had come from his going public. That was what he had to hold on to. He'd enjoyed a flood of pledges since *Matters with Maeve,* bringing the total amount of monies promised to just over eighteen thousand euro. Put the factory's fifteen thousand on top of that and he'd pulled in pledges of more than thirty-three thousand and counting for the Samaritans. Filming was also under way for his documentary, tens of families coming forward from all over the country to participate. He'd continued to drop his weight, too, and had lost a total of one hundred and ten pounds, bringing him more than halfway to his goal.

"Ah, it's yourself. What'll you have?" the red-haired, middle-aged cashier asked with a warm smile. It was like she was greeting an old friend.

He licked his lips. "I'll have the chef's salad, please, no cheese. Is it possible to get the poached salmon with that?"

"It is, of course." She smiled brightly, her face round and freckled, her shiny eyes blue-green.

He smiled back. He hadn't let the demons win.

The closer they got to their destination, the more Billy felt trapped inside a missile locked on its target. He started to second-guess the wisdom, the humanity, of doing this. He wouldn't want a trio of strangers with microphones and cameras landing in on top of him and his family, especially so soon.

The Hallorans would only just have marked their daughter's Month's Mind mass. He reminded himself the family had contacted Adam. They wanted to do this.

Adam pulled over and double-checked the map on his phone. In the field next to them, a herd of sheep watched, their wool marked with purple dye. Even now, the supersized bruise on Billy's stomach remained as dark and glaring as ever, branding him every bit as much as the purple on those sheep, showing what had owned him. The back of his neck tingled. Showing what still owned him. Adam pulled back out onto the road. The van gathered speed, zeroing in.

After stopping twice to ask for directions, they arrived at the ill-fated home. Billy felt he was being held underwater. Adam parked at the front of the house, giving himself away as a Dublin man and ignorant of the custom in the countryside of entering a home by the back door.

Beyond the two-story house, fields rolled out in every direction, a bumpy, rich green carpet edged in a maze of thick dark hedges. Dull lanes dotted with more homes also surrounded the property. Scattered everywhere, crawling briars and bands of mature oaks and sycamores. In the fields, grass waved on the breeze and several rabbits also dotted the landscape. The smell of wild woodbine, even this early in the day, filled the van. It seemed impossible, the horror that had happened here.

Billy pulled his attention back to the house, unable to stop himself from wondering where the brother and sister had done it and who had found them. The house stood tall and wide, finished in gray stone and topped with a coal-black roof. Five large windows in front stared back. The tarmac driveway bisected a large garden, one side planted with colorful flowers amid a granite rockery, and on the other side a lush green lawn with an ornamental stone wishing well. Two large flower baskets bursting with lavender and pink dahlias hung at either side of the white front door. The entire property looked as though its owners were putting everything they could into keeping as much as possible alive.

The net curtain moved in one of the bottom windows. Billy saw a flash of a woman's face before the curtain dropped.

Denis rubbed his hand over the top of his head. "Are we really going to do this?"

"You're sure they agreed to this?" Billy asked.

"I told you, I talked to the father myself," Adam said. "He understands the concept of the greater good. Now, let's get started. Take One." He clapped one hand on top of the other, channeling a director's board, and hopped out of the van. Billy struggled out after him. Denis remained in the middle of the bench seat, both doors of the van open like white wings.

Billy followed Adam around the back of the vehicle. Adam pulled open the rear doors and grabbed at the camera equipment.

"Let's introduce ourselves first, before we drag all this inside," Billy said.

"Yeah, we can show that much manners, at least," Denis said.

"He always such a charmer?" Adam asked.

The door to the house opened and a man with graying brown hair appeared on the top step, his shoulders hunched, a lit cigarette hanging from the corner of his mouth.

"Good afternoon, Mr. Halloran," Adam called out. He moved toward the house, camera in hand. Billy followed, his legs weak.

Twenty-seven

MR. HALLORAN LOOKED AT BILLY ON HIS DOORSTEP, seeming stunned. He pulled the cigarette from his thin lips, its cylinder mostly ashes. "You were the fellow on *Matters with Maeve*?"

"That's right," Billy said. "There are no words, but I want to at least try to say how very sorry I am, such an unthinkable loss for you and your family."

Mr. Halloran couldn't hold Billy's gaze. He nodded, indicating Denis still sitting in the van. "Who's he?"

"That's Denis," Billy said. "He's a dear friend, lost his father in the same way, and I'm sure Adam here told you about his nephew—"

Mr. Halloran eyed Adam's camera as if it were a wild animal. "Where are you going with that? What do you think you're doing?"

Billy, confused, alarmed, said, "I understood you invited us here today? That you wanted to take part in our documentary?"

Mr. Halloran shook his head. "I said we'd think about it, but not now, so soon." The surviving son, a young man of maybe twenty, appeared behind his father.

Adam addressed Mr. Halloran, speaking fast. "Our documentary will save lives, don't you want to be a part of that?"

The blood drained from Mr. Halloran's face. "I can't."

Billy pushed on Adam's shoulder, appalled. "Come on, let's leave these good people be."

"Wait." Mr. Halloran glanced back at his son, the young man frowning now with a mix of anger and confusion, and pulled open the door. "You'll take a cup of tea at least."

"Don't let them in!" the son said.

A stout, middle-aged woman with plum-dyed hair walked up the hall, her fingers at her chest and her hand a dappled red and white, as if marbleized. "What is it? What's going on?"

"It's the fellow from the TV, on *Matters with Maeve*," Mr. Halloran said.

"Oh, hello," she said, looking bewildered.

The son's eyes raked Billy. "At least you're not wearing that army uniform."

"I'm sorry," Billy said, addressing Mrs. Halloran. "We didn't mean to barge in. There's been a misunderstanding. We thought you were expecting us."

"Expecting you?" she said.

Mr. Halloran flapped his arm in Adam's direction. "I talked to this fellow on the phone a couple of times, said I'd think about taking part in this film they're making, to . . . to help to save lives, but I never told them they could come here."

"No, no," Mrs. Halloran said, her hand still clasped to her chest. "We couldn't."

The son moved toward Billy and Adam. "Have you no re-spect—"

"We'll go," Billy said.

"I offered them tea," Mr. Halloran said. "They've had a long drive."

"Yes, okay, all right then," Mrs. Halloran said.

Mr. and Mrs. Halloran sat at the kitchen table with Billy, Adam, and Denis. The son, Christy, moved about, fixing tea and a plate of biscuits and sandwiches. Billy felt no appetite. Several photographs of the deceased children stood on display, alongside the lineup of sympathy cards, and the scatter of burnt-down candles and holy medals in plastic pouches. A set of brown rosary beads hung from a nail next to the door, the dye faded in places from pure use.

Billy pulled himself back to the chat at the table. Despite the nerve-wracking reminders all around them, the pleasant-ries and conversation went on almost like normal—about the weather, the recession, the empty, unfinished housing estates, and the mass exodus of emigrants. Talk of all the young people leaving Ireland and of the ghost housing estates made for slip-pery subjects, though, and the chat and forced laughter started to strain. A frantic need to get out of there and home to his own family seized Billy.

"You're some man, to do all you're doing, and to be able to go on television and say all you said, too," Mrs. Halloran, Beth, said with admiration.

Billy held her kind gaze, trying to put into his face all the thanks and sympathy he felt.

"Wasn't he, Liam?" she said.

"He was," Mr. Halloran said.

"Liam," Billy said. "That was Michael's second name."

Beth and Liam smiled sadly. Then Beth managed, "We named our Rosie after my mother, and our John after Liam's father."

"That's right," Liam said, nodding sadly.

"My second son is named John," Billy said, realizing too late it was a thoughtless comeback. Beth and Liam stared.

Christy stood leaning against the range, his eyes darting about the group. Billy recognized the mounting agitation in the young man, that crazed need to do something to relieve all the ugly brewing inside. They should leave, and let these poor people get on with trying to put themselves back together.

Christy lunged at Adam, slapping at his camera. "Turn that thing off!"

Adam checked the camera, its red record light still on, and then glared at Christy. "Do you have any idea what this is worth?"

"That's it." Billy placed his hands on the table and pushed himself to standing. "We've taken up enough of your time and hospitality, thank you. We'll get going. And again I'm sorry, this is all a misunderstanding. Our intentions are only good, I promise you, but I see of course it's too soon, too much. We shouldn't have come. It's just we're desperate to stop suicide—"

"Are you for real?" Christy sneered. "Why don't you go ahead and stop cancer, then, and murder, too, while you're at it?"

"Stop, Christy," his father said. "Remember this man lost his son, too."

Beth stood up, scowling at Adam. "I'll thank you and your camera to leave." She nodded at Billy and Denis. "You two can come with me."

"What are you doing, Ma?" Christy said.

Billy, Denis, and Adam remained at the table, no one seeming to know where to look or what to do.

Christy glared at Adam. "She told you to leave."

"If you'd listen to our vision—"

"If you don't get out of here this second, you won't have any vision left," Christy said.

Adam looked at Billy, a wild, wounded look in his eyes. "Tell him."

"Just go," Billy said, drained, disgusted. He should have listened to his first instincts, shouldn't have gotten so caught up in a film at any cost. That cold feeling went at his chest and stomach. So much seemed to point to what he should have seen and done, but hadn't.

After Adam left, Liam led Billy and Denis to the living room. Billy and Denis remained in the doorway, unable to move deeper into the room. The smell of lilies choked the air, their scent undercut with the rotted taint of stems left too long in water.

Beth stood in the center of the room, facing the two shrines at either side of the fireplace, the memorial on the right dedicated to John, and the newer one on the left dedicated to Rosie. In each, a large, gold-framed photograph held pride of place, the children smiling, their faces bright. Beneath, a fake candle burned a sickly yellow. All about, a mound of cards, dried flowers, holy medals, saints' statues, plastic vials of holy water, and various smaller photographs of the two teens.

The TV, presumably moved from its usual place against the wall, stood in front of the fireplace, angled toward the doorway. There was something about the TV standing alone and out of place, blocking the dead hearth and facing the threshold, unwatched, that struck Billy as so much sadder than the two shrines. Liam rubbed his hand back and forth over the top of the displaced TV, as though dusting it with his palm. Beth followed Billy's gaze to her husband's hand in motion. She then looked at the large photograph of her daughter. "We all have our own ways of trying to keep them alive, isn't that it?"

Billy dug his nails deep into his palms, to stop himself from breaking down. Beth's blue-veined hands rushed to her face. "Both of them. How could we have lost both of them?"

Liam's hand froze on top of the TV, the pain in his face awful to witness.

"It wasn't your fault," Billy said, the hairs stirring on the back of his neck. "It wasn't anyone's fault." He spoke with an utter and almost frightening conviction, as though someone else were talking through him.

Beth inhaled and wiped at her eyes and cheeks with the flat of her hands. Liam looked from her to Billy, his lips parted and his face loose.

"It wasn't our fault," Billy said, his eyes filling.

Denis placed his hand on Billy's back, his chin quivering and his eyes watery. Billy wondered how he'd never seen before that Denis also needed to feel forgiven. "It wasn't your fault," Billy said, gently shaking Denis's shoulder.

Billy and Denis struggled to the van—neither of them fully recovered from the rush of emotion and adrenaline that had beset them inside the Hallorans' living room. Billy could barely pick up his feet and propel himself forward.

The van's engine revved, Adam scowling behind the wheel. Billy turned around. Beth, Liam, and Christy remained standing in the open doorway. Billy thought of his miniature village, of whisking the three of them away from this place and putting them in that other world, reuniting them with the two lost teens.

With a final parting wave, he followed Denis into the van. Adam reversed out onto the road and the former family of five watched them drive away. Billy held the trio in the side mirror, mindful of the two empty spaces.

Adam rammed the driver's door with the side of his fist. "Why the hell didn't you back me up?" He hit the door again, harder. "They could have been persuaded."

"You lied to me," Billy said, quaking.

"He said he'd think about it," Adam said. "I figured once he met us—"

"You trespassed on that family," Billy said. "Went against every common decency. What in hell is wrong with you? You've been through this yourself. You should know better. And they lost not *one* but *two* of their *children*, and just yesterday, practically."

"I thought you were with me," Adam said. "You're the very one who said this was a war to be waged. Well guess what? War comes at a price—" His voice cracked. "I cleaned my nephew's head off his bedroom walls. To get people to understand that, to *feel* that, you have to hit them hard. Through the camera, you have to blow up their heads, too."

"Let us out," Billy said, rattling the door handle.

"What the fuck?" Adam said.

"You heard him," Denis said. "We'll make our own way from here."

"We're in the middle of nowhere," Adam said.

"I'd rather walk the two hundred miles home than sit in this van for another second," Billy said, sickened far beyond any of the worst binges he'd ever inflicted on himself. "I'm sorry for what you went through, I am, but, Jesus, man, you can't go around tormenting people."

Adam pulled up in a squeal of brakes. As Billy exited, Adam muttered, "See how far you'll get without me."

"Would you like me to give him a thump?" Denis asked.

Billy looked up at Adam, the filmmaker's face twisted with temper and pain. All the anger left Billy, blanketed by a great sadness. "Leave him."

"If you say so." Denis slid off the seat. He and Billy stood together on the grass verge, watching Adam speed away in a screech of tires.

"Jesus, that was brutal," Denis said.

Billy saw the toll in Denis's face, saw him again inside the Hallorans' living room, his eyes wet, his chin quivering. "I know, I'm sorry."

"For what?" Denis asked.

"You've been a great friend to me and I'm not sure I've been much of a one to you."

Denis snorted. "You've been all right."

Billy sad-smiled. "I didn't realize how much you've been carrying around all this time, too."

Denis looked at the ground, nodding. "You just keep asking yourself how they could leave you?"

"I know."

"I'm sorry, of course you know, all too well."

"We better get started." They walked the road. In the ditch, golden yellow lichen bloomed from clumps of rock. Seeing life where you'd least expect it, Billy felt slammed all over again by the death he'd never foreseen.

Twenty-eight

BILLY AND DENIS HITCHHIKED TO THE TRAIN STA-
tion, rescued by a young schoolteacher in a green Honda Civic.
Alone on the backseat, Billy crossed his arms over his middle
and slyly grabbed at his sides and the rolls of loose, drooping
skin. Folds and folds that had once housed so much more of him.
Hid so much more. He squeezed his blubber, squishing the
fleshy bulges in his fist, the action strangely pleasant, calming.

He and Denis didn't admit to the schoolteacher how they'd
ended up stranded on the side of the road and, happily, the
young man didn't press them, content instead to make small
talk. Billy could just about take in the schoolteacher's words,
his head back with the Hallorans and his certainty inside that
living room, as though the departed had spoken through him.
He'd like to think that was possible.

He doubted what he'd said had helped the Hallorans or
Denis, not long term. The solace of the moment had already
gone out for him. Blame, the truth, it was something you had

to feel for yourself. He closed his eyes, asking, waiting. He couldn't feel much of anything, besides a dull ache in his stomach. His eyes opened. Maybe it was too soon. Maybe he wasn't ready. Maybe he would never know for sure. He looked out at the sky. Maybe that was one of life's great lessons—to accept that there was so much we could never know for certain, and to forgive ourselves anyway.

He gathered himself and checked the time on his phone. He texted Tricia and told her and the kids to go on into town without him. He'd never make it back now for the film and their evening out together. Another horrible, shivery feeling came over him.

Later, in the dark, a taxi drove him home from the train station, everything passing in a flash. He dragged his hand down his face, stifling a groan. All he could see was that living room and Liam rubbing his hand over the top of that displaced TV, and Beth with her hands covering her face.

In the village, TV images flickered white and blue across a window above Caroline's shop. She was likely sitting in an armchair—her slight body making shallow dents in the cushions, her black cat with the one good eye purring in her lap, her hand stroking its soft warmth. He'd known Caroline his whole life and yet he'd no clue if she had what she wanted and needed. If she felt content with her lot. How was it we could know so little about those around us, those we saw practically every day? He wished her well.

He arrived home to an empty house and stood inside the rare silence of the kitchen. This strange emptiness was what it would be like if ever Tricia and the children left him. If ever he ended up alone. Tricia had texted earlier, saying John was out with friends and confirming she had arrived at the cinema with Anna and Ivor.

He pulled his phone from his pocket, rereading the last line of her message. *John said he'd go see the film another night with you.* He held the phone tight, as if afraid the message would disappear. He couldn't remember the last time John had wanted to do anything with him. He realized he hadn't gone straight to the fridge. He crossed the room and opened the fridge door, feeling nothing. That was something, too.

Upstairs, he retrieved tiny Michael from beneath his pillow and returned outside. In the garage, he looked down at the miniature toys and village through the sting of tears, thinking of the memorialized house down in Cork. Beth's words chased him. *We all have our own ways of trying to keep them alive.* Nell Riordan's revelations also knocked about his head. Pretending, when it was only to hide the truth, was killing. With a tortured sound, he lashed out with his arm, sending the village and its inhabitants crashing to the floor. It was stupid make-believe. He was no savior. There was no bringing Michael back. No miraculous family reunion. He kicked at the toys and village on the floor, scattering them farther. He whirled around and punched the garage wall, breaking the skin on his knuckles. *How could you have done this to us, Michael? To yourself?* He gripped tiny Michael with both hands and snapped the toy in two.

He drove through the dark, the car seeming to drag, as if something were pulling on it, trying to make him turn around. He arrived at the cliffs, a place he remembered from his childhood, and parked.

He climbed the trail, his good hand gripping the heavy-duty flashlight, his mouth sucking on his bloodied knuckles. The chill evening wind bit at his nose, cheeks, and the tops of his ears. Up he climbed, it still a struggle despite all the swimming and the weight he'd lost. *I'm not fit* nipped at him.

Several times, he stumbled and almost fell on the stony gray ground. Ever since Michael's death, the earth beneath him had felt unsteady, as though at any moment it would give way and break open. How strange now to feel the actual dirt and stones slip out from underneath him, and for the real sensations to be much less worse than the instability he'd imagined. Rain fell, sprinkles at first, and then heavy on his head and shoulders, wetting and relentless. *Go ahead*, he told the heavens, *do your worst. See if I care.*

Breathless, soaked, his shoes and trousers bottoms covered in muck, he arrived at the top of the trail. Over the edge of the cliff, the sea churned white and magnificent. This high up, the air tasted different—saltier, fishier. He looked around and trained his flashlight on the path back down the trail, confirming he was alone. He tipped up his face to the black, starless sky and opened his mouth, not having tasted rain since he was a boy. He drank until his neck ached.

He dropped onto the wet, cold ground and allowed his buttocks to sink into the muck. The damp and chill seeped down to his bones, ushering in a mild and welcome numbness. His stiff hand moved to his trousers pocket and removed the two pieces of the soldier. He rubbed his thumb back and forth over its face. He pictured Michael standing in their backyard, the boy's right hand on the original red clothesline, making it dip in the middle, and his other hand on his hip. He was smiling, his left eye closed to the glare of the January sun. *Ah, no, Dad,* he said. *I didn't do it, I changed my mind. I'm still here.*

Billy slapped his knees together fast and hard, bone against bone. He remembered the night he'd arrived at the AA meeting and how badly he'd needed to get inside the locked doors of that church. He felt the strong need to knock hard on some door right now and to be let in, but he didn't know where or what. He looked up at the night sky, robbed of its stud of light. He wanted to tear the heavens open and take Michael back. "It can't be undone," he chanted over and over, rocking his upper body back and forth.

He roared. Roared till the scorch inside his throat and chest made the sting of his bloodied knuckles feel like nothing. Roared till he'd nothing left.

Breathless, spent, he struggled back to standing, his feet slipping about in the muck and the pain pulsing in the sides of his knees. He pushed himself to the farthest edge of the cliff and lowered the flashlight to the ground. In life, Michael would not have been able to stand here next to him on the cliff's edge. It would be nice to think the boy's spirit was standing alongside him now.

The sea beckoned. The curlews whistled. Billy talked in his head to Michael, telling him about the swimming pool and his lessons with Vor. He tried to tell Michael exactly how it felt to swim, suspended inside the beautiful blue. There was an enigma he couldn't articulate to the marvel of being held up, something beyond the mechanics of arms and legs and lungs. There was so much he couldn't explain, so much he hadn't said and done. "I'm sorry."

The sea roared, white and midnight-blue. The beam from his flashlight created a shimmering golden bridge that stopped midway across the sky. Inviting and glorious and terrifying. The wind slapped at his back, pushing. He understood how easily a person could go. Felt how sorry you could feel. He looked down at the broken toy in his hand, hesitating. He could no longer think of it as a tiny Michael, or think of six tiny Brennans reunited. He raised his arm, choking out a sob, and fired the two wooden pieces into the sea.

The waves raged white and powerful, their might strangely calming, working on Billy the way they did on the edges of stones. He saw Denis on the side of the road earlier, the pain contorting his face. The anorexic woman on the street a while back also returned, her body jerking in that strange way, as though she were trying to get out of herself. When he felt able, he dialed Denis's number. Denis answered on the first ring. "They don't leave us," Billy said with a gasp. "They're leaving themselves."

He heard only the clicks and swallows of Denis's throat. "Are you all right?"

"Yeah, thanks." Then, after a pause, "You're not out in this rain, are you?"

"I'm headed home now," Billy said.

"Where are you? I'll come get you."

"No, thanks, I'm grand," Billy said.

"Are you sure?"

"I'm sure."

He walked back down the trail, the flashlight's yellow-white beam leading the way, his steps slow but sure, familiar now with the slippery earth.

At home, two long arms of headlights swept through the bedroom, signaling Tricia's return. Moments later, two car doors closed in quick succession and Anna and Ivor's voices carried up. Billy had barely been able to stand the wait until they came home. Fresh from the shower, he hurried into clean tracksuit bottoms and a T-shirt. Forgetting for a moment, he almost reached for his sodden trousers on the floor, to retrieve the soldier now snapped in two and lost at sea. He moved downstairs, the sting still in the broken skin of his knuckles, in his throat and chest.

He found only Anna and Ivor in the kitchen. "Where's your mother?" Before they could answer, Tricia appeared at the back door. "There you are," he said, relieved.

She looked at him funny. "I was just closing the garage door."

"Oh," he said, embarrassed. He must have left the door open earlier, when he'd rushed out, and hadn't noticed on his way back in.

"There must have been some rain?" she said. "The Tara road was near-flooded."

"Wicked," he said, the wet and cold still in his bones. He didn't want to talk about any of that. He wanted to talk about her and the kids and their night. The small, ordinary things. "Well, how was the film?"

"Let's just say the cinema had its own fair share of waterworks," Tricia said wryly.

"Oh?" Billy said.

"The whole film was about this amazing, beautiful race-horse," Anna said. "And then he went and died at the end, right in the middle of this big race. His heart just burst, like *kaboom* and he was gone. It was horrible."

"Yeah," Ivor said. "Even John would have cried if he was there."

Billy gave a small laugh.

Ivor yawned. Anna's hand also rushed to her open mouth. "Off to bed with the two of you," Tricia said. "You're exhausted." Too tired to protest, they kissed her good night.

Anna kissed Billy's cheek. "Night, Dad."

To Billy's surprise, Ivor also kissed him. "Night, night."

"Night, Anna, night, son, sweet dreams."

They went upstairs. "Are they okay?" Billy asked.

"It was a right heartbreaker." Tricia held the kettle under the running tap.

"I'll go up to them." He turned back to her in the doorway. "Are you all right?"

She looked at him, her expression soft. "Yeah. You?"

His fingers rubbed at his forehead. "Yeah."

She noticed the cuts on his hand and frowned. "What happened?"

"Nothing, I'm fine."

"I saw your village and those toys in the garage," she said. "I picked them up and put them back on the table."

He took a sharp breath. "Thanks, but that's all finished. It . . . it wasn't real."

She nodded, her lips pressed together. "Go on up to them. I'll make us tea."

Upstairs, he tucked in Anna. "Get a good night's sleep, you hear?"

"I can't stop thinking about that poor horse."

"It was just a film," he said.

"Everything's always reminding me," she said.

"It'll get easier."

"I hope so."

"I know so," he said.

"Night, Dad."

"Do you want me to stay for a bit?" he asked.

She yawned, long and loud. "No, that's okay, I'm practically asleep already."

He smiled. "All right, good night."

"Good night."

He moved into the boys' bedroom and fussed with Ivor's pillow, just to be with the boy. "That all right for you?"

"Maybe we're supposed to keep getting reminders, so we don't forget?" Ivor said.

The knot in Billy's chest doubled. "We'll never forget Michael."

"I don't mean Michael. I mean . . . you know . . . dying."

"I don't understand," Billy said.

"We get reminders about dying, so we don't forget to make the most of living."

Once again Billy marveled at the mind of a child, his child. He kissed Ivor's forehead.

In the living room, only the TV lit the dark. From his sunken armchair, Billy watched the lies play out on the screen—actors pretending to be other people. Tricia watched from her usual spot on the couch. They sipped at the last of their tea.

Billy's arm lay on the cushion of his stomach, his fingers sneaking at his sides again, pinching and worrying a tire of fat. To hell with it. He would join Overeaters Anonymous. It needed to be done. He felt nervous, but also relieved. His almost surrendering at lunch today had unnerved him. He could no longer deny he needed more help than Denis and the nutritionist could give.

He saw himself getting down on his knees in front of everyone in his first meeting and saying, *Here I am, this is me.* The vivid image should make him think he was going crazy, but instead it calmed him. He was done with pretending, and hiding. He wanted to be seen at last, to be no more or less than himself.

"How did everything go with the filmmaker?" Tricia asked.

"Not good. I won't be working with him after all."

"I'm sorry," she said.

He shrugged. "I'll find someone else."

Their attention went back to the TV.

"Sometimes I want to die," Tricia said, her voice faint. "Just so I can see him again."

He powered off the TV, letting in the dark, and moved next to her on the couch. He risked putting his arm around her. "Don't say that, you're scaring me."

"I don't mean it, not like that at least, I just miss him so much."

"I know."

When next she spoke, he heard the ache of the young girl in her. "Right after my mother died, I hit her chest with the side of my fist, trying to make her heart work again. 'Beat,' I told it." She let her tears fall. "I pressed my hand to Michael's heart, too, in his coffin."

"Shhh, shhh." Billy tried to draw her closer, but she resisted.

Breathless, her sharp inhales made her head jerk. "'Beat,' I said, even though I knew it was stupid. Pointless. Like after all these years I'd learned nothing. I just kept saying it. Just kept begging. 'Beat. Beat.'"

She fell in on Billy, her scaffolding undone. "Tell me everything's going to be okay."

He stroked her hair, holding her to the knock of his heart. "It is. Everything's going to be okay."

Acknowledgments

My deep thanks to:

Brenda Copeland, my wonderful editor at St. Martin's Press. This book is all the better because of you.

Sally Richardson, President and Publisher, and George Witte, Editor in Chief, St. Martin's Press, for adding my book to your remarkable trove.

Lisa Senz, Dori Weintraub, Brant Janeway, Claire Leaden, Jordan Hanley, Maggie Callan, Steven Seighman, Dave Cole, Michelle Ma, and the rest of my phenomenal team at St. Martin's Press. It takes a village.

My agent, Jeff Kleinman, Folio Literary Management—you are tireless, and you went above and beyond.

The generous readers of various drafts of this book: Padraig Rohan, Danielle McLaughlin, Kirsten Menger-Anderson, Masha Hamilton, Jennifer Soloway, Rachel Howard, John Dowling, Janis Cooke Newman, Susanne Pari, Cameron Tuttle, and Lee Kravetz.

Those gifted and large-hearted writers who reached back and offered a hand: Lauren Groff, Edan Lepucki, Robert Olen Butler, Bonnie Jo Campbell, John Banville, Tom Barbash, Eowyn Ivey, Daniel Torday, and Haven Kimmel.

The owners and staff of independent bookstores everywhere, for believing. You keep books alive and vital.

The San Francisco Writers' Grotto, for tremendous support, community, wisdom, and good times. It takes a tribe.

Steve Kettmann, Sarah Ringler, and Joe Plumeri, for a month-long residency at the Wellstone Center that greatly benefited this book, and me.

My family and friends. I'm blessed to have you.

Dad. As promised. I hope I did enough.

T., this book is also for you.